A
hymn
IN THE
silence

Dark is the Night Book 2

KELLEY YORK
&
ROWAN ALTWOOD

www.kelley-york.com

Edited by Jamie Manning

Cover design by x-potion designs

Interior Design by x-potion designs

First Edition October 2018
A HYMN IN THE SILENCE

The darkness of death is like the evening twilight;
it makes all objects appear more lovely to the dying.
—Jean Paul

I HADN'T expected a brothel to be so tidy. In all fairness, I hadn't given much thought at all to what a brothel might look like from the inside; they look like any other building from the outside, save for the occasional flash of flesh from women leaning out the windows attempting to draw attention from male passers-by. Certainly, I had never thought I would have cause to actually be inside of one to find out.

"The Spirit Slayers?" James skirts cautiously down the edge of the hall before me. He speaks soft and low, but his deep voice reverberates off the walls.

"Ridiculous," I mutter.

"You're making this quite difficult, dear William."

"*You're* making this a headache. I keep telling you, we don't need some silly name for ourselves like we're some sort of twopenny-ha'penny mountebanks—"

He silences me by raising a hand and coming to an abrupt

halt. I follow his gaze to the door we've stopped in front of, which stands half-open, and I catch what he must have caught: the sound of repeated, shallow thumping coming from within, like someone rapping upon a solid surface.

We exchange looks. One would think after having done this professionally for the last six months I would be used to it, that my stomach would no longer twist itself into knots, and the heavy feeling of dread would have stopped wedging itself between my lungs, making it difficult to breathe.

Of course, James grins, because this work energises him as much as it utterly petrifies me. I want nothing more than to march right back outside where Madam Florence and her girls are waiting.

But that's the thing about a job: when you take one on, you commit yourself to it and you finish it. My own work ethic would never allow me to walk away.

Besides, who else is going to assist a house full of strumpets who are being terrorized by an unruly spirit? The police would laugh them out of town. For many of these women, this place is the only home they've ever known, and I'm not inclined to leave them huddling in fear. I know all too well how that feels.

James places his fingertips against the door, prepared to push it the rest of the way open. He lingers long enough to cast me an expectant glance. I procure a bottle of holy water from my coat pocket and hold it up with a nod. Useful stuff. I had my concerns when Miss Bennett first instructed us to utilise it, given I'm hardly a Christian man, but my lack of faith doesn't appear to dampen its effect. Perhaps James' faith is enough for us both.

With a gentle shove, the door creaks open. I follow James inside, our steps cautious and quiet. We've entered a bedroom belonging to one of the girls, where they both live and entertain

8

guests. It's an unremarkable room, the only suggestion that it's been lived in being a single framed photograph beside a hairbrush and mirror on a wash table near the window. I step over to pick up the frame, studying the woman in the portrait. It's been taken post-mortem, and I suspect it to be the mother of the girl who lives here.

Or lived here, I suppose. Past-tense. Before she had the misfortune of encountering a client with entirely too much drink in his body who saw fit to strangle her to death. He's off in a rodent-infested cell somewhere, and her ghost has been screaming bloody murder ever since.

James poises himself in the centre of the room and turns around once, full-circle. "Thomasina Beauport?" he calls. "We're here to speak with you."

A low, rumbling growl reverberates through the air. The fastens holding back the curtains fall loose, and the heavy fabric heaves shut, plunging the room into moderate darkness. I take a slow step toward James until we're back to back. He lets out a displeased huff.

"You try. They like you better."

"*Like* is such a subjective term," I mutter. But I give it a go anyway. "Miss Thomasina Beauport, please let us have a word."

The growling intensifies. James reaches back and touches my hand. I turn.

Thomasina has decided to join us after all, her naked form standing in the opposite, darkest corner of the room. Her back is to us. Long, frizzy waves cascade forward over her shoulders and give us the barest glimpse of the purpled, mottled bruising about her throat.

I step around James to approach slowly, uncorking the bottle as quietly as I can. "Miss Beauport. Thomasina. I know you've suffered a terrible tragedy, but you're frightening your friends here."

"*Get out.*" Low, rough, gravelly, like a dirt road grinding beneath carriage wheels.

Here's the thing we've discovered about ghost hunting: spirits fall into a few different categories. If we're lucky, they're merely confused and distressed. Gentle prodding is sometimes all they need to pass over to wherever it is they go. If we're unlucky—well…

Let's just say that we are rarely lucky.

Thomasina whirls with an open-mouthed shriek that paralyses my heart for a beat, long enough for her to rush at me. Her cold, bony hands connect with my chest and slam me back into the nearest wall with enough force that the bottle of holy water is knocked clear out of my grasp to spill uselessly upon the floor.

James shouts my name, and I cannot seem to get a breath in to respond to him. For that matter, I can't move. Instead I find myself losing contact with the floor as the pressure against my chest steadily increases. My ribs creak in protest. Thomasina's thin lips pull back from her teeth in something resembling a hideous, skeletal smile, mere inches from my face.

"*No more. All of you… All of you are pigs. No more.*"

"In the name of Jesus Christ, our God and Lord, strengthened by the intercession of the immaculate virgin Mary…"

Snarling, Thomasina whips toward the sound of James' voice. The weight on my chest vanishes and I slide a solid foot down the wall before I catch myself, gasping for breath. Thomasina's full attention is now on James, who has slid the crucifix from his pocket as he speaks the verses he's memorised and could now say in his sleep.

"...of blessed Michael the Archangel, of the blessed apostles Peter and Paul and all the Saints..." James' recitation does not falter, but he makes the mistake of flicking his gaze to me to ensure I'm all right, and Thomasina uses that precious second of hesitation to lunge. The same force that smashed into me moments ago now sends James clear off his feet, crashing into the dresser. He ends on his side on the floor, wincing in pain.

Before she can reach him and inflict any lasting damage, I snatch the bottle from the floor. Most of it has spilled, but there's just enough left to coat my fingers. I pitch myself forward, between Thomasina and James, and as she opens her mouth to let out another blood-curdling scream, I make the mark of the cross upon her forehead. "His enemies are scattered, and those who hate Him flee before Him. As smoke is...is—"

"As smoke is driven away, so are they driven," James picks up, voice rough as he crawls to all-fours.

Our combined efforts have Thomasina wrenching away, hands to her face as her body contorts in distress. She sinks to her knees, and the hollow sound of her screams ebbs and flows into a soft, helpless sobbing.

"Thomasina Beauport," I say, as James continues to recite without a hitch, "you've been grievously wronged, the man who did this has been put to justice, and it's time for you to rest."

She lowers her hands and turns her tear-streaked face to me. The very room around us trembles, furniture quaking and drawers rattling, and then...

Thomasina vanishes.

Everything goes silent save for the sound of our laboured breathing. I collapse to the floor and James slumps down as well. I'm almost too afraid to lift my head out of fear of discovering it hasn't worked, but I can't feel her presence here anymore. She's gone.

After a spell, James reaches out, letting his hand thump tiredly against my side. "All right, darling?"

"All right," I reply, finally allowing myself to sit up. The room is a disaster, but we aren't being paid to concern ourselves with that. We're here to remove the ghost and remove the ghost we have. "There must be an easier way to do this."

James lets out a short laugh. "That *was* easy, wasn't it? Compared to some of our other jobs." He hauls himself to his feet and extends a hand to help me to mine, which I take with the utmost gratefulness. Rather than release me when I stand, James draws me to him and ducks his head to press his mouth to mine. Sometimes, I think he does that to reward me for putting up with another merciless day of work. I never argue it because it *does* soothe my frazzled nerves a little.

We fetch our greatcoats where we left them hanging just inside the front door. The dreary London afternoon had seen fit not to open the sky and drench us on the way here, and that luck appears to be holding when we emerge to greet Madam Florence and the other women, and those who are dressed as women but I'm fairly certain are not. Given that this place caters to some of the city's elite, I suspect those who sell themselves here are prepared to service a broad range of customers with different appetites and hefty bank accounts who wish to engage with the utmost discretion.

The brothel's procuress, Madam Florence, is a steadfast woman, not easily ruffled, and commands respect with her stature and steely-eyed stare, which she levels at us as the door swings closed at our heels. "Well?"

James shoves a hand back through his ruffled hair with a

brilliant grin and descends the steps. "I believe you will find your establishment to be in order, Madam. Would you like to have a look?"

The other girls let out relieved sighs and gasps. Several of them duck past the two of us to hurry inside. Madam Florence even twitches her mouth up into the barest hint of a smile.

"We really owe you, boys." One of the girls—Margaret, if I recall her name correctly—sidles up to us. "Workin' the streets because we've been chased outta our home has been miserable. Not to mention dangerous."

"Happy to help," I offer, bowing my head, making it a point to politely keep my gaze from dropping to the swoop of her neckline, which is where I suspect she *wants* me to look. "Should you have any further complications, please let us know."

"This one's precious," Margaret says to her companions. Before I can ask what that means, she catches my face in her soft hands, and rises on tip-toe to plant a kiss on my mouth. It's a mere second of contact, but one that leaves a blush creeping up my face even as she laughs and hurries inside with her friends. James chuckles beside me and I shoot him an embarrassed glare.

Madam Florence rolls her eyes and steps closer. "Well done, gentlemen. I appreciate the hard work." She procures a coin purse from a pocket of her dress, although she hesitates before offering it out. "I don't suppose I could interest you in trade rather than coin?" she asks, taking a moment to rake her gaze over us both. "Handsome gents like you, I suspect any one of my girls would be happy to offer their services in exchange for yours."

James tips his head, rocking back on his heels and giving me a sidelong grin. "What do you think, William?"

If my face grows any warmer, I'm going to burst into flames. I manage a strained smile nonetheless and say, "As kind of an offer as that is, the coin will suit us very well, thank you."

The Madam shrugs and places the purse into James' outstretched hand, thanks us again, and excuses herself to head inside. James lets out a sharp, barking laugh once she's gone, and I have half a mind to shove him to the ground.

"What's so funny?"

"Just you," he titters, pocketing the money and briefly touching a hand to my lower back. "The girls always love your pretty face, darling. I can't keep them off you."

"Not that you ever try," I mutter. James takes great joy in watching me squirm under the attention of others. My discomfort may not be overly noticeable to most, but he knows me. He knows the twitch of my mouth and the slant of my brows and what it means. What a shame *he* is utterly oblivious when similar attention is lavished upon him, too.

We walk the few miles back to Miss Bennett's. Her small apartment serves as both her living quarters and her place of business. In the six months since we arrived at Miss Bennett's doorstep to work under her guidance, we've come to think of this place as a second home to us, as well. We certainly spend enough time here. James and I have grown quite accustomed to crowding together on a small, lumpy cot in the corner of the kitchen, fully clothed, exhausted after a long day's work.

The main room is the largest, lit by oil lamps placed on every available surface because the single window at the front does little for lighting and few homes in this part of Whitechapel have been fitted with gas. One wall is completely occupied by a hanging drapery used as a photography backdrop, and several chairs are pushed together before a camera on a tripod.

It's there that Miss Bennett does her spirit photography and her séances, a profession that gets her scoffed at daily on the street by the same people who eventually come to see her after the passing of a loved one. A medium, I suspect, only matters to those desperate enough to realise they need one.

When we step inside, those chairs are empty. Surprising for this time of day. However, I hear voices from elsewhere in the flat. Upon the coat rack is an unfamiliar overcoat, next to which we hang our own. I follow James into the kitchen, where Miss Bennett is seated across from an unfamiliar man; he's squirrelly, slight, with thinning hair and spectacles thicker than my own, and with a moustache far too thick and wide for his narrow face.

Upon our entrance, both the stranger and Miss Bennett's attention flicks to us in a manner that suggests we were previously the topic of their conversation.

Miss Bennett rises. "There they are. James, William, meet Mr. Albert Foss. He's here from Buckinghamshire on behalf of Lord Claude Wakefield to request our assistance."

Miss Bennett never leaves the area for work. In fact, one of the reasons she chose to take us on as her pupils was so that she could step back from jobs outside her home. Most of those sorts of cases are given to James and me, so it works out quite nicely. However, receiving a guest from several hours outside of Whitechapel is…different.

All smiles, James steps forward and extends a hand as Foss stands and does the same. "It's a pleasure, Mr. Foss."

Foss bobs his head into a nod and turns to me. I accept his hand because it's only polite to do so. He squeezes a bit too hard, as though he's trying to make a point, although I'm not certain what that point might be. "Gentlemen. Miss Bennett has been telling me of your exploits."

I steal a glance at Miss Bennett, who catches my eye and cocks a brow as though to convey, *you'll want to hear what he has to say.* Which is rather like the look she gives me any time someone drops a new job at our feet, because she knows I'm the one who needs convincing to take it.

"Buckinghamshire," I say. "Not often we have clientele from such a distance."

The small man clears his throat. "Yes, well, my employer felt we were running low on options."

James beckons for our guest to have a seat again and pulls out one of the other chairs to sink into it himself. "Perhaps you could fill us in on your situation?"

Foss drops back into his chair. "Murder. A family in our community was found butchered a few days past."

My eyebrows lift slowly, and I exchange a cursory glance with James, wondering if I'm missing something. Last I checked, we were not in the business of investigating murders. "Would that not be a job more appropriate for the authorities?"

Foss scoffs. "Oh, detectives have come and gone already, and an inquest was held. Not a trace to be found of the killer. My Lord is convinced it was no human who did the deed, anyway."

James' brow furrows. "He suspects spirits? Why?"

"One of the victims, Mr. Brewer, told a neighbour the day before his death that he'd come across footprints in the snow leading onto their property, but none leaving again."

Odd, to be certain, but— "Spirits aren't prone to leaving tracks," I point out. Foss frowns.

"Mr. and Mrs. Brewer also claimed something eerie was happening but couldn't explain just what it was. Our local vicar had planned on visiting to bless the home but, well, he never had the chance."

"Well, yes. I suspect it would be rather eerie if one had a person prowling their property and stalking them," James says, and I know he doesn't mean to sound condescending but, bless him, he can't help it sometimes. I find it amusingly endearing—when it's not aimed at me.

Foss exhales heavily through his nose, frustration beginning to seep into his features. "It would be easier if I could show you the location and the bodies. I can assure you, whatever did this was not human."

Miss Bennett clears her throat. "Mr. Foss' employer is, of course, more than willing to compensate you for your time, boys."

Bollocks. I can already see the cogs in James' head turning as he pins me with a thoughtful stare and says, "Allow my partner and I to consult for a moment, if you would."

"Yes, of course."

I level a scowl at Foss' back as I step out of the room with James. In the living area, I move as far from the kitchen as I can. The look I give James with my mouth pulled thin ought to say precisely what I think about this entire idea.

James pockets his hands, leaning a shoulder into the wall beside the window pane. "Oh, come now. What's the harm in having a look? At least we get a free trip."

I keep my voice low, arms tucked stubbornly across my chest. "We're not *detectives*, James. Do you really have any interest in poking about a grisly murder site?"

He bites back a smile. "That question sounds like a trap."

My expression deadpans. "Forget I asked. Name me one good reason why we should take this job. And do not say 'money' because we've been keeping plenty busy here." Granted, not always for the best pay, but we've been getting by. Some weeks are better than others.

"Adventure? Travel? If nothing else, we can take a day or two for ourselves and have a brief holiday."

"We're not likely to have time to ourselves on this little outing," I point out. We would be at the mercy of our host, rooming separately I imagine, which is frustrating enough on its own. We suffered through enough of that at Whisperwood. "Is this one of those things you want to do just for a laugh, or do you *truly* want to do it?"

James blinks those lovely hazel eyes at me as though he had not been aware there was a difference between the two. "Ah…yes?"

I contemplate shoving him out the window and settle for the most unimpressed look I can muster. Turning away, I sigh heavily.

What are the pros and cons of this? A bit of time away from Whitechapel, yes. But also, time away from our own home just outside the city. We're already away so often on work that it drives me mad. Yet again, we'd be in a place we'd need to be vigilant over every move we make, and I grow so weary of not being in the comfort of our small countryside house where I can reach out and touch James whenever I damn well please.

After a moment, I turn back to him. "One week to investigate. That's all. And if they're offering less than fifteen pounds, we're not taking it. Agreed?"

Pleased, James flashes me a grin. "Agreed."

It's a much higher bid than we would ask from any client here in the city, and it's an intentional hurdle on my part. Less of a likelihood that we'll have to accept this job, and then I won't have James pouting at me for turning it down.

We return to the kitchen. Foss looks to James expectantly as I step to the stove where a teapot waits for me to pour myself a cup of moderately warm tea. It will likely be all I have in my stomach until dinner. While I have no issues negotiating, I'll leave this one to James. He never has any qualms about asking after payments.

"Mr. Foss, how much is your employer willing to pay for us to visit and decide if this is a supernatural occurrence and thus requiring a full investigation?"

Foss doesn't seem the least bit put off by the question, at least; he was undoubtedly expecting it. "Twenty pounds for the initial visit."

Which meets and exceeds my initial bid. Damn.

"…And another sixty should you discover the cause and correct it."

I choke on my tea.

"We'll take it," James blurts, though I see him from the corner of my eye levelling a triumphant smile in my direction. Miss Bennett leans over to clap a hand against my back while I try to clear my airways.

Foss lurches to his feet, grasping James' hand and giving it an enthusiastic shake. "Oh, thank you, thank you! Wonderful news. I would like to depart first thing in the morning, if at all possible."

"At your pleasure, Mr. Foss."

"Excellent. Then I shall return tomorrow about nine, yes?"

Miss Bennett sees him out. I inhale slowly with a final cough and look to James, perhaps a bit sulkier than I mean to. "Well, I suppose you're pleased."

"I believe your demands were more than met," James says with a—yes, pleased—grin. I despise those grins. They make me want to punch him and kiss him all in the same breath because he's simultaneously obnoxious and adorable.

"You'll humour me by allowing us to return home tonight, then?" If I'm going to be forced to room apart from him for a week, then I should like to have one night sharing a bed beforehand.

His smile turns sweet. "I live to humour you, darling."

"You live to give me headaches." My voice has softened, perhaps resigned to my fate. A job is a job. All we have to do is travel to this Lord's estate, have a quick look, and inform him nothing supernatural has taken place. Better yet, perhaps we can make contact with some of the spirits of the deceased who can communicate with us who is responsible for their untimely deaths. A hit-or-miss option, seeing as spirits are notoriously rotten at communicating.

Miss Bennett returns and regards us with a thin smile. "Certain the pair of you aren't getting in over your heads?"

"No harm in having a look," James answers with a hum. "We'll be quite all right, I promise."

"I trust that you will." The look of warning that crosses her face is directed more at James than at me. "However, it isn't any spirit that concerns me. Please tread carefully."

She isn't saying as much, but I know she's referring to the fact that we need to express caution in drawing attention to our relationship. James, in particular, is about as subtle as a bag of bricks through a shop window—and Miss Bennett knows this because it's James' lack of subtlety that originally tipped her off to just how close we are. Despite it being known, it is not something she openly discusses unless it's her giving us gentle warning to be careful.

"As always," James chirps. A response that gets a snort from both Miss Bennett and myself.

2

Home is not a terribly far journey outside of the city, but just far enough that there are many nights, after a long day's work, where it's more effort than either of us care to exert to go back. Today we catch a coach home, because it's already growing late, and we need time to pack and ensure things are locked up for our prolonged absence.

Home is the one place where my nerves don't crackle on edge quite so loudly. Surrounded by nothing but fields and flowers and quiet countryside, we're quite secluded out here. I have James to myself with no fear of someone stumbling across us. No fear of judgment or ridicule or prosecution. I can wake beside him every morning and steal as many kisses as I please. We can cook and eat our meals together and enjoy the freedom of being able to sidle up to one another any time of the day and tuck a hand down the other's trousers. Not luxuries we could safely indulge in anywhere else.

So it's no surprise that I relax as we exit the carriage to head inside. The moment the door has shut behind us, James throws his arms around me and his voice is a deep, shiver-inducing rumble against my ear. "Hello there, sweetheart."

The carriage has hardly had time to exit the driveway and I can't bring myself to care. I twist in his arms, already slipping my hands into his hair and rising to kiss him properly for the first time in several days. I appreciate the way he immediately melts against me, his mouth eagerly slanting against mine in between his breathless words of, "That's *much* better."

We have things to do and it's already late in the evening. Dinner and bathing and packing…and yet I appear to be entirely distracted with pulling at James' clothes instead. "I suggest making this memorable lest I forget what it's like to have you touch me."

James laughs as I disengage. He begins shedding out of his coat. "No pressure, though."

"Plenty of pressure." I take a few slow steps back, discarding my shoes and coat in the process and donning a pleasant, playful smile before starting in on the buttons on my own clothes.

There has been the occasional night we've been desperate enough to give into our urges while crowded together on a cot at Miss Bennett's, but those are always hurried acts, often ending with my face either shoved into a pillow or James' hand across my mouth because keeping quiet is not, in fact, one of my strengths.

Here at home? We don't even make it farther than the parlour, honestly. The house is cold without a fire going and James is, as always, deliciously warm under my hands and over me and inside of me.

It's long past dark out by the time we're spent, and I've begun to think we ought to get to other things. We lie in the sparsely furnished, moonlit parlour upon the settee, windows cracked to allow in a quiet, cold breeze that ruffles the curtains. Absently threading my fingers through James' hair, damp where it rests against his forehead, I think I would like nothing more than to spend the rest of my night right here.

I'm aware we'll fall asleep if we linger much longer, however, and it's with a regretful sigh that I press a kiss to his temple. "Let's make quick work of packing our things and we'll get some proper rest."

James makes a displeased noise and noses at my throat. He hasn't shaved today; the scratch of his jaw against my skin almost tickles. "Why don't we have someone to pack for us?"

"Because one of us wanted a job which does not pay handsomely enough to afford a servant for such things."

He tsks. "Why would you do that?"

I roll my eyes and shift my hips purposefully against him in a way that makes him shiver. "Come now. I've missed our bed. The sooner we pack, the sooner I can crawl into it."

"Right, right," he sighs, moving away wearily and granting me quite a lovely view of his naked form painted with silver light. He's a fair bit trimmer and taller than he was when we met, and the misty glow from outside highlights the criss-cross of deep scars he received from Mordaunt's ghost, and a few others he's obtained since—like the narrow, upraised line cupping his left side, a reminder of the first job we took under Miss Bennett's tutelage six months ago. An unruly spirit sent a tray of cutlery flying and James, ever needing to be the hero, had put himself between the ghost and me. A butcher's knife caught him right there as it whizzed past and then lodged itself into the wall behind me.

23

Unconsciously, I flex my own scarred hand. For the most part, it's only a minor inconvenience, stiffness I have to massage loose especially when the weather grows cold. Of all the scars I now wear, it's the only one that bothers me.

James scrubs his palms over his face and turns a sullen look in my direction. Tired James is one of my favourite looks on him. Dishevelled and pouty and indignant, like some big, lazy cat who's been disrupted from its nap.

Truthfully, when I said, "we need to pack," it translates to "I need to pack because you'll end up with three trunks of absolutely nothing useful and you'll forget clean socks." Which means I set James to fetching us something small to eat from the kitchen whilst I pack a trunk of clothing, our Bibles—James' significantly more worn than my own—a few bottles of holy water, and whatever else we might need should we encounter spirits after all. James will keep my laudanum on his person. It's better that way.

It's been awhile since we've travelled such a distance. Every job we've done thus far has been in London or not far outside it, a cab ride or a short hop on the train. London is a massive place with more than enough work to keep us busy. Honestly, busier than I might care for sometimes, but it allows us to keep this house. Our home might be much less than either of us grew up with, sparse in decoration and luxuries. We've had a steep learning curve in how to take care of it all on our own—cooking and laundry were initially a nightmare—but this is the home we've created together, and there's nowhere else I'd rather be.

James returns just as I've finished packing. He places a plate of eggs, dried beef, and a hunk of undoubtedly stale bread with butter atop the dresser for me. "What are the odds this turns out to be a regular murder?"

"High." I close the lid to the trunk and thumb the latches shut. "Gruesome does not have to mean supernatural."

"I suppose it's difficult for people to think humans could be capable of such horrors."

Our eyes meet for half a breath, both of us sharing the same thought, I suspect. We've seen just what people are capable of. People like Maxwell King and Charles Simmons and Nicholas Mordaunt... We know better.

"If nothing else, we can try to put at ease any of the spirits of the victims while we're there," I say.

James smiles. "Look at you, bringing peace to the dead."

I give him a pointed look and relocate the trunk from the foot of the bed to the floor so that I can retrieve my plate and sit to eat. "For your sake only, I assure you. You're a far better man than I."

"I think you're better than you give yourself credit for."

I think James gives me entirely *too* much credit. I wouldn't be in this line of work were it not for him. Too much of a coward. What bravery I muster is always spurred on by his presence, by his courage, and a desire to keep him safe.

I don't argue the point, however, instead tucking in to eat. After which, I'll tend to a few more things about the house. Dishes, packing a few snacks for the train that will go bad if left behind anyway, washing up since it's far too late to lug water to the tub for a proper bath, a final dosage of laudanum so that I might rest easy... Only once all of that is finished do I crawl into bed tiredly beside James and curl myself against his side to sleep. It's a night before a job, and I cling to him tighter than is necessary.

As always, I sleep fitfully, plagued by nightmares of unearthly shadows that devour us whole.

25

I am not and never have been a morning person. James is even worse. Whereas I can rise with the sun and accomplish what needs to be done, James greets my morning prodding with a plaintive whine.

"Too early," he protests in a sleep-ladened voice. "More sleep."

My medicine always wears off during the night, leaving me with a restless, itching sort of buzz in the back of my skull I cannot quiet until my morning dose. It's minimal at home, but still present, especially with the prospect of a large job looming over our heads. Still, I humour James by lying there with him for just a bit, chuckling as he pulls the blankets up and over our heads.

"We'll be late, and you'll not have time for breakfast if you don't get up," I murmur.

I feel the heat of his breath on my skin, and then James gnawing lazily at my shoulder. "I have my breakfast right here."

It's somewhere between obnoxious and ticklish and gets a laugh out of me. I shove at him gently. "Come on, darling. Up."

He whimpers. "Fine, but let it be known that you're terribly cruel."

I toss back the blankets and sit up. James is adorable when he's tired and moping, and I'd love nothing more than to waste the day away lying here with him. I insist on crawling out of bed on his side, meaning I slide a leg across his hips and straddle him a moment before sliding off to the other side. "Cruel is my middle name, yes."

James cracks an eye open to watch me with calculated interest, a slow smile crossing his face. He grabs for my wrist and I dance back and out of his reach, all the while marvelling at how far we've come. Back at Whisperwood, James was very

26

particular about certain touches, about me initiating intimacy. Even after our first time together, there were days where his nerves would get the best of him, and he'd put a halt to my affections. It's been months since that's happened. I'd call that progress.

There are other things that I watch for. Letting my hands wander when he sleeps, for instance. I think waking in such a way, with my fingers or mouth in compromising positions upon his person, takes him back to a time and place he prefers not to think nor speak of. Even to me.

He sighs plaintively and sits up, his hair an incredible hedgehog of strands jutting up in every direction. "What have I ever done but love you? Why do you hurt me so?"

"Because you make me go on these jobs," I drawl, stretching my arms above my head and slipping free of my nightclothes.

"It's hardly my fault you don't find them as fun as I do."

I could point out that part of the reason they terrify me so is James' complete lack of self-preservation instincts, but I see little purpose to it. I just sigh, tossing my clothes over his face. "Up and washed, darling. We've a long day ahead of us."

For as impatient a man as people take me for, I express the utmost patience for James and his whimpering. Perhaps because I've learned to tune it out. Or perhaps because I know when he's whining for the sake of whining, or when he's complaining because something is sincerely bothering him.

We'll eat and dress and the cab will return for us right on time—the usual driver who is kind enough to venture outside of the city for those in our little community and do not have their own means of transportation.

Mr. Foss waits for us at Miss Bennett's, and he seems to be in a jovial mood despite James and I being too tired for interesting conversation because it really is still too bloody early. But, right, to the train station we go, on the ten-thirty to Chiltern Hills. A trip I would have much rather taken with James alone, because with Foss seated across from us, it means I cannot even lay my head on James' shoulder and go back to sleep.

"This is an interesting profession the two of you have stumbled into," Foss chatters as the train departs the station. "How did you come about it?"

"We attended a haunted school," James says. "We found we had a knack for dealing with such things."

Foss' eyes widen. "Fascinating."

I bite back a bitter laugh. A knack for it? More like an impetuous tenacity and refusal to give up. And a damned bit of luck, at that. I still get chills when I think back to the sensation of a spirit inside of my body, driving it about like a marionette. To think Miss Bennett willingly invites spirits to do the same to her is unfathomable to me.

Whisperwood is not a subject I care to get into overmuch. Doing so might bring up the subject of Oscar Frances, and I cannot bear to see the way such a thing makes pain flash so raw and open on James' face.

"Perhaps you can fill us in on some of the details of the Brewers' murders, Mr. Foss?" I ask.

"Oh. Yes, certainly." He clears his throat as though preparing to recite from a memorised speech. "The Brewers were a family of horse breeders. Well-known, hard-working. The community is small, so our church consists of quite the mixture of people across all classes. Hugo Brewer had mentioned to some of the other parishioners that something was off, weeks before anything happened. He said the children had spotted people watching them in the woods, but searches yielded nothing."

"And the footprints?"

"Yes. Hugo Brewer encountered them while putting out the laundry one afternoon. He divulged the information to a neighbour and they did a thorough search of the area but found nothing.

"One day, the neighbours noticed the horses had not been brought in at night, and the farm seemed unnaturally quiet. None of the children mucking about…"

Children. I know he told us this was a family, but it hadn't properly clicked in my mind that it meant these children were also dead. My stomach turns uncomfortably. James' hand, resting upon his knee, twitches, and for half a second, I think he's going to reach for mine until he remembers himself.

He asks, "I trust the house itself was searched thoroughly?"

"Naturally. As I mentioned yesterday, the police have been in and out numerous times." Foss shakes his head with a sigh, pulling a flask from his coat to take a swig. I wish I'd thought to bring one myself.

"Signs of a struggle?"

"Yes. The place is—well, it's a wreck, if I'm honest." Some of the colour falls from his face. "Blood everywhere… Something tore into those poor people like starving wolves."

James purses his lips. "Do you know if anyone who has been in the house—before or after the murders—has seen anything odd? Heard anything?"

"Before? Not so much. After, not many civilians have entered. The neighbours who found them, of course. Lord Wakefield and I escorted the police when they came to retrieve the bodies. I don't recall seeing anything peculiar, but it's difficult to say. We were rather distracted at the time."

"The police needed the escort of a lord?" I ask, eyebrow raising.

"Well," Foss takes another pull from his flask and tucks it away, "the land belongs to him, you see."

29

James says, "Ah, was he friendly with the family?"

"Lord Wakefield is friendly with everyone in the community," Foss confirms. "The Brewers fell on hard times a few years ago. He purchased the land and lowered their rent so that they could afford to stay."

"Very charitable of him," I murmur. Not unheard of, I suppose, just…unusual. I steal a glance at James.

Wakefield is a charitable and kind employer, Foss goes on to say. A good father to his daughter, a pillar in the community, and generous with his money. Perhaps I do him a disservice by comparing him to my own parents, who are most certainly not kind nor charitable with…well, anything. It's difficult for me to imagine.

The rest of the trip passed with Foss chattering away, and me wishing he'd shut his trap so that I could try to catch some more sleep.

James, however, is quite adept at filling the silence where I cannot. He knows how much socialising wears me down and never hesitates to step in, allowing me to merely exist. Although I cannot sleep, I close my eyes a few times and allow the hum of their conversation to fall by the wayside.

Trains are wretched things, as far as I'm concerned. Noisy, crowded, always too hot or too cold. Buckinghamshire is only a few hours away, thankfully. When we arrive, there's a steady snowfall and it's as cold as sin. Thankfully, a coach awaits to take us the rest of the way, so we needn't linger long at the station.

The Chiltern Hills are beautiful, there's no denying that. Sprawling hills and countryside with beautiful manor homes of some of the elite, interspersed with small specks of farms and cattle and sheep as far as the eye can see.

The driveway we pull into ends in one of the most stunning

manor houses I've seen in my life, and I feel my mouth hanging open as I lean forward to peer out the window in awe. James leans into me, following my gaze, and his whisper is meant just for my ears.

"We should have asked for more money."

"Perhaps we will yet," I murmur, biting back a smile.

A footman rushes to open our carriage door once it rolls to a stop, and suddenly I feel a little underdressed for such a lavish home. Thankfully I have some finer clothes packed, but that doesn't do me any good right now. I step down from the cab, tipping my head back to admire the architecture, snow-capped towers stretching high above our heads. Before I've had too much of a chance to take it all in, we're ushered up the steps and into the foyer of the manor, which is no less grand than the outside. High ceilings and glittering chandeliers, curtains thrown open wide over lean windows to let in as much light as possible. Along with plenty of natural lighting, there are gas lamps lining the walls. This place must be lovely at night.

"One day, we're going to live in such a fine place," James whispers to me, lingering closer than he probably ought to.

I respond with a noncommittal noise. I miss it. No, I didn't grow up in a place *this* grand, but I do miss the luxuries I once had. I miss having the finest clothes and all the books I could want. I miss going to the theatre whenever I pleased and having servants to tend to my meals and baths. More than anything, I miss having a full belly instead of the constant, dull ache of hunger because food is scarce and expensive.

And there is nothing in me that believes our line of work will ever grant us such fineries. But all it takes is one look at James to remember why I was all right with that exchange.

Foss strolls in behind us, removing his hat. From the top

of the stairs comes a loud, warm voice: "You've arrived! I'd not expected you for another few hours but leave it to Albert to be timely."

Lord Wakefield descends the stairs; he's older but quite handsome, in possession of a strong jawline and silvering at his temples, and a disarming smile. He's wearing a sack coat with only the topmost button fastened to show off a brilliant red waistcoat, the colour of which compliments his pinstripe trousers. The light glints off the chain of his pocket watch. He approaches us with the slick confidence of a man who has everything and knows it. Still, there's nothing insincere about the cheerfulness he displays as he comes to greet us, scooping up James' hand in his own and giving it a firm shake.

"Mr. Spencer, Mr. Esher! I'm positively thrilled you could make it. Welcome to Evenbury Manor."

James responds with a brilliant smile all his own. "And you must be the man we've heard so much about from Mr. Foss."

"Ah, Albert always sings my praises far too highly." He laughs and turns to give my hand the same shake. I'll admit, I'm a little thrown by him. He's very different from what I expected. "Claude Wakefield. My home is your home during your time here. Should you need anything at all, please don't hesitate to let me know. I trust Albert has filled you in on some of our predicament?"

"He has," I agree, although my gaze has strayed a bit, catching movement on the stairs.

A woman has joined us, standing upon the landing, dressed in hues of blue and gold. Her hair is pinned up meticulously, only a few stray honeyed curls are purposely let free to frame her face and tumble down the back of her neck. Everything about her is soft; her cheeks, and the gentle slope of her brows and nose...

32

She is, quite honestly, one of the most beautiful girls I've ever laid eyes on.

"I hope that we're able to be of some assistance," James is saying. Wakefield catches that my attention has wandered. He turns, smiles, and steps aside with a grand sweep of his arm. "Addy, darling! Come and say hello to our guests. Gentlemen, this is my daughter, Adelia."

Oh. Mr. Foss said Wakefield had a daughter, and it hadn't occurred to me she'd be not much younger than us. For whatever reason, I'd envisioned a small child.

Adelia Wakefield makes her way down the stairs to stand beside her father, who beams proudly. She studies us, her expression somewhere between amused and unreadable, which is intriguing in and of itself. "You must be the ghost hunters."

"The Phantom Fighters," James chirps.

I elbow him. "That's not what we call ourselves."

He gives a little sniff. "James Spencer, and this is my partner, William Esher."

I'm openly staring at Adelia like a bloody fool and even when James says my name, it takes me a moment to realise—yes, right. I'm supposed to introduce myself. I take a step forward and extend my hand to Adelia, aware a second too late that it might be entirely too forward of me to do so. "William Esher. It's a pleasure, Lady Adelia."

Adelia meets my gaze unflinchingly but doesn't take the offered hand. "A pleasure, I'm certain. But there are those who will feel much better about your arrival than I."

"Addy," Lord Wakefield sighs, a touch of warning in his tone but more exasperation than anything. "Pardon my daughter. I'm afraid she's a bit sceptical about all of this."

My cheeks warm as I withdraw my hand, tearing my eyes

away from her face. "Quite all right. As we told Mr. Foss, there may be nothing to these murders that we can assist with."

James shifts his weight from one foot to the other and clears his throat a bit forcefully. "No harm in looking, especially if it can put minds at ease."

Adelia smiles faintly at that. "Be careful not to get wrapped up in superstition, gentlemen."

"It's not superstition when there's truth behind it." I offer her a small smile that I mean to be self-assured and confident, and I fear comes across as nervous and utterly ridiculous instead. However, I can appreciate her scepticism; there are far too many simpler explanations for a great many things besides ghosts.

"Of course," she responds, though without any conviction. "Though I'm certain you will have more than your fill of those who cry supernatural."

Lord Wakefield chuckles, putting an arm around his daughter and hugging her to his side. "Well, we shall see how your investigation proceeds and what you find, hm? Allow Albert to show you to your rooms. We've quite a dinner planned this evening, so I hope you've brought your appetites."

"I'm told I have an endless appetite," James titters.

"He does," I agree flatly.

"Glad to hear it." Lord Wakefield gestures to Foss, who in turn nods to the footman who brought in our trunk. Wakefield arches an eyebrow as the footman hefts the trunk upon his back and begins to cart it upstairs. "Only one piece of luggage between the two of you?"

"We prefer to travel lightly," James is quick to say.

Wakefield only smiles and nods and, thankfully, asks no further probing questions. By his leave, James and I follow Foss and the footman upstairs. He leads us through the vast halls of the manor to the easternmost wing, which appears to consist of mostly guest apartments.

He opens a door to the left and the footman enters, placing the trunk at the foot of the four-poster bed before silently slipping away. I want to throw myself upon that gorgeous bedspread and bury my face into the plush down pillows. There is nothing about this room I don't immediately love…except for the fact that James and I won't be permitted to share it.

"Your other room is directly across the hall," Foss says, turning to us with his hands behind his back. "Might there be anything I can do for you gentlemen to help you settle in?"

"I think a bit of a rest and a quick wash, and we will both feel as good as new," James says.

Foss bows deeply. "I will have baths drawn for each of you, if you'd like."

"That sounds delightful," I say. We hadn't time for a proper bath last night, and I suspect whatever bath they can offer us here will far exceed what we have at home.

Foss takes his leave, closing the door behind him. The moment James and I are alone, he thumps me on the back of my head.

I jerk, startled. "What was that for??"

He laughs. "You know exactly what! I thought you were about to start drooling all over that poor girl and really make a mess."

A blush promptly crawls up into my face. "It was nothing. She caught me off-guard, is all."

"With what? Her *face*?"

Not just her face, but I'll keep that comment to myself. "No need for jealousy, darling. You're far prettier than she is," I offer, lifting a hand to touch his jaw.

35

KELLEY YORK & ROWAN ALTWOOD

He turns to nip at my fingers. "Uh huh."

I draw closer, taking his face in my hands. I don't get the impression he's *actually* jealous, but just in case. "You know I only have eyes for you."

A smile pulls at the corners of his mouth. "She doesn't seem to think much of us anyway. Looks like you're stuck with me."

"However shall I cope?" I sigh and kiss him, lingering a few lovely seconds, and James leans into it with an eagerness that suggests he's taking this with good humour. When I pull back, it's to slip out of my coat.

"Our rooms are across from one another. You know, perhaps we'll be able to sneak around after all. I'm always more than happy to try," James hums, watching me appreciatively.

As much as I like that idea— "We'll see. You're under the assumption the servants aren't terribly nosy and that we're capable of being careful enough."

While we wait for our baths to be drawn, I open up our trunk to fetch some clean clothes for us both. Upon opening the lid, sat atop the rest of our things, is a familiar bottle. My face warms over.

"You can't remember to pack your own bloody socks but you can remember this?" I ask, lifting the jar of oil with a pointed look in his direction.

The smile he gives is almost sheepish. Almost. "I like to come prepared."

There's a double entendre there, and I decide not to comment on it.

Before long, the servants have come to inform us our baths are prepared in a room at the end of the hall. And, in fact, the two large, luxurious tubs are not only full of water, but full of water so hot that the steam rolls off it, and I resist the urge to fall into it fully clothed. Back home, we simply haven't the means of heating water quickly enough to fill a tub. By the time it's full, we're lucky if we have it lukewarm.

As soon as the servants have left us, I flash a lopsided smile at James and quickly begin to shed my clothes. James quietly laughs at my eagerness, but he's undressed and in his tub before I am.

I sink into the water with a low, pleased groan, and drop my head back. How long has it been since we've enjoyed such a thing? I've half a mind to crawl into James' tub with him but decide it's too risky. Instead, I soak up the warmth for a while, and then open my eyes to poke through the generous selection of soaps placed at our tub-sides. I'm tempted to try all of them, honestly, because they all smell lovely.

James opens his eyes only long enough to cast a glance at me and smile. "Is the trip worth it for the bath alone?"

"That remains to be seen. The bath combined with a proper dinner just might be worth it but ask me again when we actually begin our work."

We fall into a comfortable silence, punctuated only by the sound of me scrubbing vigorously at my body and hair, and then simply enjoying the water until it begins to grow cold. James has long since washed and crawled out of his tub, got into his undergarments and trousers. He alternates between gazing out the window and watching me, permitting me to enjoy myself, and only when I've risen does he lean back in his seat with a heavy sigh.

"Soooo hungry."

So am I, actually. We skipped lunch and our breakfast was a meagre one. "Soon," I promise, stealing a look out the window. Still light out, but it must be approaching dinner. "I suspect we won't be starting our investigation until tomorrow."

"I have something you can investigate before then," James says, and although I'm not facing him, I know by the suggestive tone of his voice he is undoubtedly wiggling his eyebrows in my direction.

I towel off quickly and reach for my clean clothes. "I'd rather not push our luck on our first day here, sweetheart."

"I have something you can—"

I snatch the sponge from my bath and chuck it at his face with a laugh, although he manages to dodge it. "You're horrid. Stop that!"

He grins, which rather ruins the effect of the seductive look he's attempting to give me. "Is that a yes?"

I slip on my trousers and close the distance between us, and with a sigh I lean in to kiss him. "Perhaps later, if you're well-behaved at dinner."

"I'm *always* well-behaved."

"Oh, are you? So, all the times you talk too much and get us into trouble…?"

"I have absolutely no idea what you're talking about."

"Like the time you told Franklin Proust he was so sour because he had a face like a horse? Did I imagine that?"

James almost giggles at the memory and bites it back, attempting to maintain some semblance of a sombre expression. "Perhaps we should have you see a physician, dear William, if you're having hallucinations. Also, Proust was being a prick to you."

I snort and turn away to resume dressing. "Just keep your most charming face on tonight, hm?"

He slides from his seat, and I feel the warmth of his body behind me as he ducks down and ghosts his lips against the back of my neck. "Only so long as you do your best not to fall all over yourself like a fool for Lady Adelia."

I contemplate elbowing him in the ribs, but he moves away before I have the chance.

By the time the pair of us have dressed, shaved, and I've chased James down with a handful of pomade to make sense of his hair, Mr. Foss has returned to fetch us with an announcement that dinner will soon be served. Thankfully, a smidge earlier than usual, on our behalf because Lord Wakefield suspected we'd be famished.

When we're ready, Foss leads us to the dining hall. The sight of everything so lavishly decorated, the glitter of chandeliers and fine silver, a wine-coloured table runner, centrepieces each with freshly plucked flowers, almost makes me homesick for my parents' house.

Almost.

As far as I'm aware, it will only be us, Lord Wakefield, and his daughter dining tonight, but the entire table has been done up. James leans over to say, "If the baths were that nice, can you imagine what the food must be like?"

Lord Wakefield joins us with a bright smile. He, too, has changed clothes, and I wonder if it's on our behalf or if he really is this grandiose that he felt he couldn't show himself to us twice in the same day with the same outfit.

"Gentlemen, you look rejuvenated. I hope you're hungry."

"Always," James says predictably. "You've a lovely home here, my Lord."

Wakefield takes a seat. "You're too kind. I'm afraid I can't take credit for it, however. My late wife did most of the decorating."

My stomach lets out a plaintive growl and I press a hand to it, hoping no one else heard it. If I'm this starved, James must feel like he's dying. "Have you been without her long?"

"A number of years now. It is not a new loss." Wakefield's

mouth turns down with sadness, but only briefly before he's smiling again. "The memory of her is all around this home, and my darling daughter possesses the spirit and beauty everyone adored in her mother."

"You're too given to flattery, Father," Adelia says from the doorway, but she wears a small smile that suggests she doesn't mind the comparison at all.

Wakefield immediately rises to his feet and James and I do the same out of politeness. He steps around to get his daughter's chair for her, and she takes a seat with immense grace and not at all hindered by the bustle of her dress.

"I hope I'm not late."

"Right on time," Wakefield says with a fond smile before the three of us return to our seats.

Of course she would sit right across from me, making it difficult to avoid looking at her. Now I'm trying *too* hard not to stare and it occurs to me I have no idea how much looking at a person is *too* much—until James nudges me with his foot under the table. I steal a flustered look at him, aware I'm likely only making matters worse but unsure of how to fix it. "Judging by this hall, I suspect you often have dinner guests?"

"Indeed. Father is very social."

"Nothing wrong with that. James is much the same. Makes friends everywhere he goes, really."

Adelia regards me coolly. "Does that include spirits?"

"I'm not certain either of us 'makes friends' with the dead. Though one of the techniques we employ to help them pass over is to speak to them, sympathise, encourage them to find peace. James is quite good at that."

"And what is your strength, Mr. Esher?"

Such a question makes me slightly falter. What *is* my strength? James says the spirits seem to like me better, whatever that means. Miss Bennet says I'm sensitive to the dead, a trait I share with Benjamin Prichard and herself. It would explain why a spirit was able to take possession of me back at Whisperwood, but I'm not certain I would call that a *strength*.

"I suppose my strength would be keeping James out of trouble."

James chuckles. "William is certainly the more level-headed between the two of us."

"I merely possess more common sense," I point out with a slight smile. "Our methods of working seem to balance out well. What of you, Lady Adelia? What sort of pursuits interest you?"

The doors swing open as servants carry in platters with the first course. Soups, pies, ham, and kidney beans. This in and of itself is more than James and I have grown accustomed to eating for an entire meal, and my stomach gives another eager rumble.

"More earthly ones, I'm afraid," Adelia says. "I enjoy reading. Scotland Yard and their cases are of interest to me."

"Really? What of them?"

"The journey not only of justice, but the learning and understanding of the criminal mind." She places a napkin across her lap. "I enjoy knowing what makes people tick, whether or not a person can be redeemed after committing horrible atrocities. I also like the methodology in unravelling such mysteries."

I watch her in quiet interest as she speaks. Not the sort of thing I would have expected from a woman of her social standing. "In that case, I'd be interested in hearing your opinions on this situation with the Brewers. It sounds as though you're far more versed in these sorts of cases than we are."

41

Lord Wakefield clicks his tongue. "I'm not so sure such talk is really for a lady's ears, gentlemen."

The way Adelia's lips flatten into two thin lines does not go unnoticed. "Of course, Father."

I frown and think to argue. Adelia's knowledge would be no less useful to us just because she's a woman, but I hold my tongue and decide to file it away as a subject to approach her with later, in his absence.

"Well," I offer quietly, as Lord Wakefield has turned his attention to his glass being filled by one of the servers, "forensics is a fascinating subject, and one the world could use more sharp minds to improve upon."

The sharp edge to her gaze appears to soften ever so slightly, but she says nothing further on the subject.

"Dinner smells absolutely divine." James eyes the soup and bread as though he's ready to devour it straight from the serving bowl. A servant fills both my glass and his.

"As it should! Please, help yourselves. Eat your fill." Lord Wakefield lifts his own glass and tips it in our direction. "To new friends and, I hope, to solving the mystery of the Brewers."

We tip our glasses in a toast, and I waste no time in taking a longer drink than is probably necessary. It's past time for my medication, and that unsettled, anxious feeling has begun to set in. Not as effective as my laudanum, but it will help.

James, meanwhile, promptly digs into his food. "What were they like, the Brewers?"

Wakefield leans back in his seat, and the sip of wine he takes is far politer than mine was. "The Brewers were good people. Kind. They possessed an excellent work ethic. Almost everyone in the area has purchased horses from them; they were quite adept breeders."

"So they had no enemies?"

"None that I could name. However, their neighbours might be better able to answer that. Adelia and I rarely saw them outside of church and the occasional social function."

I take another long pull from my wine. "You're putting forth a lot of effort to assist people you were not close with. Very kind of you."

Lord Wakefield tips his head. "Our community is a small one, Mr. Esher. I'm in the financial position to help others, and so I do."

James asks, "And there were no complaints of oddities from other properties?"

"None beyond what the Brewers reported seeing to their neighbours. Oh, I do have photographs of the scene, if that would help."

I swallow down a bite of food. "Of the bodies?"

He ducks his gaze. "No. I'm afraid I hadn't the stomach for it, but I requested one of my servants to capture the footprints outside before the snowfall could cover them. I thought they might assist the police in their investigation."

"Did anyone follow them to see where they led?"

"A group of men did follow them into the woods, but the prints vanished after a time. Even the hounds could not keep on the track."

"If one were to continue in the direction of the footprints," James asks, "what would be the first man-made structure they encountered?"

Wakefield pauses and frowns, giving that a long moment of thought. "Well, trees and hills for quite some time, really. I suppose the closest structure would be the Clarks' property. Or the Marshalls'."

"Perhaps they saw or heard something."

"They were questioned, but I wasn't privy to whatever they may have told the detectives."

I glance at Adelia, wondering if she's seen the photographs or even the scene of the crime itself. I suspect her father wouldn't approve of such things. "Those photos would be most helpful. And if someone would escort us to the farm tomorrow, we'd like to look around."

"I can escort them," Adelia pipes up, though her eyes remain on her food. "I know you've business matters to tend to."

Wakefield gives her a patient smile, not unkind but entirely too patronizing. "I'm certain Albert will be happy to go." He pats her hand. "Until whatever this is has been dealt with, I prefer you not to be in harm's way."

I lower my attention to my food, nursing my guilt that I can't say anything to defend her, and unsure that she'd want me to, anyway. For the time being, I decide to coax the conversation in another direction, figuring it better for Adelia's mood to do so.

Dinner is a delicious and robust four courses, from which I try some of nearly everything placed before me. I eat until my stomach aches, because I have months of feeling hungry to make up for. I might also have had a glass too many to drink, but I still have my wits about me. James easily puts away twice the food that I do.

After our meal, Wakefield extends an offer to join him in his smoking room to take a look at the photographs. James' eyes are heavy-lidded, and we exchange glances that say we both are full and worn out and would much prefer to retire to a room and lie all over one another to sleep, but—work first. Right.

44

I've never been fond of tobacco myself, and the smell inside the room is ingrained in the walls and furniture and makes my nose crinkle. I will, however, take the offered glass of brandy, and the envelope Wakefield offers to me. I have a seat upon the settee and James joins me, hip to hip, while I slide out the photographs.

The first few images are of the farm itself, unassuming and ordinary enough. The front door stands wide open, and I can make out the small, dark splotches of footprints, and in some, the inky stains against all that white. I surmise what I'm looking at there must be blood.

I can feel James' breath against my shoulder. "Was it snowing heavily?"

"Not terribly, no." Wakefield has a seat across from us, leaning back in his chair with his smoking jacket on and a pipe in hand. "But it took the investigators quite a while to arrive, so I worried much of what was there would be gone by the time they showed up."

James makes a noise. "What did the investigators say when they saw these? Did they have any idea what sort of person they were looking for?"

"I'm afraid the police didn't determine much of anything," Wakefield says with a frown. "They believe it was a vagrant. A robbery, perhaps, and that the damage done to the bodies was the work of wild animals drawn by the smell after they'd been murdered."

A possibility, but a bit of a stretch. What sort of person— drifter or no—would break into a simple farmhouse to steal something? It sounds as though they had little to offer. James plucks one of the photos from my hand to bring it closer to his face, studying it with a sombreness he only ever displays when invested in his work. Or me.

45

James says, "May I ask your personal opinion, Lord Wakefield? I know you suspect the supernatural, but why?"

Wakefield sighs, swirling his brandy around in his glass. "I did not know the Brewers to be people who spooked easily, Mr. Spencer. When I heard they had claimed something unearthly was occurring at their home, I believed them."

"I see."

I come to the end of the photographs and look up. "We'd like to go over there first thing in the morning, just to look around. Then tomorrow night, it's probably best if we stay there."

Wakefield's brows shoot toward his hairline. "You want to stay there all night?"

"If we don't encounter anything during the day, then yes. Spirits tend to be easier to communicate with in the late hours."

He's staring at us as though we've lost our minds. "As you will. But at least allow some of my men to accompany you."

"The offer is appreciated but unnecessary. James and I are better equipped to handle this sort of thing on our own." Without novices getting underfoot, that is.

James gives an easy smile, not seeming the least bit bothered by the notion of staying the night at a murder scene. "We'll be all right."

I wish I possessed half of the confidence James does. I err on the side of uncertainty and scepticism, and at the moment, Wakefield seems to be sharing my sentiments.

For another hour or so, he keeps us there in the smoking room, refilling our glasses as we please—water for James—and chatting about the case. He explains where the bodies were found, tells us they were brought into the nearby town of Aylesbury, and that they've yet to be interred while the police try to determine what happened. Dread sinks into my stomach at the thought that we might have to pay a visit to that morgue and investigate the bodies ourselves, but one step at a time, right?

Before the hour grows too late, I politely excuse us for bed. I'm tired from a long day of traveling and socialising, I've not had my medicine since this morning, and while I've had enough to drink to make up for that it's made focusing on anything difficult. We bid Wakefield a good-night. He smiles and tips his head to us, although he makes no move to get up himself.

As I fall into step alongside James to head to our rooms, I ask, "Thoughts?"

James yawns. "I think we will find the person responsible for this. Wakefield and the rest of the community are swayed by the violence of this case and want it solved, and I feel those footprints weren't investigated well enough."

I cock an eyebrow. "You think we'll be able to figure out what the police have not?"

"Do I think I'm smarter than a group who decided the trail ended just because the tracks faded in the snow?" He rolls his gaze over to me, a smug little smile playing across his lips. "Yes."

"And you say *I'm* the condescending one."

He sniffs. "It's not often I feel intellectually superior, dear William. Let me bask in it."

"I will bow before your brilliance, darling."

When we come to our hallway, I enter my room with James on my heels. I figure he will want to change in here, give me my laudanum, and permit me to steal a kiss before we must separate for the night. He shuts the door behind him.

"However will you survive tonight without me?" he asks.

"I shall cry myself to sleep, I think." I sink onto the side of the bed to remove my shoes and shrug out of my coat. Alcohol mixed with my laudanum, which is just more alcohol and opium, tends to lend itself to a heavy sleep, but I'll not point that out right now lest he decide to withhold my dosage for the night.

He flashes me a grin as he slides the small bottle from his pocket. "That's what I like to hear."

Lashes lowering, I brace my hands upon the mattress and lean back. "Will you write poetry about how terribly you miss me?"

"Don't I always?" He plucks the dropper from the bottle, stops before the bed, between my legs, and places a few measured drops into my mouth.

Even after all this time, it never feels like enough. I'm not foolish enough to say as much to James and cause him to worry. On the very rare occasion will I beg him for more just to get through a particularly strenuous day, but now is not one of those times where I will play upon his emotions to talk him into giving it to me. Once he's replaced the bottle back into his pocket, I snag the front of his shirt and drag him down for a kiss.

With a pleased sigh, James leans into me, and I wonder if he can catch the traces of laudanum on my tongue. When he finally draws back enough to speak, he asks, "Are you *sure* I can't stay?"

"It would be unwise," I murmur against his mouth. "But do believe me when I say I'm tempted."

His lips twitch into a smile. "What if I got naked? Would that tempt you more?"

I bite back a laugh. "Well, you *do* need to get changed."

"I'll behave for now." He grins, stealing another kiss. I catch his lower lip between my teeth gently when he pulls away.

"Yes, yes, go on. Try to get some rest."

After James has fetched his nightshirt and departed, I strip out of my clothes, wash, and change before crawling into bed.

And, oh, it's a terribly comfortable bed. I sink into it with a groan, face buried into the pillows. Still, as comfortable as it is, it's been quite literally months since I've slept without James beside me and it feels downright unnatural. Repeatedly, I reach for him only to find him not there. Were it not for the laudanum working through my system and the fact I am a touch drunk, I fear I would not be able to sleep at all.

I wake feeling surprisingly well-rested and far too comfortable to crawl out of bed immediately, preferring to savour the moment a bit longer. I'm tempted to stay here and feign sleep for a few hours.

Except we have things to do. I drag myself from the warm cradle of blankets and ready myself for our day, washing and dressing before crossing the hall to James' room. He is, of course, still asleep. At least, until I open the door and announce, "Up, James." At which point he groans and pulls the blankets over his head and mumbles at me to go away.

"If you want breakfast, you'll need to get up."

"No, sleep time."

He's impossible. I glance either way down the hall, step into the room, and shut the door behind me before moving to kneel upon the edge of the bed. "I will eat your share if you don't get up."

"No." A wayward hand darts out to grab at me and I lean out of its reach.

"We have work to do, darling. Unless you would send me off to a murder scene alone?"

That hand thumps to the mattress. "Have fun."

I scowl. Then I grab the edge of the blankets and yank them right off of him. James responds with a sharp, hollow whimper as he blindly gropes for the covers. "Why?!"

"Because you're being terribly rude," I say, flinging the blankets as far to the bottom of the bed as I can. "Please get up."

"You're terribly rude," he whines. "I was having the loveliest dream."

Well, that must be nice. I take a seat upon the bed and fold my hands in my lap. "You can tell me all about it while you dress."

He does sit up, albeit slowly. "But it's cold. Why am I being punished for you taking this job?"

My mouth thins out. My patience is running thin. "Hm."

"Let me get dressed, you brat," he relents, chucking his pillow at me, which I catch and tuck behind my head. *I'm* already dressed so I can afford to lounge a bit while he prepares for his day.

"What did you dream about?"

James gives a pitiful sniff and shuffles over to his wash table. "I dreamt that I used our payment for this job to buy the most delicious cake in the world."

"That dream can become a reality if you continue getting up on time."

"I take that as permission to use all of our earnings to buy cake."

"If you do, you'll be finding yourself a new lover to keep you warm at night."

"After all that cake, I shall be large enough to warm myself, thank you very much." James glances over his shoulder, beaming, positively chuffed with himself.

There's little I can do but to tip my head back and let out a long, suffering sigh.

We tuck in for breakfast alone, as Lord Wakefield is a late sleeper. No surprise there. I recall being at home with my family and how normal it was to stay up all hours of the night and sleep late. Before Whisperwood, my days rarely started before noon. Such is life for the well-heeled. I'm fine with that; it means no pressure to make casual conversation. Filling my belly for a second meal in a row is heavenly, and I will miss this when we return to London.

After we're done, Foss is ready and waiting to take us to the Brewers'. He greets us with a curt bow, holding open the carriage door. "Good morning, gentlemen. I trust you slept well?"

"Like a dream," James responds, slipping inside.

"Excellent." Foss steps in after me, settling in the seat across from us. Momentarily, the driver flicks the reins and the carriage lurches forward. "Lord Wakefield wishes to extend an invitation to join us for mass today, by the by. He loathes the idea of you missing out on the Lord's day for work."

I grimace and look out the window to avoid being the one to answer that. Church is an uncomfortable place for an atheist, a discomfort I only suffer through for special occasions when James wishes to go, because I'm not heartless enough to make him go on his own. I hardly believe in God, and even if I did, I would find no comfort in the walls of a place that believes us and what we share to be sinful.

"That was very kind of him." The amusement in James'

voice is evident to me but goes unnoticed by Foss. Despite it not being any sort of a commitment, Foss smiles and seems to take it as one.

"Wonderful. It will also grant you the opportunity to meet several other families who knew the Brewers."

I must grudgingly admit that it would be convenient to have everyone in one place to speak to but, ahh… I push the thought aside for now. I suppose we're going to church after all.

The Brewers' farm is about fifteen minutes down the road. Not far, really, though it's slow-going due to the snow. The carriage comes to a halt at the end of the long driveway, which has not been shovelled and therefore is in no shape for the carriage wheels to make it through. Foss steps out and holds the door for James and me to exit, and he seems prepared to accompany us.

I hold up a hand. "We're all right on our own, Mr. Foss."

He frowns deeply. "Are you certain?"

"Quite. If we have any questions, we'll file them away for later." We don't need someone getting underfoot, after all. "If you'd mind sending the carriage back for us in a while, that will do just fine."

He glances to James but nods reluctantly and fishes a key from his pocket, which he hands to me, and then clambers back into the carriage to return home.

It's cold and the farm is so eerie in its silence that my stomach is already in knots, but I offer a tight smile to James and begin heading through the snow. He falls into step alongside me, hands crammed into his coat pockets.

"Are you well?" he asks.

I glance askance at him. "A question better served for

after we've looked at the house. I imagine this is going to be a bit…messier than our usual jobs."

"Would you prefer if I went in on my own first?"

My insides somersault at the mere thought, making me feel ill. "Over my dead body."

He chuckles. "Well, I offered."

"You do enough reckless things even when I'm present." I survey the area. The horses and whatever other animals the Brewers possessed are notably absent. No doubt the neighbours took them in to avoid them starving to death, left here alone.

Under Miss Bennett's guidance over the last several months, I've grown quite good at attuning myself to the atmosphere of the places we work. Here is no different. The uneasy sensation rolls off the Brewers' farm in waves, making my vision momentarily blur and my stomach roll. Needing to give myself a moment, I slide the key to James. He unlocks the door and steps inside without hesitation, and as I always do, I keep on his heels.

Before we can even take in the scene, the smell crashes into us in one overwhelming wave. I clamp a hand over my nose and mouth. It's cloying, nauseating. The source being the copious amounts of blood soaked into the flooring amid the overturned furniture and dishes strewn about. It looks less like the scene of a murder and more like a pack of wolves tore through a herd of sheep. "Christ…"

James wheezes, yanking a handkerchief from his pocket to cover the lower half of his face. "Did the thought of airing this place out occur to no one?"

"Clearly not." I leave the door open wide and promptly move to the nearest window to shove it open. James follows suit.

"Should we examine the outside for a bit?" he asks.

Although I think he's attempting to be kind for my sake, I say, "No point. Everything happened in here."

Beyond the smell and the horrifying smear of gore and blood all over the kitchen, I try to remember my training with Miss Bennett, closing my eyes and focusing. It's difficult to describe, like the subtle tug of a single thread wrapped around someone's finger, except that thread is tied about my ribs and sometimes figuring out the direction it wishes me to go is nigh impossible. This time, however, it leads me out of the single large, main room that serves as a living space, kitchen, and dining area, and into a bedroom.

A children's bedroom. Which, at first glance, appears to be in mostly decent shape—save for the crudely made bassinet in the corner, with its blood-soaked blanket hanging half out.

Immediately I turn away, and James is right there, his shoulders tense as he takes in the sight before us.

"Whoever did this deserves a far worse fate than any law is capable of doling out," I whisper.

"I'm not certain there's any punishment worthy," he softly agrees.

I place a hand against James' chest, the feel of him there helping to ground me and slow my racing heart. "What sort of monster kills a baby?"

James covers my hand with his own. "One we're going to find."

I'm glad one of us is confident about that.

Before I can respond, the flicker of something on the edge of my sight snags my attention. The hair along the back of my neck stands to attention. "James."

His grip on my hand twitches tighter. He turns to follow my gaze. "What did you see?"

I don't know. Something. Nothing. It doesn't *feel* malicious, whatever it was, but I'm hardly as adept at telling the difference as someone like Miss Bennett. "Something back in the other room."

James' jaw tightens briefly. He releases me and moves out of the doorway. In the main room, a small, silent wisp of a shadow slips through the front door. There's no mistaking it's a young boy, which gives me pause because I'm not so certain my stomach can handle seeing the ghost of a mangled child—especially if it turns out to be an angry one.

We follow it back out into the cold. The pale boy nearly vanishes against the snowy backdrop. He does not halt, however, moving toward the treeline. My heart lurches into my throat. This is too reminiscent of Whisperwood, of following dead boys in the woods to hidden tunnels…

Except we don't get more than a few paces from the house before the child ducks behind one of the trees, out of sight, and a long, low wail pierces the air and makes my spine go rigid. It even serves to still James for half a second—and then he's dashing forward, heading straight toward the sound. Because of course he does. I shake off the chill settling into my bones and give chase, swearing under my breath.

However, the spirit seems to have left us. Upon reaching the trees, we halt, turning full-circle, searching the towering trunks and branches and endless grey-and-white and find... nothing.

James scowls. "Damn it! Do you see anything?"

I grab his arm, lest he try to run off on me again. "No, nothing. We've lost him."

"There's a reason he ran out here," he mutters, beginning to move further into the woods. I tighten my hold on his arm to halt him. The last thing we need is to wander into unfamiliar territory in the cold and get turned around without lanterns or any means of finding our way back.

"We'll have better luck making contact at night. We'll try to speak to him next time, now that we know they're still here."

For a few heartbeats, James lingers, and I worry he's going to insist on giving chase to ghosts we cannot see. Finally, he sighs. "Let's head back inside."

I permit myself to relax and ease my hold on his arm.

Back inside, the smell is still strong, but dissipating slowly. The last, unexplored room we check is another bedroom, looking to have belonged to Mr. and Mrs. Brewer themselves. A lone bed is shoved against the wall. It is the only space here that appears free of blood and gore, so I suppose this is where we'll sleep tonight, although we will need to take turns keeping watch.

The blood on the floor has long since dried, but I still hesitate to walk where it has soaked into the floorboards. I put the kitchen table upright again, stooping to pick up objects that were scattered in the struggle; a few eating utensils, bowls, knives, potatoes. I don't know why I do it, just that seeing everything in such disarray is too unsettling.

James leans against the doorframe as he watches me clean up, arms folded across his chest, the cogs in his head no doubt working a mile a minute. I can always tell by the look on his face. "I'm still convinced a human is responsible for this."

I frown at that, leaning to draw shut the kitchen windows. They had the house locked up when we arrived, and it seems only proper we leave the place as we found it. "What makes you so certain?"

"Because a spirit would make no sense. How long had they complained of strange sightings? A few weeks? They've clearly lived here awhile, not just some family who moved in without knowing the house had a bad history. I've not heard tell of a spirit just…showing up and slaughtering a family."

"It could have been something lying dormant, but…" He has a point. This farm doesn't look particularly old, not like Whisperwood was, not like some of the manors and homes we've worked in. I wouldn't be surprised if Mr. Brewer himself built the place. "But just one person, though? You think one human was capable of slaughtering an entire family? It's obvious they put up a struggle."

James shrugs. "It wouldn't be the first time. Case in point, a man by the name of McConaughy, some years back… He killed an entirely family of six, all on his own."

Despite myself, I can't help but smile. "Look at you, doing your research."

He grins and bows. "I do what I can."

What a charming brat he is. "We'll see what the spirits have to say tonight, hm? For now, let's lock up and await Foss' return. Perhaps we can get some more information from the neighbours at mass."

He chuckles, straightening up and turning to shut the remaining windows. "I had been attempting to drag things out so you wouldn't have to go, you realise. I know you do worry about bursting into flames upon entering a church."

I sniff indignantly. "I could feign illness and make you go alone."

"By all means." He smiles sweetly.

I give his arm a shove as I move to the door. "Why are you so eager to leave me behind?"

"I'm not, but I do enjoy your adorable indignation."

Would he whine at me if I shoved him face-first into the snow? Likely. I settle for casting a sullen look his way instead.

We trek back up the path, taking our time to examine the outside of the house as we go. No sign of someone breaking in anywhere. Once we reach the road, it's a waiting game for the carriage to return. When it does, there's only the driver to greet us and no Mr. Foss. He hops down from his perch to open the door for us.

"Sirs, am I taking you to the chapel, or returning you to Lord Wakefield's?"

James steals a look at me. "To church, please."

I don't mope over it, at least not much. I did say it was a smart idea. My only regret is that I didn't take more of my laudanum this morning to get me through this.

Since we have the closed carriage to ourselves, the moment it's in motion, I wrap my fingers about James' and squeeze. He turns his head, lips brushing against my temple and his voice low. "Would you like a little more medicine, darling?"

My gaze snaps to him, unable to help the hopefulness creeping into my expression. "You've brought it?"

He smiles a little. "In case the house was too much for you, yes."

A relieved sigh finds its way past my lips. "You're an angel. Please."

James slides the bottle from his pocket, doling out a dropper full for me. I swallow it down and rest my head against his shoulder, feeling infinitely grateful for him in that moment. No matter what the situation, James is always concerned for me, always a step ahead in trying to ensure my comfort as much as he's able for a person who is never comfortable in their own skin.

His cheek comes to rest atop my head. "So perhaps now when you burst into flames, you'll not feel it as much."

I chuckle. "Mm, a possibility."

"Hopefully it won't last long."

"It's mass. It always lasts forever."

I can feel his mouth curve into a smile as I nestle my face into his throat. "You're always so dramatic."

The drive to church is not terribly long. The chapel's bell tower stands tall, but otherwise, it's a quaint little building, far smaller and simpler than the churches I'm used to in London. A number of people are in various stages of arriving. As we exit the carriage and follow them inside, my chest begins to tighten in that familiar ball of tension and nervousness that nothing but my laudanum knows how to untangle.

James takes the lead, as he's prone to do when he senses my discomfort; with him as a barrier between me and the world, it makes things a little more bearable.

Inside, small as the church might be, it's quite lovely. Well-lit, and the sunlight through the stained-glass windows casts everything in a beautiful prismatic glow. A brief scan of the chapel reveals that, while there are indeed quite a mix of people here, only the richest of the bunch are seated up front.

I spot Lord Wakefield and Adelia in the front row. Wakefield is chatting amiably with the occasional parishioner who stops by to greet him, and I nudge James in the right direction. When Wakefield spots us, he rises to his feet with a smile. "Glad you could make it."

"I'm glad we aren't late," James says pleasantly.

Wakefield beckons to the empty seats beside Adelia. James has a seat; however, he leaves the spot between Adelia and him open, and I'm not certain if he thinks he's doing me a favour or if he's getting back at me for making eyes at her before. Either way, I sink slowly down between them, wishing I could be in James' spot so that I might tuck myself as far back into the corner of the pew as possible where no one will notice me. I do offer a tight-lipped smile to Adelia and a *good morning*, because nervousness does not make me abandon my manners.

In return, Adelia offers a smile and murmurs under her breath, "You had the chance to avoid this; you should have taken it."

Such a response is understandably startling, and I glance at her with a brow cocked. "Well, I thought it might be rude to turn down the invitation."

"I don't know why it would be rude. You're not here to save your soul, you're here to work."

The smile her words coax out of me is a little more relaxed this time. "I *am* working. Which is also why I showed up."

Her eyebrows lift, and she seems to understand that I'm referring to needing to question people. "They'll talk you dry."

"That's all right," I chuckle. "I have a secret weapon."

"Your friend?"

"James could out-talk every person in this room."

Adelia looks about to respond, but from the front of the church, the vicar begins to speak, and she falls silent. I turn my attention to the altar.

The Reverend Bernard Thomas is close to Lord Wakefield's age. He's a thin man, just beginning to go grey, and possesses a kind smile that one would expect a man of the cloth to have. He greets everyone warmly, and if he happens to notice the unfamiliar faces in his front row, he either doesn't care or doesn't let it show.

Instead he delves right into his service, and I do try to pay attention. Really, I do. James humours me so often by not dragging me to church that I feel I owe it to him to not tune everything out this one time. But I'm certain, at some point, my eyes have glazed over in boredom and I'm biting back the urge to yawn.

KELLEY YORK & ROWAN ALTWOOD

When it comes time for communion, I freeze in my seat. Do I participate? It was something I sat out at Whisperwood, much to the displeasure of our school's chaplain. But here in the presence of strangers and our employer, I wonder if it would provoke too many awkward questions. I might very well be overthinking it; surely others will be sitting it out, too.

James touches my knee briefly as he rises and gives a reassuring nod of his head to let me know it's all right for me to stay put. I sink back against the bench, keeping my eyes downcast to avoid any curious or disapproving looks I might be receiving.

Only once Reverend Thomas concludes everything for the day do I finally relax.

Thank God.

Of course, the end of that just means the beginning of work for us, doesn't it?

Reverend Thomas bids each of the parishioners farewell from the front door. As we approach, Lord Wakefield greets him jovially. "Lovely sermon, as always, Reverend." He then beckons to us. "Mr. Spencer, Mr. Esher, this is Reverend Bernard Thomas. Reverend Thomas, James Spencer and William Esher."

"You must be the ones here investigating the Brewers." Reverend Thomas smiles and extends a hand, first to me and then to James. "Thank you for coming today. It's always a delight to see new faces in our church."

James sports a sunny smile. "I never turn down a good sermon. I hope we can be of some help."

"I certainly hope so. The Brewers were an important part of our community." A troubled frown crosses his face. "If there is anything I can assist with…"

"We do have questions," I say, glancing back at the other parishioners and wondering if we'll have time to catch them before they leave.

"Any information you might have about strange occurrences, people behaving oddly, anything the Brewers might have said, would all be immensely useful."

Reverend Thomas ducks his head into a nod, pausing only long enough to bid farewell to a few passing families. "About a week before their passing, Mrs. Brewer came to me. She said the children had been speaking of seeing strange things around the property. Shadows, people watching them. They brushed it off as overactive imaginations at first, until Mrs. Brewer herself woke one night to someone outside her window."

"And yet no suspects?" James asks.

"They couldn't offer any descriptions," he says, shaking his head. "Just shadows."

"What of the footprints?"

"Ah, yes. Mr. Brewer told me of those. The children found them. The tracks came toward the farm, but not away. Mr. Brewer took two of his neighbours and tried to trace them to their origin but lost them about half a mile into the woods."

"Because of the snow?" I ask.

"Yes. Even the hounds could not keep hold of the scent, the men said."

That the hounds were able to find a scent at all means we are, in fact, dealing with a person. Or people. As far as I'm aware, dogs cannot track a spirit.

James asks, "No one who lives nearby has seen anything since?"

"Not so far as I've been told," he says apologetically. "Their neighbours would be the Griggs and the Clarks, if you'd like to speak with them."

I purse my lips, looking to where he points to a group of people conversing nearby. "Someone mentioned you were asked to perform a blessing on the farm."

The vicar's gaze drops, guilt overtaking his features. "Yes. I was scheduled to go over there, but—well."

James' expression softens. "Honestly, Reverend, if there was something there strong enough to do what it did, then I'm not certain anything you could have done would have helped."

"It's kind of you to say so, Mr. Spencer, but I can't help but wonder if I'd gone to see them sooner..." He draws in a deep breath, letting it lift his slumped shoulders and raise his head. "Does this mean you believe this was caused by something supernatural?"

"That means I wouldn't rule it out. It would be foolish to lean in one direction or the other so early on."

I glance at James, knowing better. "Thank you very much for your assistance, Reverend. I believe we'll catch the other families before they leave and see if they can offer us anything further. James?"

Without waiting for a response, I dip my head in a polite nod and turn to descend the steps of the church. I think the Griggs and the Clarks must have been waiting for us, because they cease their conversations and turn our way as we approach.

Unlike the talkative friendliness of Wakefield and Reverend Thomas, these families are quieter, eyeing us with uncertainty. I can't say I blame them. It was Mr. Griggs who found the Brewers, and as such, most of our questions are for him. He recounts the day in a sombre voice and with a haunted look upon his face, eyes downcast. He found Mr. Brewer first, face-down in the kitchen. Three of the children were there with him. Meanwhile, Mrs. Brewer had fled into the children's room in a desperate attempt to retrieve the baby, and it was there they found her and the infant in similar states of mutilation.

James lowers his gaze. "We'll do everything in our power to apprehend whoever—or whatever—is responsible."

Mr. Griggs' jaw tenses. "You find whoever did it, boy, I suggest you hand 'em over to those that knew those people. No need for law enforcement after what we'll do to 'em."

"Thank you again for your assistance." I bow my head as he turns to follow his family. But left alone again, I turn to James with a sigh. "So, they had no enemies, this is not a pattern, and we have no suspects."

James scratches a hand back through his hair. "A vagrant would be rare, but not unheard of."

"To what end?" I mumble. "Why kill a family who had so little? Nothing seems to have been taken. No money, no possessions. Even all the horses were accounted for."

"And to what end a haunting? The house has no history we've heard of, and I haven't heard of any member of the family disturbing a spirit. There are also the dogs. If they followed a scent, it couldn't have been a ghost."

I sigh, folding my arms against the cold. Wakefield and Adelia are lingering nearby, conversing with some of the other parishioners, but I see them steal glances at us now and again, clearly waiting for us so we can depart as a group. "Well, I suppose we only have one way to find out. Let's return to Lord Wakefield's and prepare for tonight."

4

THE hours at Evenbury tick by, but at least they include another full meal and a brief tour around the estate. It's an impressive place. The gardens themselves are vast and undoubtedly stunning during the spring and summer. Even now in the snow, they're quite enchanting.

An hour before sunset, however, we request to be returned to the Brewers'. Wakefield again asks if we're certain we don't want company and I politely decline. While there is strength in numbers, having novices underfoot will only serve as a distraction. James and I have spent months honing our abilities, learning to be more in-tune with the spirits, learning how to defend ourselves against them. Even so, we still have much to learn.

James seems as unbothered as always at the prospect of facing not one, but an entire family of the dead. He pats my leg during the drive and says, "If we can handle Whisperwood, we can handle anything."

Wakefield's driver returns us to the farm with a long, almost solemn look, as though he suspects he's never going to see us again. Not a settling feeling, to be certain. I grab our bag of supplies and a lantern, and hop out, unable to help a shiver that sends gooseflesh across my skin. It certainly looks much more ominous in the dark, doesn't it?

The carriage creaks away back down the road as the driver departs, leaving us standing on the side of the road, alone. Moonlight casts its haunting glow on the glittering blanket of snow.

James murmurs, "It's remarkably quiet."

"Too quiet," I agree.

Even the woods back at Whisperwood were never this silent. There'd been the wind rustling the trees, the low, haunting hoots of owls, and crickets chirping. Out here, everything is impossibly still. I find myself searching the shadows for any signs of movement, because I can sense *something* is off, but cannot for the life of me place what it is.

Inside is no more comforting. Everything is as we left it a few hours ago, but the blood on the floorboards looks black in the absence of proper light and the cloying scent is still noticeably present. We don't dare open the windows this time. The goal is to be locked in here with the spirits, and not give them an easy access to slip through our grasp again. While it is not a hard and fast rule, ghosts—for the most part—seem to abide by the same rules we do regarding barriers. Perhaps it's the memory of being alive that makes it so.

The moment the door is shut, I light our lanterns. James cups his hands and huffs a warm breath against them. "So, what's the plan?"

"This is your job and you're asking me?"

67

He laughs. "What are you, then? Merely an onlooker?"

"I'm here to ensure you don't do something stupid." Someone has to be the voice of reason when James gets ahead of himself, after all. I shut the lantern hatch and straighten up. "If you want my opinion, we should take turns keeping watch and see who, or what, shows up."

James arches a brow. "You want to be left on your own for any length of time?"

"You'll be asleep right next to me, won't you?"

"Asleep," he agrees, "unaware if something should happen."

"I appreciate you worrying, but I'm all right." No, I don't *like* having to face things on my own, but I've proven more than once that I *can*.

James ducks in to sneak a kiss. "You've come a long way, dear William. Do you want first or second shift?"

That simple gesture of affection eases some of the tension in my back. "I'll leave that up to you, although I'll not find sleep easy for a while yet." My laudanum would remedy that, but on a job like this, I've little choice but to forego it. I can't risk something happening and me being too drugged to respond appropriately. I wish I'd had more to drink at dinner to take the edge off.

We take some time to search the house, looking in closets and cupboards, seeking reassurance that we are, in fact, alone. A trip around the perimeter of the farm is also conducted, checking the windows from the outside. Once James is satisfied it's just the two of us, he slips out of his coat and settles upon the Brewers' bed with a yawn. "Enjoy your first shift."

I have a seat beside him, legs stretched out before me, a hand in his hair to help coax him to sleep. "Sweet dreams, darling."

He rests a hand upon my thigh, and it's no surprise to me that despite the surroundings and the circumstances, James is quick to drift off. I might envy him, that ability to sleep anywhere, were it not for the nights I've seen him hardly sleep at all due to nightmares. They're a less frequent occurrence these days, but still as vicious when they do happen.

As James rests, I pluck a book from our bag to read by lantern-light. I alternate between focusing on the words upon the page and remaining idly aware of the house around us.

I'm not certain whether I doze off, or if I've simply lost concentration, but a dull *thud* from the other room kicks my heart into my throat and my spine goes rigid. Gaze snapping up, through the doorway, I spot something rolling across the floor of the kitchen.

Should I wake James? It could be nothing. It could be something.

Slowly, I place the book aside and slide out of bed. James sighs plaintively and rolls onto his other side but does not wake. I step to the doorway first, and then out into the main room, stooping to pick up the object that has come to rest just beneath the dining table.

A ball. A child's toy.

When I look left, to the direction it came from, I spot a boy crouched in the corner.

In as far as I can tell, it's the same child we spotted before. He can't be any older than five or six. His wide dead eyes are locked right onto me, and the gashes raked down the side of his face and the front of his chest make my stomach turn. The initial kick of fear is not more overwhelming than my sadness, and to be honest, he looks as frightened of me as I am of him. That fear could easily turn into anger and prompt him to attack.

I drop slowly to a crouch and roll the ball back to him. The child catches it, smiles with the side of his mouth that isn't a mangled mess, and rolls it back to me. Progress. Excellent.

Wakefield told us of the Brewers' children. They had four. Three daughters and only a single son, so— "Are you Douglas?"

He nods, opening his hands in a silent plea for me to return his toy. I do so.

"Hello, Douglas." I sink forward to my knees, keeping my voice low and easy. "My name is William. Do you know who came into your home and hurt you?"

Something akin to uncertainty flashes across the boy's face, but again, he nods.

"I'm here to help you. But to do that, I need to know more about who hurt you and where to find them. Can you tell me that?"

Douglas' face screws up into something pained. A shudder courses through his small body, and he heaves the ball in my direction forcefully enough that I have to duck aside to avoid being struck.

And then he's beside me, hand upon my shoulder, his voice a gargled whisper against my ear.

"*She's under the bed.*"

Cold floods through every fibre of my being. I plant a hand to the floor and twist around toward the bedroom.

Just in time to see the vacant eyes and bared teeth of a face appearing from beneath the bed James is sleeping on.

5

THE woman's nails drag across the floor with the most ungodly sound. As she hauls herself from beneath the bed and crawls to her feet, I'm doing the same, painfully and purposefully slow. In part because fear has closed its hands around my throat and momentarily paralysed me. In part because I know from experience that running from anything supernatural draws its attention.

She's dressed in nothing but a nightgown, soiled around the hems, and her feet are bare. Her hair hangs about her hollow face in matted blonde ringlets.

James stirs, sighs, and the woman begins to turn. Panic surges hot in my chest. Defenceless, he'll never stand a chance if she can tear into him the way she did the rest of the Brewers. But if I shout for him, if he startles awake, the movement might only further divert her interest to him.

The ball is still in my hand, my fingers gripping it so tightly my knuckles are mottled white. Without knowing if it'll do a spot of good, I slam it down to the ground. It gives only the dullest of bounces before rolling away, but the sound of it thudding to the floor at my feet is enough to regain her attention. She whips toward me, dry lips pulled back in a terrifying grimace, and I've forgotten every single bloody verse I should be reciting right now to try to quell her. I have just enough time to grab the phial of water from my coat pocket when she rushes at me.

The kitchen table is enough of an obstacle between us that a swift side-step on my part makes it a barrier. It does not hinder her. She leaps atop it and lunges at me, knocking the table and every adjoining chair aside.

When spirits grab you, the sensation is unearthly—a cold vice against your skin. Tangible but not. I brace myself just in time for impact, unable to open the holy water before she's slammed me to the floor. The feel of her, the weight of her atop me, is feverish and scorching.

Something is different. The fingers that begin to dig at my flesh are very, very warm and very, very much alive.

The burn of jagged nails rakes across my cheek and then through my shirt over my chest as she begins to tear at me. The blossoms of pain are only just bearable as I struggle to uncork the phial. A task that is abandoned when she sinks her teeth into the side of my throat, sending white-hot pain flashing into every inch of my body and ripping a scream from my chest.

The phial clatters to the floor. It's all I can do to wedge an arm against her throat to hold her at bay, her bloodied teeth snapping inches from my face.

I can scarcely think through the pain.

The water. I need the holy water.

72

Groping blindly with my free hand, I can't locate it. Instead, my fingers close around an object that must have fallen from the overturned table—a kitchen knife.

I swing up with as much force as I can, wedging the small blade into the woman's throat. It slides easily into the meat of her neck, glancing off her clavicle.

She snarls, but she does not stop.

Dimly, I hear James' voice shouting my name, but it does little to draw the woman's attention away from me. She's far stronger than she ought to be; she's a slight, bony thing, and yet it's taking everything I have to keep her from ripping into my face or throat again. Blood—my blood—drips from her gaping mouth, and I can feel my arms aching with the effort of trying to shove her away. "*James!*"

Not a moment later, James has his arms around her middle. The weight of her atop me finally vanishes as he heaves her off me and stumbles back. I suck in a sharp breath of air, shaky and dizzy. I roll to my side, again feeling around for the holy water, although I haven't the faintest where it's rolled off to, or if it even survived the fall.

The woman gnashes her teeth at James, one hand lashing out to catch him across the face. He's just a step ahead of her, holy water in hand. The second the water splashes across her skin, she shrieks and rears away. Rather than attack again, she shoves past him and makes a wild dash for the door, somehow having the intelligence to unlock it before fleeing outside.

For half a heartbeat, I fear James is going to give chase. But in the next second, he's scrambling to my side, bloodied scratches upon his cheek. "William! Are you all right?"

It hurts. God, it hurts. I'm shaken and largely in shock, so I haven't any idea how bad the damage is. I'm aware of the blood from the bite in my neck, the scratches along my jaw and chest where she tore right through my shirt. Mostly, though, I am frightened.

The moment James is close enough, I lock my arms around him, equal parts afraid and yet relieved, because he's all right. I'm completely useless at formulating any kind of answer to his question.

He drags me to him, stroking my hair and voice whisper-soft. "It's all right, darling. You're all right. She's gone now."

I tremble in his arms, a combination of fear and my heart racing as fast as it is, and I'm unable to tear my eyes off that door lest she return and catch us unawares. "She was—James, under the bed. She—"

"Christ." He sighs, placing kisses across my forehead. "I'm so sorry. I hadn't thought to check there."

It's hardly his fault; neither of us did. I drag in slow, deep breaths to steady my shaken nerves. As much as I want to bury my face against his chest and hide there awhile, I force myself to pull away, still jittery as I get to my feet and head for the door. In part to look outside to see if the girl has gone, but also because leaving the door gaping wide open is asking for trouble. "I stabbed her. She didn't even flinch."

James keeps close to my side, still watching me in concern. "She was human, wasn't she?"

"I… I don't know." I touch a hand to my bleeding throat, lightheaded. "What sort of human gets stabbed in the throat and keeps going?"

"One not right in the mind," James answers. "You can't stab a ghost, however, so what else could it be? Come, let me clean that and bandage it."

"Shouldn't we…" *Go after it*, is how I mean to finish that statement, but the words catch on the back of my tongue because I honestly, truly, do not want to. Not in the middle of the night in an unfamiliar place. I swallow it back and nod, shutting the door and locking it. How in the world did she get in here in the first place? *When*? Has she been hiding under that bed since before we arrived?

James ushers me into the bedroom where I shed my jacket, waistcoat, and bloodied shirt, and have a seat upon the edge of the mattress. He joins me in short order with a small medical supply kit we keep on hand and sets about tending to me. The sting of antiseptic against the open wounds makes me hiss between my teeth and he grimaces with a murmured apology.

I do my best not to squirm beneath his efforts. The scratches are flesh wounds, they'll heal fine. The bite is deep enough that it's likely to permanently mar my skin, but fortunately, she didn't bite deep enough to do any real damage. I'm still alive, after all.

My nerves are still alight, something unlikely to change until I sleep or medicate myself into a calmer state, although James' gentle attentions do help.

"Should we try to track her down?" I ask.

"In the dead of night, in a place we don't know?" James finishes wrapping the bandages about my throat and reaches into his pocket for my laudanum. I let out an audible noise of relief at the sight of it, refraining from grabbing it from him. James opens the bottle to dole out my dosage, which will not be enough to fully steady the racing of my heart, but it will help. "We'd only succeed in getting ourselves lost in the cold. We can search in the morning, perhaps ask around town. For now, you should get some rest."

It occurs to me only after I've swallowed the medicine that I probably should not have taken it for the very same reason I didn't take it earlier. "I'm not certain I should leave you to keep watch alone."

"I won't leave the room without waking you."

I could point out how useless I would be if woken after being medicated, but I don't have much of a choice. I extend a hand to touch his jaw, minding the scratches upon his cheek. "Let me clean those before I lie down."

It grants me a few moments to focus on something other than my own discomfort, to fuss over James while my medicine has a chance to take hold. I clean the wounds, and then lean in to press a kiss to his mouth. When I lie down, I take his hand in mine.

"I did see one of the children. The boy. He said that woman was the one who attacked his family."

James folds his hand securely around mine. "We'll have to ask around to see if anyone knows her."

"Mm. You promise to wake me if you see or hear anything?"

His expression softens. "I swear it."

"Thank you." I draw his hand to my lips, kissing his knuckles. "I love you."

Even with my eyes closed, I can practically hear the smile in James' voice as he says, "I love you, too."

As worked up as I am, my exhaustion coupled with my medicine will work quickly to put me to sleep. As I always do when medicated, I sleep like the dead, scarcely budging throughout the night. The most I do is reach out for James when I stir, insisting on holding onto him for dear life.

WHAT jars me awake some hours later is a rapping sound elsewhere in the house. Blinking blearily, it occurs to me that James has fallen asleep beside me, and that my head was resting upon his chest.

It also occurs to me that I *hurt*. The pain radiates all throughout my neck and into my shoulder. I sit up, touching a hand to the bandages as I inch to the edge of the mattress. The rapping appears to be someone knocking. Foss must have come to retrieve us.

"James, someone's here."

He makes a low noise. "Tell them to go 'way."

"I'm not sure that's an option." I brush his hair back from his face and push myself to my feet. If he wishes to stay put a bit longer, I'll not force him out of bed. Instead, I pull on my shirt and make swift work of buttoning it, and then head into the other room to open the door. Surprisingly, it is not just Foss standing there, but also Lord Wakefield himself.

Wakefield's eyes widen at the sight of me in my crimson-stained clothes and bandages. "Good Lord. Mr. Esher, what's happened?"

"It was a long night." I step aside to let them in. Wakefield hesitates, and the way his gaze darts about the room makes me wonder if this is the first time he's been inside this house since the murders. He did say he hadn't the stomach to see the bodies, and none of the photographs he showed us were of the interior of the farm.

The kitchen is a disaster from last night. I right all the furniture so at least everyone has a place to sit, and it's with a grimace that I realise some of the blood on the floor is now mine. "I encountered one of the ghosts last night. The Brewers' son."

Wakefield sinks slowly into one of the chairs, eyes locked onto me and expression unreadable. "He couldn't possibly have done that to you, did he? What did he say?"

I proceed to explain the events of last night, up to the point where the woman fled the house. Foss and Wakefield stare at me in silent horror and disbelief, sharing looks now and again as though they aren't certain what to make of this.

After I've finished speaking, James chimes in, "We were hoping someone would be able to recognise the woman based on her description."

I glance over to where he's leaned against the doorway with his arms across his chest. He's not even bothered to button up his shirt, and were we alone, I'd be inclined to pause and admire the lovely line of exposed skin.

Wakefield looks to James, seeming to take in the wounds on his face, as well. "What did she look like?"

"Small," I say. "Your daughter's height, perhaps. It was difficult to tell. Long, blonde hair." I couldn't tell him the

78

colour of her eyes, seeing as she looked half-dead, clouded irises and all.

Wakefield's brows furrow. "I mean, that could be any number of women, really."

"Given that she was in a nightgown, I suspect she was a local girl not terribly far from home. Know of anyone who's been acting odd as of late?"

Foss shakes his head. "You said she ran off. Did she leave footprints? Could we attempt to track her?"

"That was our next plan. We were just waiting for daylight," James says as I rise from my chair. "Which we have in abundance now. If it didn't snow too heavily in the night, we ought to be able to follow her tracks."

I step back into the bedroom to slip into a fresh shirt. The collar rubs stiffly against my damaged throat and I wince, deciding to forego my usual tie. I pull on my coat and toss James' to him before heading for the door.

It doesn't appear to have snowed much or at all, so the tracks are still prominent leading away from the farm. James shrugs into his jacket and off he goes, leaving me to fall into step alongside him and with Lord Wakefield and his assistant at our backs.

It's early enough that the sun is still low in the sky. Honestly, I'm surprised Lord Wakefield is even up at such an hour, though by the way he's yawning, it's clear he'd rather not be. Early or not, it's for the best that we be on this trail before something can disturb it.

The trees stand far enough apart that traversing the forest is not particularly difficult. I lose track of how long we walk. The prints, which began further apart as the girl ran, begin to close in distance, signifying when her gait slowed. It's only then that the blood becomes noticeable against the forest floor.

I'm so focused on those details and studying the prints that I damned near trip over the body.

James grabs my shoulder to steady me as I suck in a breath. We find ourselves staring at the woman lying face-down and motionless in a stain of red snow, her head angled toward us. Any doubts I may have harboured about what we saw last night being human are certainly dashed now. I needn't even go to her to see if she's breathing. Her eyes possess the glazed look of a corpse, and she's been here long enough that ice has begun to crystalize on her skin, glittering in her long lashes. The knife that was embedded in her throat when she fled is gone, which would explain the blood. Either it dislodged during her escape, or she extracted it herself.

Foss and Wakefield catch up to us, slightly winded from our trek.

"What is—oh, oh my goodness." Wakefield halts beside me. Foss hesitates, but crouches beside the girl, grimacing as he touches her shoulder to roll her onto her side so we might get a better look at her face.

I'm attempting to work through this in my head. She was alive last night. I felt her. Her skin was warm—too warm—and she was breathing. A living, breathing human being. Now she's dead and that is…

My fault. I'm the one who stabbed her.

I have never killed anyone before.

A small favour that my stomach is empty, else I fear I might lose my breakfast. As it is, I have to take a step back and turn slightly away. James keeps his hand on my shoulder, squeezing, studying my face, and I suspect he knows exactly what is going through my head.

"Isn't this… Isn't this Madeline?" Foss says to his employer. "Phineas' girl?"

Wakefield frowns, but he appears reluctant to get too close for a better look. "Now that you mention it, it might very well be."

"Who is that?" James asks.

Foss says, "Phineas Edison. Lives not far off from the church. His girl went missing a while ago."

I push a hand through my hair and force myself to turn back to the conversation, although I attempt to keep my eyes off the girl. Madeline. "A girl was missing? That would have been helpful to know when we asked if anyone was acting odd."

Foss shakes his head. "It was three, maybe four months ago. Her family thought she'd run off with a boy from another family."

"So, *two* people went missing?"

"Together, yes. Young lovers run off together all the time when their families don't approve. He was of a much higher station than she. No one thought much of it."

A frown pulls at James' features. "Who was the other?"

"Abraham Fletcher," Wakefield says.

"Sounds like we need to be looking for him, then."

Wakefield folds his arms across his chest. "To what end? We know now that this girl is responsible for the death of the Brewers, yes? If she's a murderer, then it's likely she ended that poor boy, too."

James gives him a sideways glance. "Forgive me, but somehow I doubt a woman of that stature could have slaughtered an entire family on her own."

"By the sounds of it," Foss interjects, "she was in possession of some impressive strength and did not even respond to being stabbed." He looks to me as he says this. "If she caught Mr. Brewer unaware, then the children and Mrs. Brewer would have been easy targets."

81

That is true, I'll grudgingly admit. But it still doesn't sit right with me. I cross my arms, huffing and looking to James. "We'll not sort any of this out standing here. We should have Miss Madeline here transported to the undertaker, see if we can't better tie her to the victims."

James purses his lips, still looking as though he wants to argue his point, but— "Yes, that would be for the best."

Foss waits with the body while the rest of us return to the farm and the driver. The next few hours tick by at a snail's pace; the police are summoned, which takes time, and James and I are questioned extensively to recount the attack of the previous night. Having to divulge our purpose for being at the Brewers' in the first place gets us several long, unimpressed looks…and a few uneasy ones. That's how you tell the believers from the non-believers, I suppose.

The part I prefer not to be present for is when the Edisons arrive to identify the body of their daughter, and thus I duck back into the farmhouse. I've no words of comfort to offer these strangers, but the sound of Mrs. Edison's wailing from outside near the road confirms well enough that the girl is— was—the missing Madeline.

And she's dead now because of me.

Exhaustion is settling in fast. We've not eaten, and it's still early in the day but I'm already feeling exponentially worn down and irritable. I press my fingers against my eyes.

"Let's follow the police into town," I say to James. "The undertaker is still in possession of the Brewers' corpses. We ought to see if they'll let us in. Any thoughts on this newest development?"

James has seated himself at the table and is watching me worriedly. "I don't think Madeline is the one who did this. Or, if she did, she was not acting alone. She was too wild to be focused enough to overcome an entire family."

"I agree. I think Wakefield is eager to lay the blame and call it done to bring closure to the community. Do you suppose that boy could have been her accomplice rather than her victim?"

He shrugs. "Anything is possible. I would like to speak to his family and hers. Try to get a feel for what kind of people they were, what they grew up in."

I sigh, pinching the bridge of my nose. Our line of work is not to follow leads to solve a murder mystery. However, I promised a week's worth of work, and I'll not back out of that now. I know what I saw, and what I saw was a living, breathing woman with the eyes of the dead.

Madeline's parents are still outside, but rather inconsolable at the moment. It might benefit everyone involved to give them some time before questioning them. "Very well."

The front door opens, and Foss pokes his head in. "The police are about to leave if you've any further questions."

Lord, I've the worst beginnings of a headache building behind my eyes. "No, but if Lord Wakefield doesn't mind, we'd appreciate the use of a carriage and a driver."

In short order, we're bound for town, following behind the wagon transporting Madeline Edison's body to the mortuary. It's going to be a bit of a drive, I'm restless and anxious, and the best cure for that just might be laying my head on James' shoulder and trying to sleep through it. James touches my cheek briefly and remains silent to allow me to rest, yet I sense his unease. The few times I steal looks up at him, he's gazing out the window, brows knitted together as though he's puzzling over something.

I do manage to doze along the way, but it's a fitful, uncomfortable sort of sleep so I'm not certain how rested I feel upon waking. The carriage has brought us to the morgue, which is a significantly smaller building than the morgues of London. While the police circle round to bring the body through the gates into the yard, our carriage has stopped on the street in front to let us out.

We've been to morgues and funeral homes a few times before, but it was only for identification purposes, not for actually *investigating* the corpses. My stomach rolls at the thought.

As we head inside I ask, "How much are we looking forward to this?"

James pockets his hands and wrinkles his nose. "Terribly much."

"Ah, have we found something that's distasteful even to you, darling?"

"Are you asking if I'm human after all? It's possible." He grins.

Inside the building, a burly, balding man—likely the mortician's assistant—greets us. After explaining who we are, he looks almost relieved.

"Does this mean we'll be able to move those bodies out of here soon?" he asks, leading us down a hallway dimly lit with gas lamps.

I frown. "I'm afraid I don't know. Where will they go when they leave here?"

He shrugs. "Not my concern. If they've no family left to claim them, and no one wishes to foot the bill for a burial, they'll go into pauper's graves."

Well, that's remarkably depressing.

The man opens a door at the end of the hall and gestures. The room within is large and chilly, likely kept cool for preservation purposes. While the morgues back home would have contained row after row of bodies, lined and stacked and some set out for viewing, this room contains maybe a dozen. A number of them belong to the Brewers.

"Have at it," he says. "Give a shout if you need anything."

"Thank you," James says, sliding the handkerchief from his pocket to cover his nose and mouth as the door shuts behind us.

I do the same as we move to the Brewers' bodies in the corner, although the smell is not as horrible as I anticipated. There's an undercurrent of something—lemon, I think— used to combat the stench of decay. I linger a few paces behind James, eyes roaming over the shrouded bodies with uncertainty. They're the only ones in the room who are covered, a testament to how badly they've been mutilated. The smaller shapes of the children are evident, and I plan to avoid them if I can help it. Instead, I draw back the sheet on one of the adults.

There is nothing to keep Mrs. Brewer modest beneath the sheet. She's already progressed in stages of decomposition, her honey-coloured hair matted with blood. She possesses ugly claw marks across her arms and abdomen and face, and her throat is ripped wide open in a way that makes me touch a hand to my own neck with a grimace.

James draws in a slow breath. "Poor thing..."

I have to look away for a moment while an unpleasant shudder flows through me. This could have been either of us last night. Had Madeline got to James before I'd distracted her...

Christ, I hate this job.

I turn to the neighbouring table and draw back the sheet. If Mrs. Brewer was in bad shape, Mr. Brewer is almost unrecognizable.

Together, we step back and stare at the bodies, as though some answer will magically make itself known to us. What are we searching for? What are we hoping to find? How could any living creature commit such an act against an innocent family?

I say, "I don't begin to understand what sort of insanity a person could possess that would have prompted something like this."

Beside me, James goes perfectly still for a heartbeat before his eyes snap wide and his chin lifts. "Possession."

My skin prickles. "Pardon?"

"The look on that girl's face… I've been trying to determine where I've seen it before, and it was *you*, William." He looks at me. "When that spirit took you over at Whisperwood. The clouded look in your eyes, the fever… Staring into your face but knowing you weren't really there? It's the exact same."

Of all the things James could say, this is on the more unnerving end of the spectrum. I shiver. "So she was, what, under control of a spirit? Not acting of her own accord?"

"It makes more sense than a girl going missing and popping up again just to slaughter an entire family."

This is not the answer I wanted to arrive at. Dizziness washes over me, that anxious, tight sensation in my chest rearing its ugly head and making it difficult to breathe. I brace my hands against the edge of the table.

"So, I murdered an innocent girl."

James frowns. "What—*no*. William, don't be foolish. She was trying to kill you!"

"Had I attacked any of you back at Whisperwood and someone killed me," I begin, not even needing to finish it. He knows damned well he would not have forgiven anyone for that.

"I would have been devastated," he admits, "but still— self-defence."

I'm not certain I agree with that. If Madeline Edison was possessed, then we could have done something. We could have *saved* her.

Ducking my head, I take a spell to try to shake it off. It's done, isn't it? I must stuff my guilt deep down because there's nothing I can do about it now. "All right. Possession, then. That would be a logical answer for her behaviour."

James' jaw clenches, and I think he means to lecture me because he knows I'm blaming myself. Instead he says, "The question now, then, is why and by what."

This changes the game. Most certainly, it places the job back into our realm of expertise. I rack my brain. "If we could figure out if that missing boy was still out there, then he might have answers." Or if he's dead…well, another dead end. No pun intended. I study Mr. Brewer, the bite marks upon his neck. "Lady Adelia said she's studied many unusual crime cases. She might have some insight for us, perhaps?"

James arcs an eyebrow. "We can ask her, I suppose."

"Unless you have a better idea. We're not anatomists, so this might have been a fruitless trip."

"You've got me there."

I replace the shrouds over Mr. and Mrs. Brewer with a sense of relief at not having to look at them anymore. "Then let's be gone. This place is unpleasant."

As I turn to go, James catches me by the elbow to draw my attention back to him. "Are you all right, William?"

Am I? I've been worse, certainly. "Ask me that again once we're out of here."

He squeezes briefly, the smile on his face an attempt to be comforting. "Let's go, then."

The carriage is still waiting for us outside, and I'm grateful for some peace and quiet during the trip back. Yet even in the silence, even in the calm, the nervous itching inside of my chest becomes all-encompassing and too much to bear.

"James, please," is all I murmur. He knows me well enough by now. Indeed, he does not even ask, merely produces the laudanum from his pocket.

It isn't an immediate fix, but to know the relief is coming does help. I take James' hand in mine, squeezing it tight, infinitely grateful for him and his endless patience. His lips press to my forehead, and that in and of itself is a gesture that helps to soothe me.

Upon returning to Lord Wakefield's, my stomach is a mess of protesting growls and hunger pangs. I can hear James' now and again, too. We ought to be just in time for lunch, so there's that. James even mumbles as he disembarks the carriage, "I'm going to eat everything in sight."

My medicine has had the opportunity to kick in during our journey, which leaves me blissfully relaxed and wanting a nap more than food now. I offer James a lazy smile. "You usually do, darling."

Foss greets us in the foyer, thin mouth curved down in its usual serious manner. "Welcome back, gentlemen. How did your adventure go?"

James pockets his hands. "I think we're getting a bit closer to finding an answer."

He tsks. "I worry you two are overthinking this. You've found the culprit, what more is there to find?"

I frown. "The how and the why are rather important, are they not?"

"Miss Edison is dead, regrettably. I doubt any answers will make anyone feel any better about that fact. However…" He beckons us, thankfully, toward the dining room, which hopefully means toward food. "Lord Wakefield is immensely pleased with your progress. He's holding a gathering tonight in your honour."

James pauses. "Pardon?"

"A party," Foss says. "Of course, if you both are not fully convinced the mystery is solved, perhaps it will be a good opportunity for you to meet and speak with more of the townspeople?"

Joy. I'm not the sort for parties. Oh, I love the idea of them. I love the dancing and the music, in particular, but it's the whole *people* bit I find distasteful.

James purses his lips, eyes sliding to the side to watch me, and I suspect he's thinking this is utterly ridiculous. "Of course."

Foss claps his hands together. "Wonderful. Everyone will be here, and they're undoubtedly looking forward to meeting you."

Somehow, I doubt *everyone* will be here. Likely, just the upper echelon. I'm far too medicated to care much at the moment, so I just roll my gaze briefly ceilingward. "Lovely."

James swallows a laugh and keeps his voice low. "I'm sure there will be plenty of drink to get you through."

Never as much fun when I'm drinking alone, though that never stops me. Medicated enough or drunk enough, I can put on quite a charming front.

Besides, I know well why James does not drink. It came about a few months after we began living together, one of the first times I found myself well into my cups after a job and, regrettably, a little persistent in wanting James to enjoy it with me. Bless him, he'd been so patient with my ineptitude, and he'd finally taken my hands in his and leaned in until our foreheads touched as he whispered, *What if I'm like* him *when I drink?*

That simple sentence had sobered me immediately, pierced to the quick of my heart to let guilt bleed right out. Never had I considered such a thing would cross his mind and, of course, I tried to reassure him. He is not his uncle. He is a good man with a good heart, and his uncle—that foul, disgusting, monster of a human being—had a dark soul and no morals.

Since then, I've not pressed him on the matter. Perhaps it's something he'll come to terms with someday. If not, that's all right, too.

Even now, he has a smile upon his face. "One of us has to keep our wits about us."

Foss pauses before the double doors to the dining room. "Lord Wakefield is attending to some business this afternoon to prepare for tonight, so he will not be joining you." He pushes open the doors, revealing a fine spread of food, and Lady Adelia seated there, already enjoying her meal, looking lovely in a blue dress, a few spirals of her neatly done hair purposely left cascading down the back of her neck. Just the person we wanted to speak to without her father present.

She lifts her head at the sight of us. "Good afternoon, gentlemen."

"Good afternoon, Lady Adelia," I say, having a seat. "Glad to have you joining us."

"There are whispers you've solved the case," she says, peering at us curiously.

"Whispers are often slivers of truth blown out of proportion." The food is already on the table, and we waste no time in beginning to serve ourselves, not inclined to wait for a servant to do it for us. "We've found a lead, but there are still a number of unanswered questions."

"Questions such as…?"

"How much did your father tell you?" James asks.

"That it was Madeline Edison who killed the Brewers… and that she attacked the two of you." Her eyes dart to my bandaged throat.

I nod. "All true. Miss Edison, we believe, was under possession at the time she committed the murders."

The look Adelia gives us can only be described as patient. "Possession."

"That's what I said." I pick up my glass to have a drink. "Now our goal is to find out what, precisely, possessed her so we can be rid of it lest it repeat the process with another unwitting victim."

"What makes you so certain it's possession?"

"Because James has seen it before."

Her gaze swings to James, who shrugs. "It's…a certain vacancy to the eyes, and she felt feverish to the touch. She also had some incredible strength and seemed to not feel pain."

I don't particularly care to get into the details of how James knows what he knows, so I'm quick to add on before Adelia can question it. "Suffice it to say, it's our best guess right now. We're also looking into whether Miss Edison's companion, the boy she was thought to have run off with, is still alive or if she killed him, too. Which…actually brings us to you."

Adelia blinks. "Me?"

"You study unusual crime cases, yes? I had hoped you might be able to offer some insight." I smile.

She seems to consider that. "Do you have specifics?"

It feels awkward to explain the state of the bodies to anyone, let alone the daughter of a Lord, but I picture Miss Bennett giving me the most unimpressed look if she were here to see my hesitation. "Whoever attacked the Brewers mangled their bodies quite viciously. Bite marks everywhere, tore into their torsos with their bare hands. Mrs. Brewer's throat was ripped into by teeth—which is precisely what Miss Edison tried to do to me last night."

Adelia doesn't so much as flinch at the description. "What do you want to know from me, then?"

"Is there a way to determine if the murders were committed by only one assailant, or if she had an accomplice?"

Her eyes drop half-closed as she thinks. "Ideally, one would be able to confirm the alibi of the one suspected. Failing that, you said there were bite marks. Those could be compared to Miss Edison's teeth to see if they match up."

"You can do that?" I suppose it makes sense. If one could determine the sort of animal that caused an injury, then…

"*I* cannot, no. One more intimate with the human body might be able to. There's quite a difference in reading about techniques and ideas in books and actually applying them."

Well, there goes that idea. If the coroner here had any knowledge of such a process, surely he'd have done it already, but…

I pause and tip my head toward James. "I say…"

James, who has been busy stuffing food down his gullet, pauses to look at me. "Hm?"

I scarcely resist the urge to dust a few crumbs from the corner of his mouth. "Perhaps a letter to Virgil is in order. He may know of someone who can help."

His face immediately wrinkles. "Must we?"

Not that James minds Virgil, but I think he still views him as a voice of authority, despite that we're no longer in school. Virgil is, however, one of the few people I've found myself calling a friend outside of Whisperwood. Alexander and Prichard are good fellows, but they are more James' friends than mine.

Virgil and I… We're similar in our awkwardness, I suppose. He's one of the only men I've ever met who takes things more seriously than I do. More than that, he's sharp, and he's always been fascinated to hear from me about our work. "I'm certain he'd be happy to come and lecture you over something."

James sniffles. "No, thank you."

"Who is Virgil?" Adelia asks.

"An acquaintance from school," I say with a smile. "His father is a physician, and he seemed to be following in those footsteps. He may have some advice."

"He's a pain, is what he is," James laments.

"He's no more a pain than you are."

"I'm certain Father would be happy to allow a companion of yours to stay here, even if he's insistent everything is solved."

Virgil ought to be in the middle of a term at university, so I doubt he'll drop everything to show up himself, but... "I'll speak with your father about it. I suspect tomorrow we'll be returning to the house again. If you'd like to accompany us, you might glean a little more information."

Adelia scrutinises me, as though trying to determine whether or not I'm toying with her. "I might."

"It would be appreciated," I say in all seriousness. Then I look down to my plate and blink in confusion when I find it far emptier than it should be considering I've only had a few small bites.

James asks, "What's wrong?"

I frown. "I apparently ate more than I thought I did."

He reaches over and slowly takes another forkful of food from my plate. "That's a shame."

"James Edward Spencer, I will remove that hand from your person!" I give his arm a slap. He recoils with a pitiful whimper.

"But I'm still hungry and you weren't eating!"

"I was *talking*," I say, scooting my place from him. "You have a table full of food."

93

A pout takes over his face. "Yours always tastes better."

I give him a glare, almost slipping by saying *at least give me a kiss first*, just barely catching myself. Instead, I scoop food onto my fork and take a bite, never breaking eye contact with him.

"How long have you two known each other, exactly?" Adelia asks. I'd almost forgotten we weren't alone.

"Since our third year at public school. So, more than three years now." I flash a sugary sweet smile at James, whose pout deepens.

"What drove you to work together in this…unique line of work?"

While my attention is upon her again, I'm well aware of James attempting to steal more of my food, but I pretend not to notice. If he's entertained, it isn't hurting me any, and given that there is plenty to eat, it doesn't really bother me. "James lost a friend there. We were…caught up in some things that required us to have dealings with the spirits there. After graduating, James insisted we continue it as a profession."

"And you're working under someone, I've heard?"

"Miss Eleanor Bennett. She's a medium in Whitechapel. Brilliant woman, and she was kind enough to take us under her wing and teach us what she knows."

Adelia arches a delicate brow. "It sounds as though you've quite a story to yourselves. Does your business have a name? I thought you mentioned something about that when we met."

"Paranormal Punishers," James pipes up.

I slap his hand away again. "Please, Lady Adelia. Don't encourage him."

"Ghostly Crusaders," James says, all with a straight face. Adelia frowns in puzzlement.

I sigh. "We don't have a business name. As you can see, we are…undecided on one."

94

Adelia purses her lips. "…Fishy Occurrences."

James' face lights up in a grin. My expression deadpans. "I'll never hear the end of it now."

"Ghost Farmers," James says.

"Undead Collectors," Adelia adds.

"I am not medicated nor drunk enough for the pair of you," I sigh, taking one last bite of food before pushing my chair back. "I'm going to see about a bath before the party tonight."

"Paranormal Poachers," Adelia bites back a smile.

"Spirit Tamers."

"Phantom Fighters?"

James clutches his chest, eyes wide. "That was one of my ideas!"

With a groan, I wave them both off as I head for the door. "Or maybe I shall drown myself and be spared having to listen to this further. Thank you for a lovely meal that James ate."

Their ridiculous suggestions follow me out of the hall. I head upstairs, stopping a servant along the way to request a bath to be drawn for me. I will need to change my bandages and get into some clean clothes that don't smell of blood and sweat and a morgue, I think. And if I have time for a nap before the gathering, all the better.

A hot bath coupled with the laudanum in my system only serves to make me wonderfully drowsy. I intend to dress and do my hair after bathing, but upon returning to my room, the call of a soft bed is too much, and I find myself crawling beneath the covers, entirely naked, and falling right to sleep. Even the knocking upon my door some hours later does little but drag a noise of complaint from me.

"Rise and shine," James says as he steps into the room.

Another fitful sigh, and I roll onto my side and force my eyes open. "Must I?"

He shuts the door behind him with a smile. "Well, do you want to be late to your own party?"

"I would be willing to be fashionably late if you were to keep me in bed, yes." I hide a smile behind my arm.

James chuckles, crosses the room, and throws himself upon the bed—and me. "Nap time!"

I yelp but can't help a soft laugh as I roll onto my back and get my arms around him. "You big oaf."

He shoves his face against the crook of my neck. "Shh, sleep now."

My hands find their way into his hair, effectively mussing it up, and I breathe in deep. God, I want to go home to the comfort and privacy of our house. Falling asleep again would be quick, easy, except after a few moments tick by…James begins to nibble at the uninjured side of my throat, just above my pulse point.

I sigh. "Is that my cue to get up?"

"They'll have food at the party," James hums, nipping again. "I don't want to miss it."

"You're impossible." I squirm free. "All right, all right, I'm up."

He sits up and slides a hand through his hair. He's actually done a nice job of dressing for the occasion; his gold silk waistcoat and garishly coloured checkered trousers—which I've always thought looked ridiculous but seem to be all the fashion these days—and the tie that matches those trousers, are all something only James could pull off.

"Did you sleep well?" he asks.

I bite back a yawn as I slide from bed to dress. "As well as I ever do when you aren't here to lie all over me and drool in my hair."

"I was thinking it looked a bit dry."

96

I smile sleepily as I begin to dress. "And how did you enjoy the rest of my lunch?"

"Quite delicious. Oh, and how about Haunted Enforcers?"

I groan, chucking a shirt at him. "Don't start that again."

He catches it with a laugh. "She's right, you know. We do need a name."

"Spencer and Esher Spirit Specialists. Simple and professional."

"*Bo-ring.* Two Men and a Ghost?"

"You give me a headache."

"Give me about fifteen minutes and I can take that headache away," he says with a suggestive grin.

I snatch my coat and turn to him. "By medicating me? How kind of you."

His brows lift sharply. "Goodness. We're calling that medicating now?"

My cheeks warm as I step closer, carding my fingers through his hair. "You're an absolute beast, you realise. Be on your best behaviour tonight and perhaps we'll sneak away early."

James gives me his best 'good boy' smile as he stands. "On my mother's life. Do I look presentable?"

I take a moment to admire him, smoothing the lapels of his jacket. "You look like the sort of man I could fall in love with."

His eyes widen a fraction and then narrow. "I'm going to kick my own arse."

It takes significant effort not to laugh at that. Instead I take his face in my hands, bringing my forehead to his and lingering there a moment. He truly has no idea how precious he is, and the way his idiotic sense of humour warms me to my bones. I draw back, beckoning him along. Undoubtedly the party will begin soon and, as the guests of honour, it would be rude if we were late.

James doesn't offer my medicine, and as much as I want to ask for it, I refrain. Past experiences have proven that being medicated *and* drunk makes for a bad combination. Namely, me passing out or coming close to it, and remembering nothing the next day. The last time such a thing occurred, James damned near had a heart attack, swearing he'd witnessed my breath stopping. I've no interest in worrying him like that again.

We sweep through the house, locating Mr. Foss giving instructions to various staff members, who are scurrying about decorating the ballroom. I had figured a party would simply involve a group in the parlour, not something quite so large. The thought of so many people has me already itching for a drink.

James turns in a full-circle, admiring the room with its towering windows, each cracked open, curtains swept aside, the tables placed out for parlour games, and a grand piano in the corner that I would love to get a better look at. We could not afford one, and it's been so long since I've had the chance to play.

"This house is really quite lovely," James says.

Foss skims over a checklist in his hands. "Of course it is. Lord Wakefield and his late wife were quite insistent on creating such an environment. I fear Lady Adelia does not share the same interest."

I choose not to point out that not everyone has a love of such frivolous things, and Wakefield likely wouldn't listen to her opinion anyway. "Speaking of Lady Adelia, she'll be joining us tonight, I trust?"

"While the lady would rather be in her room with a book, her presence has been requested."

The sound of Adelia's voice from the doorway makes me turn. To no surprise, she looks stunning in a forest green gown with golden embroidery fanning up the skirt and spilling down the sleeves like waterfalls. It compliments her green eyes and makes the dusting of freckles across her cheeks and nose that much more noticeable.

"You look lovely, Lady Adelia. You've done your hair differently," I say. It's piled high atop her head, and I can only imagine the time and effort such a style took.

She sighs, a hand flitting up to touch it. "I've been assured it's the latest fashion in London, for whatever that nonsense is worth."

"Never fear. By the time the night is over, the latest fashion will have changed twice already."

A fleeting smile passes across her lips. "How are you two doing this evening?" As though we didn't see each other a few hours ago.

"Hungry again," James replies.

"James is a bottomless pit, I'm afraid. He insisted we not be late lest we miss out on the *hors d'oeuvres.*"

"I'm a growing boy."

Adelia looks almost amused. "There will be plenty to eat. Poor Mr. Esher might even be able to sneak in a bite or two."

I scoff. "Unlikely. I waste away so that James can eat his fill." Besides, I spot a server wandering by with a case of wine bottles, and that looks far more appetising. "What are your father's parties like? Mr. Foss says 'everyone' is invited."

"I believe he intends this to be more a village celebration than any dinner party you might be used to. Not terribly stuffy, if that's your concern."

I raise a brow. "So, he really does invite the entire community? Not just those within his own social circle?"

"The entire community, yes. Those who wish to attend and have the time to do so."

James and I share a look, equally impressed. Not the sort of thing either of our families would do. Or…any family of means, for that matter. "I suppose we'll have our opportunity to speak with the Fletchers after all. I suspect the Edisons won't be in attendance."

"A party more or less celebrating that their deceased daughter was a murderer? No, I can't imagine they would want to join the festivities."

Fair enough. "We'll talk with the boy's parents. But for now…" I trail off as Wakefield himself strolls into the room and makes his way over to us. He gives his daughter a smile, of course complimenting her on how beautiful she looks and slipping into the conversation that plenty of single young men will be in attendance. He asks James and I about our injuries, and the concern appears sincere.

Before long, guests begin to arrive. The women are shown upstairs to leave their wraps and adjust their hair and faces before joining us in the ballroom. Wakefield leads James and me from family to family. He knows every single one of their names and, for those without titles of importance, he tells us what they do for a living. The interest he displays in those below his status is both impressive and admirable, I'll admit.

But, oh, I swiftly grow weary of being swept about the room, introduced to far more people and given more names than either of us could possibly memorise. This is a situation in which I *can* smile and be acceptably charming, but it quickly wears me down. James notices my fatigue and does his best to carry the burden of the conversations.

The sound of people talking, enjoying the food, drinking, laughing and—after a while—dancing, ignites mixed feelings within me. These are the sorts of atmospheres I enjoy in theory, and hate in practise, because I desperately wish I were better equipped to be a part of it. I would love to have a seat at the piano and play a few songs for the dancers, except...

I steal a glance at James. Not for the first time, I lament how depressing it is that I cannot simply take his hand and have a dance with him in front of everyone.

Thankfully, there is drinking. I snag the first glass I can from a passing server, downing half of it in one go and finishing it off not long after. A few drinks in, surely, relaxing will be easier. At some point, I slip away from James, seeking solitude near the doors with my back pressed to a wall, willing my head to stop spinning with the noise in the room. I scarcely hear Adelia beside me.

"Mr. Esher, would you care to have a dance with me?"

It's hardly appropriate for a lady to approach a man and ask for a dance, so at first, I'm taken aback, and my expression shows it. Rather than look offended or scolding her for her demeanour, I give a lopsided smile and place my now-empty glass aside. "I would love to," is my warm reply, extending my arm out to her.

"Do you always enjoy parties so much?" The sarcasm is evident in Adelia's tone. She takes the offered arm and we walk to the other side of the room where couples are dancing.

"I enjoy the atmosphere. It's just that I find them...a bit overwhelming." I glance around, wondering if James is watching, if it will bother him that I'm dancing with a woman. I hope that it won't, but I cannot seem to locate him.

Adelia peers into my face. "Your companion asked me to come dance with you, in case you're looking for him."

My eyebrows shoot up at that. "Did he now?"

"He did. He said you looked like you weren't having fun."

That sounds like James. "Well, he's correct, I suppose. And I do enjoy a good dance." I take her hand and draw her to me. "Thank you, then, for humouring me."

KELLEY YORK & ROWAN ALTWOOD

"You're doing me a favour, too." Adelia's other hand settles delicately upon my shoulder.

"Is that right?"

"Naturally. You heard Father earlier—plenty of young suitors here vying for the attention of any unattached women. He'd be insisting I pay them attention."

We begin to fall into step with the music, and it's an utter delight to have a dance partner who clearly knows what she's doing. The Christmas parties at Whisperwood could be entertaining, but those girls' knowledge of dancing was usually limited to what their teachers taught them just for the party. "None of the gentlemen have caught your eye?"

She scoffs. "I've no interest in marriage or being wooed, Mr. Esher."

"Why not?" I tip my head, not intending the question to be anything more than simple curiosity. "Too constricting?"

"Too constricting," she agrees with a faint smile. "If I wanted to have a man tell me what to do for the rest of my life, I needn't look further than my father."

I can imagine that, and it would be disheartening to see a woman with Adelia's spirit be pinned down by the rules and expectations of society. "Then the idea of falling in love and spending your life with someone, in and of itself, is not unappealing?"

"No. I'm only human, after all."

"Then perhaps a gentleman who has no interest in controlling you will come along. I promise, one is out there who will treat you the way you deserve to be treated."

She chuckles. "I'm not a believer of fairy tales."

I didn't used to be, either. "You'll see. If you've no interest in marrying, what is it you hope to do with your life?"

"Realistically?" She considers. "Spend my days reading and learning."

"Just learning? No goal in mind to apply your knowledge to?"

That earns me a patient look. "I said realistically, Mr. Esher."

"I'm not asking for realism."

Her lack of hesitation suggests she's spent a long while thinking about this. "I would be a detective."

A smile pulls the corners of my mouth. "You should do that, then."

"It's your privilege that allows you to say such things as though it's easy," Adelia says mildly.

"Perhaps, yes. Or perhaps I think you're an extraordinary woman, and if someone had the ability to challenge the status quo, it would be someone like you."

Her chin dips, long lashes brushing her rosy, freckled cheeks. "Such faith in someone you barely know."

"I like to think I'm a good judge of character."

"If I didn't know better, I would say that you're flirting with me, Mr. Esher."

Am I? That was certainly not my intention, but—were this another time and place, had I never met James, had I survived school, Adelia would have been the kind woman to capture my attention. Someone sharp and brilliant, someone who knows what she wants in life.

How do I convey that? How do I say that I'm not flirting, but it isn't any failing on her part? "You're a fascinating woman, Lady Adelia. I believe I would be flirting were my own heart not otherwise claimed."

"I did say if I didn't know better."

She pins me with such a knowing look then that my heart damned near stutters to a halt in my chest. It takes everything I have to keep my eyes on her and not immediately look around for James. We try to be so careful, but of course it's possible someone observant would take notice.

103

KELLEY YORK & ROWAN ALTWOOD

Adelia squeezes my hand, not breaking eye contact. "Don't look so worried. I'm very good at keeping secrets."

I will myself to calm my nerves. James and I...it is not something I discuss. Not with anyone. Certainly, there are people who *know*. Preston Alexander, Benjamin Prichard, Miss Bennett, Virgil. But knowing and speaking about it are entirely different beasts. It's easy for people to turn a blind eye to something and feign ignorance, after all. "Thank you. I believe that solidifies my earlier opinion of you."

She shakes her head. "It's simple decency."

"Thank you, all the same."

We fall into companionable silence, enjoying one another's company, enjoying the music for a time. When Adelia speaks again, it's to inquire, "Would you like a break from dancing, Mr. Esher? A drink, perhaps?"

I believe I've lost track of time. "William. Please. At least when your father isn't within earshot to lecture us about propriety. And a drink sounds wonderful."

She smiles. "William. Let's get a drink, then."

I take a polite step back and bow before leading her from the dancers. As we go I finally spot James, speaking with a couple across the room. The conversation appears to be heavy.

"Who are those people with James?"

Adelia follows my gaze. "Those would be the parents of that missing young man."

The Fletchers. I had a feeling. I wonder if I ought to join James, but he's good at speaking to people. Perhaps sometimes he runs his mouth more than he should, but he's good at empathising and people like him. I snatch a glass from one of the servers. "All work and no play."

Adelia also claims a glass, but her sips are small and polite. "What do you hope he learns from them?"

"I'm not honestly sure they'll have anything of use for us. I suppose we're hoping to find out more about their son and Miss Edison. If they did, in fact, run away together. Did they encounter trouble after leaving? Is he the cause of her possession, or did he fall victim to her, as well?"

"I suppose we won't really know until you find him."

"We're going to try. Your assistance tomorrow will hopefully help lead us to him, if he's still alive."

"You realise it may be more difficult now," she murmurs. "If everyone is pushing back because they consider the mystery solved."

The smile that pulls at my face is because it doesn't bother me in the least. "I assure you, we've dealt with much more resistance than I believe we'll face here."

"Resistance?" another voice says.

I turn to see Reverend Thomas nearby, nursing a glass of something I suspect is not alcohol. When he sees the sharp look upon my face, he blushes. "I'm terribly sorry, Mr. Esher, Lady Adelia. I didn't mean to eavesdrop. I merely meant—I hope no one is giving you a difficult time about your investigation."

I will myself to relax. "Not at all, Reverend."

He gives us both a quiet smile and nods, stepping closer. "Lord Wakefield had made it sound as though you'd found our murderer, but you don't sound so sure."

I glance at Adelia, whose expression has slipped back into the tight, polite mask she typically wears. It occurs to me that today, I've begun to see beneath that mask, in her conversation with us at lunch and again while dancing.

I'm not sure anyone is privy to details about our case, either, but… "There are some loose ends we need to wrap up. It would hardly be professional of us not to ensure all avenues have been fully explored, though I suppose I could ask if you knew anything about Miss Edison and Mr. Fletcher and their relationship."

He hesitates, smile waning. "That's a difficult question to answer. Some things are told to me in confidence."

Adelia tips her head. "Would God not want you to do what you could to help those in need?"

Reverend Thomas heaves a sigh. "That is… Yes, I suppose that's fair. I do know Mr. Fletcher and Miss Edison were very much in love, despite their parents' disapproval." He casts a wary glance around and moves in close to us, so that he can lower his voice without fear of being overheard. "They had a very set plan to run away together. I debated whether I ought to divulge this information to their parents, as they were both still children, but I felt it wasn't my place."

I drain the rest of my glass, already feeling like I'm going to need another for this conversation. "A plan, you say?"

"They went missing prior to the date Mr. Fletcher told me they were set to depart, but perhaps something happened. Perhaps their parents found out about their intentions and they sought to flee early to avoid being caught."

Adelia touches my arm. "Then perhaps Mr. Spencer will have heard as much from the Fletchers."

I nod in absent agreement, bringing a hand lightly against her back. "Thank you, Reverend Thomas. If it's all right with you, we may stop by the church sometime soon to inquire further about this. For tonight, I'd hate to spoil the party with such serious talk." Which isn't true, but my anxiousness is making me eager to hunt down James and keep close to him and to find out what information he received. Not to mention, the alcohol has begun to go to my head, and I can't fully focus on such a conversation.

Reverend Thomas bows his head in a gracious nod as I steer Adelia away, searching the crowd for James. "Things always get more complicated."

I spot him across the room and he catches my eye and makes his way toward us. "There you are. Done dancing?"

The act of being near James is enough to calm me a bit, even if I cannot reach out to touch him like I want to. I am, however, beginning to feel tipsy enough that it almost seems like a good idea to slouch against him and shove my face against his throat, but I refrain. "Lady Adelia has helped me salvage this otherwise dismal evening, yes. How did your talk with the Fletchers go?"

"Uneventful," he sighs. "They refuse to believe their boy would have left willingly, which is what I figured they'd say."

"Well, to add another voice to the mix, Reverend Thomas proclaims the pair confessed to him they had plans to run away together."

James' eyes widen. "He betrayed confidences? He shouldn't really have done that."

"Adelia managed to convince him to spill a bit. God would want him to help bring them peace, after all."

Still, a scandalised frown tugs at James' face. "He's not supposed to, regardless of reason."

"Then I suggest not telling him any secrets while we're here," I say gently, suspecting this is more upsetting for him than it ever could be for me. "For our purposes, it's a good thing he did."

He sniffs. "Yes, well. The information doesn't help us anyway. We have two different stories and proof of neither."

"I think…" I trail off because my focus is rapidly diminishing. "We will… We will figure it out. At some point. Is that not what we're good at?"

James' gaze slides from me to Adelia. "How much has he had to drink?"

She pats my arm. "More than enough."

I roll my eyes. "It's only been a few." I've lost count, but whatever. "I shall have another when I can find a server."

James' smile makes the corners of his eyes crinkle. "Of course you will."

I give an indignant sniff. Just out of spite, I whirl away from them and seek out another drink.

And then another.

By then, I'm feeling good—*normal*, I daresay—and conversing and socialising becomes easy. I needn't cling to James or Adelia's sides for comfort, although habit has me returning to James periodically anyway.

Being like this, it's freeing. I can chat to almost anyone in the room with ease, even Lord Wakefield himself, who seems delighted with the conversation.

James never once attempts to reel me in. I hear him murmur to Adelia at one point, "Watch him go. Remarkable, isn't it? Two entirely different people."

He could not possibly understand, I think. For at least tonight, I can pretend I am normal.

EVENTUALLY, the hour grows late, and many of the lower-class party goers have begun to leave because they need to rise early for work the next morning. The elite, of course, have no pressing schedules and I know from experience they'll stay until the small hours if Wakefield permits it.

However, even as I flit about from person to person and have my share of dances with any woman who looks as though she might want to, I find my attention diverting back to James more and more. He stands there with that lovely smile upon his face, looking absolutely delectable. I could eat him up. I believe I shall tell him as much, too.

I make my way back to his side, doing my best not to look entirely obvious as I lean in to murmur against his ear. "I would very much like to take you back to my room and have my way with you."

James nearly chokes on his drink in his attempt not to laugh. "Goodness. I think we should call it a night."

He smells nice. I want to bury my face against his neck and run my hands through his hair. "Yes. Please."

James nudges me into straightening up and turns to Adelia. "It would appear dear William has had too much to drink. I'm going to help him to his room."

Oh. Yes. Right. I turn to Adelia with my most charming smile in place, taking her hand and bringing it to my lips to kiss the back of it. "Thank you for gracing me with a dance tonight."

Adelia bites her lip, amused. "You're most welcome, William. Do get some rest."

"I believe I shall," I announce, turning to saunter off. James catches me by the elbow after a few paces, gently informs me I'm headed the wrong way, and directs me out by the proper door.

As we exit the ballroom and head upstairs, I hum a tune beneath my breath. James ushers me into my room. "Here we go. Let's get you to bed."

He's scarcely got me inside before I'm smiling and catching his tie in my hands, leaning into him. "Only if you're coming to bed with me."

His mouth twists up into a grin. "What happened to being careful?"

"I'll lock the door." I lean in to ghost my lips against the corner of his mouth, while reaching behind him to twist the deadbolt. "Everyone is preoccupied at the party, and if I don't have you right now, I just might die."

He laughs even as his arms loop around my shoulders to draw me closer. "You are ridiculous, and utterly adorable."

I catch his lower lip between my teeth, drawing a shiver

from him, before I slip free of his embrace and take a step back with a slow, sultry smile. I back away and begin to undo my tie, attempting to toe off my shoes as I go and damned near toppling over my own feet until I reach the sofa near the windows and sink onto it. I'm attempting to look seductive, but I'm entirely unsure whether or not I'm managing it. "Is that right?"

James smiles, slow and warm, and he bends to remove his shoes before following after me with the most gentle, adoring gaze. "That is entirely right."

I drape myself upon the couch, watching James and beckoning to him. "Come show me just how much. I miss having your hands on me."

"I would be happy to oblige." He slides his coat from his shoulders and lets it fall to the floor. It's only been a few days. Ridiculous, then, that I feel as though it's been months. I reach for James as he nears me. He touches my face gently, ducking down to press his mouth against mine.

There is nothing in the world quite like James' kisses. They possess the ability to be so careful and loving while eager and passionate all at once. I can feel every ounce of love and desire, warming every inch of my body. I sigh against his mouth, clutching at his sleeve with one hand and sliding the other to the back of his head, fingers threading into his hair and I hold him there to me. Slowly, I lean back, wanting to drag him down to the chaise longue with me.

He goes without protest, settling himself atop me as his hands smooth through my hair, down my jaw. "My sweet William…"

I'm dizzy with the effects of alcohol combined with the warmth of James' mouth, and I find myself tugging at his shirt, the buttons, his tie and waistcoat, eager to free him from them. I don't give a damn about the party in full swing downstairs. All I care about is getting James out of his clothes, getting my hands all over him, getting him inside of me. My eagerness seems to be contagious, because James' movements become just as hurried.

No sooner has he unfastened his trousers than there is a knock at the door, and Adelia's voice calls out in a hushed whisper, "William, James? Are you in there?"

I freeze at the sound, fear seizing hold. I've got James' waistcoat and shirt off him, and my own is half-undone, and there is absolutely no way either of us is fit for company. I stare widely at James as I call, "Just—just a moment!"

James yanks his trousers up, attempting to straighten his hair. But his clothes are all over the floor and he appears to panic because in the next moment, he dives under the bed.

I push a hand through my hair and scramble for the door, pausing when I realise what James is doing and—well, whatever, I've already got the door open, adjusting my crooked glasses and peering at Adelia out in the hall.

She blinks back at me, though if she's startled by my ruffled appearance, she doesn't comment on it. "I'm sorry to be a bother, but I felt I should warn you that father was looking for you."

I lean against the doorframe, doing my best to look sober and not as though I've just had my tongue in someone's mouth and my hand down their trousers. "Ah...right. Yes. I will—um." I clear my throat. "I will make sure I'm presentable."

One corner of her mouth ticks up. "Mhmm," is all she says before she turns away.

I lean out the door. "Wait, do you know what he wants?"

She turns back. "He wanted to discuss you finishing out your week here. He has a mind to ask you to find that

A HYMN IN THE SILENCE

missing boy. I just thought you might appreciate warning so he didn't…" her gaze rakes over me, "…interrupt anything."

Heat floods to my face. I can't help the sullen look that I'm undoubtedly wearing. I just wanted to drag James to bed and this is preventing that from happening. "Of course. Thank you, Adelia."

She dips her head in a nod and heads down the hall. I retreat to the room and shut the door, slumping against it with a low, whining groan. James giggles from under the bed and pokes his head out, earning him a scowl. "Oh, stop that," I sniff sadly, stooping to retrieve his clothing from the floor.

He smiles sweetly. "Should I stay under here until you're free?"

"He wants to speak to us both, and if he finds you're not in here, he may go to your room to look for you."

James slides out from beneath the bed and stands. "Well, that's no fun."

"He had better make this quick." I hand over his clothes, give myself a once-over in the wash table mirror, and turn back to James to fuss with his hair while he pulls on his shirt.

"Very insistent tonight, aren't you?"

"Have you seen yourself? No one could possibly blame me."

"Flatterer." His eyes are positively shining with want as he ducks in to kiss me. It drags some of the annoyance right out of me and I lean into him, head swimming.

"Not at all; I'm just a man hopelessly attracted to the love of his life," I mumble.

"You're so sweet." His lips travelling across my cheek, down my jaw, mouthing lazily at my throat. I begin to lose myself in that, eyes shut, head tipped. A part of me is forgetting just why James is dressed again.

113

At least, until someone knocks upon the door again and I heave a heavy, frustrated sigh and drop my forehead to his shoulder. James only muffles a quiet laugh against my throat and pulls away.

"You should answer that."

I give his shoulder a shove and step to the door to open it. "Ah, Lord Wakefield." As though I'm surprised.

Wakefield has clearly had a few drinks of his own, but hardly as many as I have. He gives a slightly crooked smile. "Oh, good, Mr. Spencer is here with you. Might I pop in for a moment?"

Reluctantly, I step aside, stealing a glimpse around to ensure we've not forgotten any articles of clothing on the floor. "I apologise for ducking out early. I'm afraid we aren't accustomed to these late hours."

"No, not at all." He waves a hand dismissively. "I merely wanted to ask, before you two made plans to return home… Would you be willing to stay, just a bit longer? To investigate the missing Fletcher boy."

That's what we wanted to do anyway, isn't it? More time. "I think we would be agreeable to that," James answers.

Wakefield's face brightens. "That is most excellent news. I will, of course, ensure you're compensated for your time. Any resources you need are at your disposal."

I hadn't expected more money, but I'm not going to argue it. From our conversation during the party, I know Wakefield is not a man hurting for money and hasn't a clue he's really overpaying us. I bite my lip sharply to keep from smiling like a bloody loon. I've had far too much to drink. "We have a few leads we'll begin following up on tomorrow."

"I don't know what I would do without the both of you." He claps us on the shoulders. "Please, get some rest."

As the door swings shut behind him, James turns to me with his face split into a gigantic grin. "We'll be able to buy *so* much cake."

I allow myself to laugh, re-locking the door. If I have any response to that, it's to simply throw myself back into James' arms, kissing him senseless.

Should we have any more interruptions, I will pitch an absolute fit. I despise the feeling of sneaking around, of worrying someone will overhear or walk in, but I'm drunk and James is beautiful and little else matters.

I'm the more reserved of the pair of us, but when the mood strikes me—*well*. James is compliant about getting us undressed again, stopping only long enough to retrieve that bottle of oil he brought along from home. I suppose I ought to thank him for being the prepared one for a change. Once we're out of our clothes, I push him down to the bed and crawl atop him, the feel of his skin against mine sending shivers and sparks all along my insides. And it's only then that I pause, breathing quickly, remembering myself.

James normally tenses up at this positioning, at having someone looming over him, and even in my alcohol-induced haze, I have no interest in crossing a boundary that will sap his enjoyment of this moment.

My hesitation makes James open his eyes, tongue swiping across his upper lip as he gazes up at me. Rather than lock up or give me that *look* that I know means I need to stop, he slides his hands up my thighs. "Hello, dear William."

A breath catches in my throat in delightful, hopeful surprise. I lean down, hands planted against the bed on either side of him. "This is all right…?"

He smiles as he slips a hand between my legs. "Mhm. So far, so good."

My lashes flutter closed, hips jerking down against his in response. If it's all right with him, if he continues to be all right, then I have no qualms in kissing him, in taking him inside of me with a sharp intake of breath and an edge of pain that is tolerable only because we have become quite familiar with this. I brace my palms against his chest, nails biting gently into his flesh.

Any lingering hesitation James seems to have had vanishes. He watches me in fascination, unable to keep his hands off me, and I welcome every touch. Being silent is a chore. I don't enjoy having to bite back the sounds James drags out of me. Every trembling muscle and repressed whimper and moan is because of how lovely he feels.

Release crashes over me all at once. My hands fist into his hair, and I let loose a moan against his mouth, unable to help myself, unable to keep quiet because he isn't far behind me. This is my favourite sensation in all the world, the exact moment where James is kissing me, and his hands are gripping my hips and he's panting and spent inside of me.

I draw up slowly, head tipped back, granting myself a moment to catch my breath. "Much better…"

"Much," James agrees, breathless. He drags me down to hold me against his chest, his breath warm against my ear. "I do love you, so very much."

Those words send a jolt right down my spine and I smile. My eyes feel impossibly heavy now, and rested with my cheek to his chest, it occurs to me how terribly I already miss sleeping like this. "I love you. Although I suppose this is the part where I banish you back to your room for the night."

He chuckles against my hair. "I wouldn't argue if you wanted to test our luck."

I'm conflicted. I sleep worlds better when James is with

me, but is it risking too much? I bite my lip, wondering if my willingness to throw caution to the wind is a result of drinking. "I fear I'm not in a position to ask you to go anywhere."

James grunts a little, fingers trailing down my spine. "How about I stay until you fall asleep?"

"Mmm, just like school?"

"Just like school."

James prods me gently from bed long enough to wash us both up a bit before falling back into the covers. With a pleased noise, I wrap my arms around him, tucking my head against his shoulder. "When we've been paid, we should take a holiday."

"Where to?"

"Anywhere. France? I hear they've delicious cakes there."

"I do adore cake."

I tip my head to nip at his collarbone. "More than me?"

"Almost." He grins. "But not quite."

"Tsk."

James presses a kiss to my hair. True to his word, he lies there with me, and the sound of his heartbeat and the warmth of his skin lulls me quickly to sleep.

8

THANKS to the drink and the lovemaking, sleep comes easily. After James has left, I reach for him, disturbed awake when I find him not there. But— right. He would have gone back to his room, of course. So, I sigh and lie my head back down, eyes drifting shut, and try to resume sleep.

There's something off about the room, though. A prickling along my skin that has my eyes opening and scanning every dark corner, every shadow, with my heartbeat kicking up a notch. I've woken like this many nights during my years at Whisperwood.

I slide out of bed, nursing the beginnings of a headache. I step to the window, fumble my glasses on, part the curtains, and gaze into the night.

Standing in the snow, I make out the faint shapes of several figures, motionless, their marred faces twisted, and their dead eyes lifted to Evenbury Manor. Goosebumps race across my skin and I hold my breath.

Flora Brewer and her children.

I throw on my nightshirt and a robe, ducking into the hall and racing through the house, nearly getting turned around in the dark and unfamiliar halls. In the foyer, I throw open the front doors to dash outside. I should have grabbed James but thought I might not have time. Standing there at the bottom of the front steps, barefoot, shivering, I can no longer spot the Brewers anywhere. Surely, I did not imagine it.

Frustrated, I linger a few moments longer before retreating into the house again, my feet having gone numb. I decide not to rouse James over it; short of dressing and venturing out into the night, we'll not find them now.

I attempt to go back to sleep, but it comes in fits and starts. I end up dressing early and heading outside to search around the property as the sun rises. There are footprints in the snow in some peculiar places but given the number of people who were here last night, it's impossible to know if these didn't belong to one of the attendees.

Near the gardens, close to where I spotted the Brewers, are a set of stone benches, one of which I take a seat upon. What should have been a delightfully restful night has turned into me being exhausted and with a headache pinching behind my eyes.

"There you are."

I start only for the half-second before my brain recognises it as James' voice. "Good morning," I mumble, slouching as he sits beside me. "Sleep well?"

He yawns. "Well enough. Why didn't you wake me?"

"I figured one of us ought to get a proper night's rest." I tip my head toward him and point. "I spotted the Brewers outside my window last night."

There's an inquiring twist to James' mouth. "Did you go and say hello to them?"

"An attempt was made. By the time I got outside, they were nowhere to be found."

He leans his shoulder into mine. "You should have woken me."

"There was little to be done. I didn't want you running off into the night to look for ghosts."

"Well, I think we should return to the farm."

I sigh. "I suppose so. Virgil ought to receive my letter today. Hopefully we'll hear from him in short order."

"Don't sound too excited."

"I'm quite ready to return home, if I'm honest. I miss our bed."

James' smile is sympathetic. "The money will be good for us. We can take that holiday."

I know, just as I also know I'm unjustifiably cranky this morning and a fair bit hungover, and there's no reason to mope about and take it out on James. I imagine he's - hungry and it's about time for breakfast, and as much as I do not have an appetite, I need to eat to keep my strength up. "Let's go see about breakfast."

James catches my elbow and rises, drawing me to him. "Before we go…" He holds up my bottle of laudanum, and the agitation itching inside my chest releases at the mere sight of it.

"We should have purchased more before leaving Whitechapel," I observe, opening my mouth. I feel like such a child when James has to dole out my dosages to me, but it's really my own fault that I can't be trusted to do it myself.

"We can nip into town to get more, if necessary," James assures, administering the drops to my tongue before pocketing the bottle. "Come now, I'm wasting away from starvation."

We head inside for breakfast. Unsurprisingly, Lord Wakefield is still asleep. What is surprising is that Adelia is absent; she knew we had plans to return to the house today, and Foss explains she left early to go and visit a friend. Odd, but little we can do about it. I'll not hold off our investigation.

Rather than request the aid of a driver, Foss grants us the use of a cabriolet and a horse so we can drive ourselves. I give the reins over to James, having no interest in driving now that my medicine has kicked in and my throbbing headache has begun to fade.

"At your leisure, m'lord," James teases, but he takes the reins and navigates us to the Brewers' farm. I keep the hood of the carriage down, wanting to enjoy the weather which, while still chilly, is a fair bit warmer than it has been the last few days. I tip my head back, eyes closed, and enjoy the ride.

Upon arriving at the farm and pulling down the long driveway, I spot a horse tethered near the house, not visible from the road. I slip from the cab with a frown. "James."

He hops down beside me. "We appear to have company."

Unsettling, that. I square my shoulders. We march to the door, determined to catch our guest unawares in case they try to flee. Before we get too far, the door swings open from the other side, and I find myself face to face with Adelia, who greets us with an unimpressed stare.

"You two took your time."

I lean back with a surprised twitch of my eyebrow. "Lady Adelia, you—What are you doing here so early?"

She steps aside to let us enter. "Father and Mr. Foss would never have allowed me to come, so it only made sense that I slip away on my own."

"I would have got you out. It's dangerous to be here alone." I slip inside, noting she's already opened the windows to air the place out.

Adelia scowls. "I'm sorry if you think I'm in need of an escort."

"While I appreciate your bravery, I would request that *no one*, male or female, be in this house without us right now." I pause, gaze roaming over her. She's dressed quite differently than I've seen her before. Flat shoes, hair pulled back in a practical, easy style, and a simple, homely dress more befitting a house servant than a lord's daughter.

Adelia catches me staring and frowns. "I thought it wise to wear something that lent itself to better mobility. I borrowed it from one of the maids." She turns away. "Anyway, I've searched the house top to bottom, so I know we're alone. However, someone has obviously been lurking about because there were footprints outside when I arrived."

My stomach turns. Had someone, or something, been here and Adelia had fallen victim to it… I dread to think of what we might have arrived to find. Still, I doubt lecturing her on it now will do anything but annoy her, so I take a deep breath. "Footsteps where?"

"Around the back, oddly enough," Adelia says. "I saw none that led away or indoors. It looked as though…someone appeared, paced back and forth, and then vanished."

Something about that makes me shiver. I glance at the spot on the floor where the Edison girl nearly tore out my throat and remind myself she is dead and gone and no more a threat than the people standing here with me. "Right. Well, is there anything you can discern from the crime scene?"

"With the amount of blood and damage, I don't feel it was the work of a sole attacker."

I lean against the wall by the door, arms crossed. "Not even a supernatural one?"

She cocks an eyebrow. "How would I know? There aren't many studies on the matter."

"All right. But not your everyday, run-of-the-mill human being, then. One of them being a woman about your build."

She answers with certainty, "Absolutely not. Even in a frenzy, perhaps one or two victims taken by surprise—but an entire family? No." She steps to the centre of the room. "Recalling what the neighbours told the police, Mr. Brewer was found here, along with three of the children. I suspect when the attackers entered, they took out the children first. Easy targets. They had no chance to run. Mr. Brewer engaged them, while Mrs. Brewer ran into the bedroom to get the baby. One of the attackers followed her. Or perhaps both, once Mr. Brewer had been dispatched."

She turns back to us, hands clasped loosely before her. "Had there only been Madeline by herself, Mrs. Brewer or any one of the children would have had a chance to flee. We would have found their bodies elsewhere."

I study her, impressed. It's all common sense, but I suppose I'd not given it that much thought before now. "Nicely done."

"Thank you."

James clears his throat. "Let's have a look at those footprints outside."

The three of us venture back into the cold and locate the tracks. We follow their lead, into the sparse trees, just as James and I did the other day. The snow has thinned out, grass peeking through in wet dewy patches, which—for our tracking purposes—is not necessarily a good thing.

We arrive at a clearing where the lack of tree cover has permitted the early morning sun to melt the snow, and I can't make out the tracks anywhere.

James stands in the centre of the clearing. "Another dead end."

I swear quietly under my breath and cross the clearing, hoping for some sign of where the footprints pick up on the other side. They have to be somewhere. Whoever made them did not simply disappear into thin air.

As I approach the edge of the clearing, I feel it: needles in my skin, ice in my veins, that invisible string that tugs at my insides, telling me to run because something dangerous is coming.

A siren-like shriek pierces the air as I whip around, just in time to see the ghost of Mrs. Brewer emerging from the forest.

The form that straightens up before Adelia is both human and not. A face I have seen close-up only on a morgue table, horribly twisted and beaten. The colour to her skin is all wrong, sickly pale and splotched with decay. Adelia scrambles back, mouth agape, but no sound emerges.

Before any of us can register anything, Flora Brewer rushes at Adelia and slams her to the ground.

I wrench a bottle of holy water from my pocket and yank the stopper as I dash toward them, prepared to throw it on the ghost as soon as I'm within range. The moment the droplets land on her skin, Mrs. Brewer recoils with another shriek. James wastes no time in snagging Adelia's arm to haul her to her feet and shove her behind him.

Flora rears back. I push myself between her and Adelia and James. Christ, I can never recall any of those fucking verses when I need them. "Mrs. Brewer, we need your help! Stop this!"

The water only works to deter her for so long. Flora drops to all fours, another ear-piercing shriek tearing from her blackened mouth. She scurries to the left, joints twisting and cracking. I brace myself in anticipation of her charging at me, only just barely managing to find my voice. "I command you, unclean spirit, whoever you are, along with all your minions now attacking this servant of God—"

But Flora seems to have no interest in me, or James, for that matter. She circles us, her dead eyes never leaving Adelia.

I trust James to keep her safe, but I don't trust the ghost not to hurt James to get at Adelia. I circle along with her, keeping myself a barrier between her and them, fishing out the small crucifix from my pocket to hold it out in front of me.

"—by the mysteries of the incarnation, the—the…" *Damn it.*

Whether it's the cross, the holy water, my clumsily spoken verses, or a combination of all three, Flora finally begins to crawl backwards, and I advance. If we must force her to cross over, then so be it. But it would mean one less source of information if we can't get her to regain some semblance of sanity.

Flora brings her hands to her face, a scream melting into a sob and then—she vanishes into the trees. Not banished, simply fled.

I drag in a shaky breath, stumbling back and dropping down into a crouch.

James straightens, turning to Adelia. "Are you all right?"

Adelia's face is pale and her wide eyes look from James to me and back again. "What—What on *earth* was that about?"

I scan the trees, just in case the ghost's retreat was only temporary. The creeping sensation has faded so I'm confident we're alone again. "She certainly seemed to have an interest in you," I say as I turn back to them. They both appear unharmed. Good. "Did you and Mrs. Brewer have any sort of disagreements when she was alive?"

Adelia attempts to dust off the back of her dress. For as calm as she's trying to appear, I think her hands are quaking ever so slightly. "I think not. I never spoke much to her, but on the rare occasion we did, it was pleasant enough."

I squint. I'm not getting the impression she's lying. It's possible Flora mistook Adelia for Madeline Edison, but that seems a stretch. Aside from being similar in height and age,

125

they really look nothing alike. "Another unanswered question, then. We've definitely lost the tracks. I don't see them anywhere. This was your first time seeing a spirit. Are you all right?"

She looks to me, eyes still a touch wide in alarm. "It was… It was something. I don't really know."

"There's no sense in lingering in the cold." James removes his hand from where it was, still on Adelia's upper back. "Let's return to the farm."

Here's hoping we can communicate better with whatever spirit we encounter next, but that's likely going to require us staying overnight again. "I'm running low on holy water," I tell James on our way back. "How many do you have left?"

"Two," he says, which is one more than I have. "But we might as well keep our stock full. We'll stop by the church and see if Reverend Thomas can replenish our supply. Is it time for lunch yet, do you think?"

I roll my eyes. "I'm sure we can return to Evenbury if you're hungry."

He gives an indignant sniff. "I worked up an appetite, thank you very much."

James manages to stave off his hunger so that we can head straight to the church, with Adelia leading the way perched side-saddle on her horse.

The church is quiet at this time of day, devoid of the Sunday crowds. I hop down from the carriage, intending to offer a hand to Adelia to help her from her horse, but she waves me off and insists she can wait for us there.

Inside, the church is quiet. The pleasant smell of Damascus rose incense and the twirls of smoke above the candles creates a lovely atmosphere. I may dislike religion, but I'll admit, churches are beautiful places.

It looks as though no one is here at a glance, but then

Reverend Thomas steps into view from a back room, and he smiles. "This is a pleasant surprise. Mr. Spencer, Mr. Esher."

James strolls right down the aisle, perfectly at home. "Reverend Thomas, we were hoping to request your assistance."

He meets us halfway, hands clasped before him. "Certainly. How may I help?"

"We seem to have run short on our supply of holy water," I say. "We'd hoped you might have some we could use."

He blinks. "Holy water?"

"It's effective against the spirits."

"I see." He looks startled by that but smiles again easily enough. We take the empty phials from our pockets and offer them up. He excuses himself to the back room again to refill them. While he's gone, I look around, thinking the church— while small—is certainly well-maintained for a countryside chapel. I wonder if Lord Wakefield's money is to thank for that.

"What else is on our agenda today?" James asks, hovering close to my side.

"We need to prioritise speaking with the Edisons," I murmur. "See if they have more information than the Fletchers did. Perhaps they'll have an idea if Madeline and Abraham had plans on where to run off to, or if they were in talks with anyone who might have been helping them." Not that I'm looking forward to speaking with Madeline's family. Do they know I'm responsible for their daughter's death? My throat constricts at the thought.

A touch to my cheek startles me into looking over at James. His fingertips linger there against my skin.

"You're worrying about something," he says.

"Aren't I always?" I cover his hand with my own, grateful

127

for the comfort his affection offers. "I was just thinking that the Edisons might not wish to speak with us if they know Madeline is dead because of me."

"We'll figure that out when we get there, but it would be foolish for them to hold it against you. That wasn't their daughter anymore, and it was either you or her." James leans in, pressing a kiss to my forehead. "And I'm glad it was you."

As much as I'd like to close my eyes and keep him close, we're hardly in a place for such things. I draw back. "Thank you, James."

Reverend Thomas returns in short order, offering our refilled phials. "Here you are. Should you require more…"

"This should do for a time. Thank you very much." I pass half of them over to James and pocket the rest. Since I'm far more coherent today, I feel I should ask— "Reverend, can you shed any light on whether Miss Edison and Mr. Fletcher had specific plans of where they were going when they ran away together?"

He shakes his head. "They told me they had plans, but didn't divulge what those plans were, I'm afraid."

Well, damn. "Thank you again. If you think of anything else…"

He thanks us for stopping by and we take our leave. Adelia offers to escort us to the Edison place a few miles up the road, saying that they're more likely to speak with us with someone familiar present.

The Edisons live in a home much more along the lines of the Brewers' than Lord Wakefield's. From what we've been told, it was their daughter's lowly social status that made her a poor match for Abraham.

A ridiculous notion to me, really. Had James grown up in a poor family, I cannot imagine him being so different a person that I wouldn't have fallen in love with him. If they made one another happy, should that not have been all that mattered to their parents?

When we disembark from the carriage, Adelia instructs us to wait while she approaches to the door to speak to them alone.

James pockets his hands as we wait. "How well do you think this will go?"

"There's no telling. We can hope. Work your charm on them; you're good at that."

He grins. "I'm just a likable person, dear William."

I can't help my expression softening toward him. "Yes, well, I'm afraid they can't have you. You're mine."

"Oh, possessive!"

"You say that as though you're at all surprised."

"I say it as though I find it remarkably attractive."

I laugh at that, planting a hand over his face. "*Honestly.* You're too much."

"You adore me." He takes a playful bite at my palm covering his mouth.

From the corner of my gaze, I notice Adelia returning to us and swiftly jerk my hand back, feeling like a child caught sneaking sweets. She approaches without any look on her face to suggest she saw us horsing around. "They've agreed to speak with you, but strictly on the basis that you're investigating this under the assumption that the murders were not Madeline's fault."

James shrugs. "Fair enough. We can do that."

Phineas Edison is a tall, broad-shouldered man with the golden skin of one who spends far too much time outdoors. His eyes are cautious, and his mouth pulled taught as we approach, the intensity ruined by the way he shrinks back to avoid tripping over several children barrelling past him to go outside to play.

I step into the house and extend a hand. "Mr. Edison, thank you for meeting with us."

"Lady Adelia tells us you don't think Madeline was responsible for what happened," he says gruffly, taking my hand and shaking it. His skin is warm and calloused. "We know our girl. She wouldn't hurt a fly."

My eyes adjust slowly to the dim, musty interior of their cluttered home. I haven't a clue where they keep all those children. Two more little ones are inside, one toddling about with its hand fisted in Mrs. Edison's skirt, and a new-born fast asleep in its mother's arms. Mrs. Edison regards us with the same impassive stare as her husband, but when I attempt to smile at her, she drops her gaze.

"We're terribly sorry for your loss," James says. "I know this is a difficult time for your family, but we're trying to piece together precisely what happened to Madeline and Abraham Fletcher."

Mr. Edison gestures for us to have a seat at the table. He himself leans against a counter, arms folded. "We don't know much, but whatever we can do to help."

James has a seat, but I find myself wishing to stand. Adelia remains at my side. James begins, "I suppose I should start this off by asking what you thought of Abraham Fletcher. You knew of your daughter's interest in him, I presume."

He sighs. "Yeah, we knew. Good lad, a little too hopeless."

"What was your opinion on his relationship with your daughter?"

"As I said... The lad was hopeless. I've no doubt he loved Madeline, but it never would have worked out."

I purse my lips. "Do you believe Madeline ran off with him, then?"

Mr. Edison's gaze sharpens. "Absolutely not. She'd never have hurt her mother or me like that."

All right, not a line of thought we'll travel down if he's so prickly over it. Let's try this again. "May I ask, what do *you* think happened to your daughter?"

"I haven't the foggiest. But I tell you, Madeline's done nothing to hurt anyone. Something took hold of her, or someone made her do it."

James' voice is gentle. "I assure you, your daughter was not acting of her own volition. It's our intention to find out just what it was that had sway over her, and to find out what happened to Abraham."

His words do the trick to relax Mr. Edison, who inhales deeply through his nose. "Thank you. Most people around here...well, I'm sure you know their thoughts."

We don't. Not truly, but that statement tells me what I need to know. Mrs. Edison has been quite silent during this conversation. Her eyes remain downcast, her face tired and worn. I recall the sound of her sobbing over her dead daughter's body, and guilt lights up in me anew. "One last question. How did Madeline feel about the church?"

"She was a good, God-fearing child," Mr. Edison responds. "She spent a lot of time visiting and doing what she could to help Reverend Thomas."

Funny. Somehow, I doubt all that time away from home was spent assisting Reverend Thomas with anything; he certainly never mentioned it. It was likely a cover-up for her to spend time with Abraham, but this isn't something I'll say to a set of grieving, defensive parents. I wonder if Mr. Edison understands his refusal to think his daughter *might* have run away could be hindering our progress. I could really use a drink right about now.

We thank the Edisons for their time and Mr. Edison sees us out. It feels like a wasted trip.

YET again, we're left with conflicting stories. The
Fletchers believe Madeline and Abraham ran off. The
Edisons do not. Then we have Reverend Thomas'
bit of information, which could be shared with the families,
but… No. I'm of the opinion that what they shared with him
should be kept secret. We've no idea yet if they did manage to
leave, or if they were caught up in something else before they
had the chance.

The three of us make our way back to Evenbury, worn
out and more than a little discouraged. It is not, however,
the first time James and I have run into walls during our
investigations. How many times did we encounter dead-ends
back at Whisperwood? Perhaps we need to step back. Start
from the beginning. Really analyse what we know.

I do that very thing over a late, light lunch of sandwiches
and tea, scribbling down in neat, organised lines the various

facts we have. Sadly, doing this makes me realise that most of what we 'know' is assumption. Theory. We *think* Madeline was possessed, and it's a solid theory, but not a proven one. We *think* she did not act alone. We *think* Abraham might still be out there somewhere, though what state he is in, there's no telling.

It isn't until later in the evening that Foss finds us, a letter in hand, and offers it to James. There are only two people it could be from all the way out here: Virgil or Miss Bennett. I sit up straighter.

James slides a thumb beneath the envelope flap to break the seal and remove the letter, scanning it. "Virgil says he'll be here Tuesday afternoon."

"Wait, he's coming himself?" He ought to be at school right about now. Well, whatever. Perhaps he has a holiday. I don't exactly keep up with his schedule. At this point, a fresh set of eyes certainly won't hurt.

I take a sip from my tea, then, and pause. "…Isn't today Tuesday?"

James peers back at me. "Is it?"

I'm losing track of our days, so I turn to Adelia, who clearly wasn't paying us any attention over her tea and book. "What day is it?"

She raises a brow. "Tuesday."

So apparently Virgil's letter arrived…after he did. I groan, rocking to my feet as James does the same. I never did get my drink, and I've still a while yet before I think James will give me my medicine. "Will you be joining us, Adelia?"

Adelia considers it for only a second before smiling and rising. "Well, Father *is* always after me to socialise more."

"I'm afraid Virgil is not the best at socialising," I say, fetching my coat.

"Virgil is not good at much except for making people go to bed by curfew," James counters.

I give Adelia a smile that lets her know James is being terribly over-dramatic. Virgil is one of his favourite people to endlessly needle.

For this trip, we make use of one of Wakefield's larger carriages, a four-seater, so that we've room to bring Virgil back with us should he not have plans to stay in town. Adelia insists lodgings there are not the best.

It takes longer than last time on account of it being so dark out, and I almost wish we'd asked for a driver. I can't see ten feet in front of my face. Then again, my eyesight is hardly the best even in broad daylight.

The dark roads lit only by the feeble light of the carriage lanterns make my heart start and stop at every peculiar noise and shadow, and I find myself more than once nearly reaching for James' hand.

At least the town is not so intimidating. Although it isn't as well-lit as Whitechapel at night, it's early enough yet that the streets are still moderately busy, businesses are only just beginning to close, and the morgue's "open" sign is still present upon the door.

When we step in, triggering the bell, it takes a few moments before anyone comes to greet us. It just so happens to be the coroner's assistant from the other day, although he's got a mile-wide scowl upon his face. The moment he spots us and recognises who we are, his eyes widen. "Oi, you there!"

James, completely unabashed by that glare, smiles. "Good evening!"

He huffs, pointing down the hall he emerged from. "That your friend in there?"

My mouth twitches down. "That depends. What is he doing?"

"He swaggered in here sayin' he was a coroner from London, and he's been cuttin' into that Edison girl's body. I'll have 'im arrested if you don't get a handle on 'im!"

Ah. Well. I'm surprised this gentleman allowed it, but then again, the image of Virgil swanning in here and granting himself permission to do as he pleases is immensely entertaining. I wonder if a bribe was involved.

"We'll see to it," I say, ducking past his broad form to head down the corridor with James and Adelia at my back. At the far end of the hall, I push open the same door we were brought to before.

Inside is Virgil, working by the light of the gas lamps. He's discarded his coat and his sleeves are shoved to his elbows, tie swept back over one shoulder as he hunches forward. When he hears us enter, he doesn't so much as glance up. "I told you to stop rushing me. It'll be just a few moments."

James scoots around me. "The bloke in charge is doing the rushing."

Only then does Virgil pause, just a brief flick of his eyes up to our faces before he returns to what he's doing, ever so focused. "I was beginning to think you wouldn't show up."

"You arrived before your letter did." As loath as I am to advance and get a better look at his work, James marches right on over and I fall into step beside him. I have never seen an autopsy performed before, and I daresay I could have died happy never doing so. I stop at Madeline's feet. One look at her ribcage split wide open is all I need before I'm turning away, stomach rolling with enough force that I'm concerned I'll lose my lunch.

Adelia, however, seems completely unbothered. She steps up to Madeline's shoulder, directly across from Virgil, a look of fascination upon her face. "What are you hoping to find?"

The new voice does the trick of distracting Virgil from his work, and his head lifts. His eyes lock onto Adelia opposite from him, his mouth parts to speak, and…he promptly drops his scalpel into the woman's open chest cavity. "Ah."

James snorts out a laugh. "Slippery hands there, Virgil? You're going to embarrass dear William; he told Adelia you were skilled."

Virgil continues to stare wide-eyed, although even in the lantern light I can see his cheeks beginning to redden, which is quite fascinating. I don't believe I've ever seen him flustered. "You, ah. I'm sorry. I had not expected…"

"Virgil Appleton, this is Lady Adelia Wakefield," James introduces. "Her father is our employer. She's been helping us with this investigation."

"Oh," Virgil says, which is most unlike him because he's always such a polite fellow that for him to forget himself is unusual. He seems to shake off his surprise, however, straightening his bent posture. He starts to offer a hand, seems to realise he's been wrist-deep inside a corpse, and refrains. "Lady Adelia. It's a pleasure to meet you."

"And you." Despite James' snickering, Adelia smiles, resting her fingertips upon the table. "What is it you're hoping to learn from Madeline's body, Mr. Appleton?"

"I was…" He blinks a few times and snaps himself out of gawking at her like some ridiculous schoolboy. "I was merely studying Miss Edison here. William wrote that she was possessed, and I was curious to see if there were any lasting effects on the body. I never got a thorough look at William when he was possessed—" I shoot him a sharp glare to shut him up, but he's so focused on Adelia he doesn't catch it. "—So, this seemed like a prime opportunity."

Adelia snaps her eyes to his face. "William was possessed?"

Virgil raises an eyebrow and slowly slides his gaze to me. "Um. Maybe?"

My look turns scathing. "Why don't you remove your tool from that poor woman's ribcage, Appleton?"

Adelia frowns, and I can see her lips part with a hundred questions, but she lets out a breath and seems to decide against letting them loose for now. "Is there anything I can assist with?"

As always, Virgil's expressions are tricky to read. He watches Adelia appraisingly a moment before dipping down to, yes, retrieve the lancet. "Most people would not want to dirty their hands, my lady."

Adelia scoffs. "I'm not interested in what most people would do."

Virgil plucks the scalpel free and wipes it on the shroud covering Madeline from the waist down. From the tray beside him, he picks up what appears to be a chunk of clay and offers it to Adelia. "We need imprints of her teeth."

My face blanches, but Adelia scarcely blinks as she takes it. "All right."

James chuckles at me as I roll my gaze to the ceiling, feeling squeamish at watching the pair of them work. Virgil does not seem to notice my discomfort in the slightest.

"I've noticed during my examination," he says, "Miss Edison, is it? She's quite emaciated. Was she always like that?"

"Not at all." Adelia studies Madeline's ashen face before gingerly prying her mouth open. "Their family wasn't rich, but they never went hungry."

He hmm's, lifting one of Madeline's wrists. I do turn enough to watch this and, yes, I suppose I'd not given it much thought before, but she *does* look quite skeletal. More so than a girl only a few days dead ought to look. Virgil runs a thumb across the prominent bones of her wrists. "How long was she missing? A few months?"

137

"About that, yes," James answers.

"Wherever she was during that time, she wasn't eating well."

Adelia considers. "She couldn't have gone terribly far just to wind up back here."

"Unless she was being held somewhere against her will." Virgil lifts her arm. "Look, abrasions on her wrists and ankles." That coaxes James and I both closer to get a better look. The marks are faint in the poor lighting, but there are, in fact, bruises and raw, worn skin, particularly upon her ankles.

"Christ," James breathes.

"If she was being held prisoner somewhere, then is it possible Mr. Fletcher is being held, too?"

James lingers by my side. "If he is, we might find him yet."

"I would love to share in your optimism," I say.

Adelia completes her task of meticulously getting the impressions of Madeline's teeth into the hunk of clay. Virgil sets his tools aside, rinses his hands in a nearby bucket, and steps around the table to the other draped bodies, beckoning Adelia to join him. He draws the sheet back from one of the bodies. Mrs. Brewer.

"Look for a bite mark with clean enough edges we can compare to the ones taken from Miss Edison," he instructs Adelia. Which appears to be easier said than done. Not all of the damage is from teeth, and many of the bite marks involved shredded flesh rather than simple puncture wounds.

Adelia sets to investigating the children, and I see her pause as she unveils them, a flicker of sadness settling into her features. After a few moments of searching, she straightens up and looks to Virgil. "I might have found one that works."

Virgil doesn't look away from his own task, studying Mrs. Brewer's lacerated throat. "Go on, then. See if you can't match it up to the print you took."

He seems to have every bit of faith she can do it without him hovering over her shoulder. After some time, Adelia speaks up again. "It's not lining up no matter which way I turn it."

I glance over, curious. Virgil straightens his spine and moves to her side, dropping to a crouch to put himself eye-level with the wound on the boy's arm. Unlike the other injuries, this is very much a single bite, something chomping down and then releasing. Virgil moves so easily and with such comfort around the dead and I cannot understand it. Has a year at university really desensitised him so much, or has he always been this way?

"Mm. Miss Edison has quite straight teeth," he finally says. "Whoever made this mark has canines that didn't quite align with his premolars, and their left incisor is crooked." He tips his head to look up at Adelia. "Well spotted."

Adelia offers a genuinely pleased smile. James leans over to murmur to me, "Uh-oh, is that competition I see?"

"I'm certain Virgil still only has eyes for you," I mutter dryly, then, louder, "Virgil, how positive are you?"

He rises to his feet and turns to us. "As certain as one can be when they've not done this sort of thing before."

I pinch the bridge of my nose, thinking I really ought to have had a drink before we came here. "All right. So that confirms she wasn't acting alone, but that means we have *two* possessed people carrying out a murder? That's almost as unbelievable as her doing it by herself."

"Or one possessed person and one madman," Adelia says.

"A possibility, but what would have stopped her from attacking her companion?" I point out. "And what sort of common criminal takes a bite out of a child?"

Adelia looks down to the little boy, touching her fingertips to the back of his hand. "The sort insane enough to have command over a possessed person."

That gives me pause and I turn to James. "That's not possible, is it? Actually *controlling* someone under possession?" Miss Bennett has never said anything of the sort, although I can't say the subject has ever arisen, either.

James scrapes a hand through his hair with a sigh. "I don't know."

"Well, it would make sense, wouldn't it?" Adelia asks. "All the tales of people summoning demons to control, trapping spirits to do their bidding…"

I cross my arms. "I can't say if any of those stories are true, but I suppose we can't rule any of it out."

"We've seen spirits have an effect on people before, if you'll recall," Virgil says. "We've long suspected Headmaster King was pushed over the edge by Mordaunt's ghost."

Fair enough. Thinking on it too much is giving me a headache. I drop my gaze to Madeline's body, feeling the wound in my neck aching with memory. "Maybe you ought to…ah, put her back together? It's growing late, and I suspect you'll be in a pinch of trouble if the coroner's assistant returns."

James laughs. "Oh, we got rather distracted. We were supposed to come in and drive you out."

Virgil's face twitches into a frown. "William summoned me here to assist with the bodies, did you not?"

"To be perfectly fair, I wrote asking for your advice. I'd not meant you needed to drop everything to actually come here."

He gives a bit of a sniff, stepping back to Madeline's body. "If my friends require my help, then that is where I should be."

"We're not friends." James scrunches up his nose, and I promptly jab him between the ribs, because Virgil is a man who takes things quite literally and I can tell by the flat expression he casts at James that he isn't entirely sure whether or not he's joking. James rubs at his side. "It was a jest, you miserable bastards."

"No cake for you," I mumble at him.

"I shall have my cake! And yours, and Virgil's, since none of you are any fun."

Virgil seems to have brushed it off. He begins the task of returning Madeline's organs into her body and stitching her up, although he pauses halfway through, as though debating, and flicks his gaze to Adelia. "…Would you like to try?"

Adelia startles, glancing to us like she expects us to object. Otherwise, there isn't a moment's hesitation. "Certainly."

He graces her with a bare smile, which is about a hundred times more of a smile than he gives anyone else, and coaxes Adelia closer to place the needle in her hands. "Just follow the stitches I've done."

As they work, James leans over to me. "Do you think he's going to throw up out of nerves? He looks pale."

"I think that's just his face, James."

He pinches my side and I squirm with a slow smile.

Once the pair of them have finished their task and washed up, we take our leave. The coroner's assistant casts scathing looks in our direction as we depart, undoubtedly angry at the implied notion that the original autopsy was not performed well enough, but I pay him no mind.

With him, Virgil has brought only one small case of belongings and his bag of medical tools, so stashing them upon the carriage is easy enough. I cannot help but dwell on the fact that it's late, I'm tired, hungry, and in dire need of my medicine. The smell of the morgue will not leave my sinuses.

If James notices my squirrelliness, he doesn't comment on it. At some point during the trip he asks Virgil, "You're sticking around, then? Are you accompanying us on our overnight excursion?"

Virgil has busied himself attempting small-talk with Adelia. Thankfully for him, getting on the topic of crime scenes seems to do the trick. He appears sincerely interested in her opinion on all manner of things; I'm not certain I've ever seen him speak so much to a person before.

To James' question, he blinks. "Excursion?"

"To the Brewers'," I say, head tipping back and eyes closed as I fend off the nervous constriction building in my chest. "Are we really doing that tonight?"

"Yes," James responds. I feel him shift, and I suspect he's watching me. "I can go on my own, if you'd prefer."

My eyes snap open. "Absolutely not. But it's growing late, and Virgil's been travelling all day. Perhaps it would do us good to regroup and attempt this tomorrow."

His brow furrows a little. I wonder if he sees it, that I'm at my limit for the day. "All right."

Thank God. The last thing I needed was to argue with him. I'm well aware of how cranky I am when I get like this, and I'm prone to letting my tone be far harsher than I mean it to.

It's pitch-dark out by the time we arrive back at Evenbury. Wakefield himself hurries down into the foyer to greet us, relief flooding his features at the sight of Adelia.

"Good heavens, child! You could have at least told me you'd be off gallivanting around today! Had one of the servants not seen you leave, I'd have been worried to death."

Adelia takes this lecture in stride, an amused smile playing across her face as she leans up to kiss his cheek. "You were busy when I left. I apologise."

Wakefield sighs, but seems placated enough. He looks to James and me. "Where did you go?"

"Lady Adelia was merely introducing us to some of the

people we wanted to question," James says easily and with a sweet smile. "They were far more receptive to our inquiries with her accompanying us."

Wakefield frowns, but the answer seems to work. Were we to inform him Adelia spent her evening sewing up corpses, I doubt he'd be pleased.

Adelia pats his arm. "And we've a guest with us. Mr. Esher and Mr. Spencer's colleague has arrived to help find Abraham Fletcher."

"Oh?" Wakefield looks up, only then just seeming to notice Virgil standing there, which is rather ridiculous given how tall Virgil is. He's difficult to miss.

Virgil takes the prompt and steps forward, extending a hand. Once polite introductions are made, Adelia manages to get us all excused to head upstairs. A servant sees Virgil and his luggage off to another guest room, and James slips into my room right behind me.

No sooner are we alone and I've undone my tie than James steps up behind me, arms around my middle and face tucked against my throat. "Hello, pretty."

Normally, such an affectionate gesture would serve to calm me. And I do lean into it for a moment, but I feel I'm about to crawl out of my skin and I cannot for the life of me get comfortable. I make a soft noise, reaching back to touch my fingers to his jaw before I slip free from his grasp to begin undressing for bed. "I imagine tomorrow will be another long day."

"Undoubtedly." From the periphery of my gaze, I spot him reaching into his pocket.

Damn it all, I can't help it; the moment I realise what he's reaching for, my posture straightens and relief edges in to stamp down my nervousness. I abandon my shirt and waistcoat upon the settee and turn to him. The smile he gives me along with my medicine is sympathetic.

"Better?"

A tricky question, isn't it? A nagging sense of shame goes down right along with the laudanum. I duck my head to rest it against James' shoulder. "Yes, thank you."

His fingers slide through my hair, reassuring. "Just remember, once this is over… Holiday."

"Holiday," I repeat with a sigh, shoulders slumping beneath that gentle petting. Spending a week or two alone with James in some French villa? That sounds heavenly. "You should go and get some rest, darling."

"Yes, sir." He ducks his head to steal a warm, sweet kiss from me before he takes his leave. As much as I would like him to stay until I fall asleep, I know myself enough to be well aware that I'll not be sleeping for a bit yet.

For now, it's simply a waiting game for the laudanum to take hold and to banish this insufferable restless itching in my bones.

'M up as early as I ever am but remain in bed, lethargic
and unwilling to rise just yet. Habit has me reaching to
the empty spot beside me, aching for James' familiar,
snoring figure to be sprawled out all over three quarters of
the bed, and heave a sigh when, of course, he isn't there.

I almost debate going back to sleep when a knock at the
door makes me pause. I don't think James would knock, so I
drag myself slowly up to sitting, shoving a hand through my
hair. "One moment."

"It's just me," Virgil calls.

Ah. Yes, I'd forgotten he was here. If it's just him, though,
I'll slouch back against the pillows. "Come in."

Virgil lets himself in, already tidily dressed for the day,
which almost makes me laugh. That's usually me, isn't it? As
much as I hate mornings, I'm typically up and dressed early
unless James sweet-talks me into remaining in bed. I don't

know what's got into me the last few months that maintaining my schedule has grown so difficult.

"Good morning, Virgil. Sleep well?"

"Better than I have in ages, actually." Virgil surveys my room, although I suspect it looks just like his, and he has a seat only once I've beckoned to the chair near the window. "Home is much draughtier than this. Not to mention the quality of the beds is much nicer."

I contemplate teasing him about the company being better, too, but decide against it. I won't pretend to know if Virgil's apparent interest in Adelia is anything more than two like-minds seeking companionship or if it's something more, and I'll not make him self-conscious over it, either. "Speaking of home… Shouldn't you be busy with school right now?"

Virgil's expression falls flat, unreadable, though his eyes drop, and he plucks at the arm of the chair. "I'm no longer attending medical school."

"What? Why not?"

"It's a long story." He sighs when I only watch him expectantly, waiting for him to elaborate. "Do you have any idea how many students there are studying in the medical field and anatomy these days?"

"I…cannot say I do, no."

"Well, there are a lot. Enough that there aren't enough bodies to go around for studying. Of course, the larger schools can afford the higher costs and get first pick of cadavers, and so my school often went without. I can't count how many days I attended class and all we had were old Greek texts and diagrams to look over. Performing necropsies on dogs and pigs is no substitute for the real thing."

I shudder a little at the thought. Virgil has a much stronger stomach than I do. "And post-mortems are what you've found yourself interested in?"

He shakes his head. "What father does as a physician is important, don't get me wrong. But he's not a surgeon, and the medical field is changing. Rapidly. I've no interest in prescribing medicine and herbs for ailments that I'd be better served studying myself to find new, improved cures for."

"So, you felt school was wasting your time, in other words. Fair enough. But what are you doing now?"

His fingers still, a muscle twitching in his jaw from clenching his teeth. "I met a surgeon that has taken me under their wing. We are…studying on our own."

Peculiar. If his school can't secure bodies for scientific purposes, then how in the world would Virgil be doing it on his—

Oh.

Oh.

I damned near lurch out of bed, eyes wide. "Virgil, *please* tell me you haven't got yourself mixed up in body-snatching."

His face colours. "Keep your voice down. And no, I haven't. I mean, not—not *exactly*." He runs his hands over his face. "It's complicated."

"I'm listening. Intently."

I've never seen Virgil look so uncomfortable in a situation, shoulders hunched, face flushed, mouth downturned. "*I'm* not doing any body-snatching. However, the bodies brought to me—well. I don't always know where they come from."

"Bloody hell, Virgil! You do know how much trouble you'll be in if you get caught?"

"Please. It's not as though the schools procuring bodies by entirely legal means, either. And *you're* hardly one to lecture me about things that could get me in trouble."

Reflex has me quickly spitting back, "I've no idea what you're talking about." It earns me a most unimpressed look and sets a nervous fire in my belly.

Virgil knows about James and me. Of course he does. Unspoken, but there. After Whisperwood, there was no way he, Prichard, and Alexander could not have known, especially when we proceeded to live and work together post-graduation.

It does not mean Virgil and I have ever spoken of it. I wouldn't even begin to know how to or where to begin. I'm ashamed of many things in my life and myself, but my love for James is not one of them. No, my reflex to remain so tight-lipped stems from the desperate desire to *protect* James. To protect *us*. An unfair thing, perhaps, to presume Virgil would ever turn us out for our relationship, but it's not something I've wanted to risk.

Now I feel rather silly when he's staring at me like that, with a flat expression that clearly reads, *Really, William?* "You needn't insult my intelligence. As an aside, I meant to inquire in one of my letters and couldn't figure out how to word it, but…"

"But?"

He taps his fingers against the arm of the chair. "Your laudanum use."

Ah. Hell.

"What of it?"

"You *are* still using it, aren't you?"

There's no sense in lying; I wouldn't put it past him to have already asked James about it anyway. Still, I stamp down the immediate surge of defensiveness the topic stirs within me. "You know I am."

He arches an eyebrow. "And…? Are you maintaining it well enough?"

There's a dangerous question if I ever heard one. How do I begin to answer it? *I'm trying?* Some days, I feel I'm managing it quite well. Other days, I find myself silently begging James to let his guard down, just for a bit, so I might sneak an extra dose when he isn't looking. The immediate swell of shame makes me look away from Virgil. "I'm doing fine. Thank you for your concern."

That raised brow morphs into a frown, as though he knows I'm lying and just exactly how much I'm lying about. "William…"

"I'm doing my best. What more do you want me to say? James doles out my medication and I've not bought any on my own."

"I recall one of your letters from your fourth year saying you were attempting to quit completely. I don't believe you ever told me what happened with that."

"Because I hadn't thought it anyone's business." The venom in my voice makes me wince. I don't mean to lash out, I don't mean to dismiss his care so flippantly, but the words press against the inside of my ribs, desperate to drive him as far away from this topic as possible.

Not that his expression reflects if any of this is bothering him or not. Save for a brief tick at the corner of his mouth that might be akin to a sympathetic smile, his face remains unchanged. "If you're struggling with this again…"

I throw back the blankets and slide from bed with the sudden desire to be up and moving and, frankly, not having to look at him. "I'm *fine.*"

As I peel out of my nightgown before the wash basin, unbothered by his presence a few feet away, the silence hovering in the room is stifling. Now and again he takes in a breath and I brace myself for whatever wise words of wisdom he's about to spout at me, but…

Nothing.

When I steal a glance, Virgil's gaze is downcast, studying

his folded hands in his lap. Instantly, the guilt returns ten-fold. Here is my friend—one of the very few I have—concerned for my well-being, and I'm being quite a bear about it. I don't want him to know how miserably I failed at trying to function throughout my fourth year. Bad enough that James had to deal with me through it all, and I was such a miserable wretch that even he deemed it appropriate for me to go back onto the laudanum after graduation.

I brace my hands against the edge of the basin, water dripping from my chin, and take a few deep breaths. This was not how I wanted to begin my day. "I'm sorry. I'm crabby in the mornings."

"Mhmm. I wonder why that is?"

I think it's meant to be a jab rather than a question, likely to do with craving the drugs when I wake, but when I jerk my head up to peer at him in the mirror, he's turned, gazing off out the window, and I wonder if I'm being over-sensitive.

I finish washing and dressing and, thankfully, Virgil changes the subject to the case at hand so that I can fill him in. When we emerge from the bedroom, he heads downstairs for breakfast, and I stop into James' room to drag him from bed and get him dressed.

I'm still feeling rankled from my conversation with Virgil, however, so when James attempts to offer my laudanum, I give a curt refusal. I've proven before I can deal without it, it's just harder. A *lot* harder, sometimes.

James pauses, the bottle still in hand, his expression one of concern. "Everything all right?"

I give him a tight-lipped smile meant to be reassuring but turn away to avoid my eyes flicking longingly to that bottle. "Quite. I just don't think I'm in need of it at the moment."

His hands come to rest upon my waist and he leans in, his

lips brushing against the shell of my ear. "All right. Are you hungry?"

"Do you mean am I prepared to pretend to eat while you steal my food? I suppose so."

He grins. I can feel it even when I cannot see it. "As long as you're prepared."

I twist in his grasp to nip at his jaw with a smile. "You test me, darling."

11

FOR the moment, irritation toward Virgil (and myself) aside, I'm feeling well enough that I have faith I can get through the day just fine. I've little appetite but do my best to eat a full breakfast anyway, knowing I'll need the energy.

Wakefield joins us for breakfast this time, which adds a layer of tension to the room because, I suspect, none of us wish to discuss the case in front of him. I'm not certain why that is; we've given more information to Adelia than to him, and there's nothing keeping her from sharing any of that information with her father. I wouldn't blame her if she did.

Wakefield does enough talking on his own, at any rate. He speaks of the original inquest the coroner performed on the Brewers, on the politics surrounding the entire thing. This community hardly has the communal funds for a large, proper inquest, and although many people were questioned, no one was present at the time of the deaths and so what information could anyone really offer? Law enforcement was not going to entertain the idea of an otherworldly reason behind the murders, after all.

After our meal, Wakefield informs us he's leaving overnight to travel to London for some business. He asks Adelia if she's positive she doesn't wish to go along with him—"You could visit your cousin! It's been awhile since you saw her last."—and I wonder if he's nervous about leaving her in the company of three men he does not know well.

His leaving, though, will make our work easier if Adelia wants to accompany us tonight. It would mean she need only slip away from Foss' watchful eye instead of her father's.

"I'll be fine, Father," she reassures him with a smile. "Albert will keep an eye on me, and I'll spend my evening with a good book."

He hesitates, and I chime in, "We'll be at the Brewers' again tonight, I believe." If he knows we'll not be here, perhaps he'll feel more at ease.

As suspected, his shoulders relax ever so slightly. He pats his daughter's hand. "Very well. If you insist."

Once he's excused himself from the table, I glance at Adelia with an amused twist of my mouth. She's quite good at catering to his over-protective nature to get what she wants. Adelia only gives me a patient, innocent little smile in return.

Lord Wakefield departs Evenbury after lunch, which means the rest of us linger about in the meantime. Of course, we still have the servants and Foss to contend with, and Foss seems to be a more prevalent presence in his master's absence, checking on us repeatedly.

As the day rolls on, I rapidly grow to regret my decision of foregoing my medicine. I could ask James for it and he would give it to me without question, but I'm unwilling to cave in just yet.

But as lunch comes and goes—I've no appetite now—and we begin discussing our plans for that night, I'm aware that attempting to work like this, as I am, will not play out in my favour.

I excuse myself from the group for a bit, citing a desire to get a bit of fresh air, and duck down the halls. Mostly, I just want a moment of silence to get my head on straight, but the quietest of places I find happens to be Wakefield's parlour, where I sink into one of the chairs and find myself staring right at the table against the far wall, lined with alcohol.

Surely, a quick nip would be better than my medicine, wouldn't it? It will blunt the edge of this scrabbling, gnawing feeling in my insides.

I've no time for puttering about and enjoying a drink, so I down a few shots of brandy, which is not my favourite by any means, and that may be why I choose it, to prove it's a matter of *need* and not *want*.

When I return to the others, Virgil inclines his chin in my direction. "We've come up with a plan for this evening. You and James will head to the farm after dinner. Once Foss has retired for the night, Lady Adelia and I will sneak out past the servants and meet you there."

Bonelessly, I slump down into a chair beside James', already relishing the calmness in my head. "All right."

Adelia's eyes practically twinkle when she smiles. "Mr. Appleton is going to ensure nothing dark and evil eats me along the way."

I chuckle at that, catching the slight colouring to Virgil's cheeks. "I suspect you'll be the one protecting him. Please, travel safely." Still, it's a wise idea for us to all travel in groups.

We have a few hours left before heading to the Brewers'. Before James and I depart, I steal away for another quick drink or two, then join him outside to load into the carriage. No sooner have we started out on the road than James asks, "How are you feeling, sweetheart?"

At the moment? I think I'm feeling quite all right. The alcohol has dimmed everything to a pleasant hum. I give him a smile and lean into him a bit. "Prepared for a long night and hopefully some answers to all of this."

James turns his head toward me. A pause. A brief kiss to my hair. "Let's hope it's our lucky night and the spirits decide to grace us with their presence this time."

Lucky to me would be not to encounter anything at all, but I won't say as much. We need to finish the job, get paid, and then…holiday. Right. That's my end goal now. Having that end in sight makes me more compliant toward ghost-hunting.

It isn't quite dark by the time we turn into the Brewers' driveway, but it's getting there. The horse whickers nervously as we approach, coming to a halt sooner than expected and refusing to go any further. I look around but see nothing that could be causing her distress. Not that that necessarily means anything.

"And the fun begins," James murmurs, dismounting. "Let's check around outside before we head in."

I hop down after him, steadying myself before catching the mare's reins and prodding it off the side of the driveway enough that I can tether her to the nearby fence post.

Trailing after James, I study at the ground around us. It hasn't snowed all day and the sun has been out, so there's more slush and mud than anything else. We do a thorough sweep around the perimeter of the farmhouse and the stables, decide everything looks fine enough, and head inside after I fish the key from my pocket.

Something does feel off, something akin to the first night we were here, which makes my pulse quicken a bit. It's for that reason I express caution when I ease inside, immediately going to the table to get a lantern lit so we aren't standing around in the dark. James doesn't even wait that long before he's moving about the rooms, peering around corners and under beds, and I scramble to hurry after him, unwilling to let us remain split up for long.

Only once I've seen for myself there's nothing lurking in the shadows do I allow myself to relax. Attempting anything to try to summon the Brewers outright ought to wait until the others have arrived, and we've no idea just how long that will be.

I reach for James' hand, fingers gliding against his. "It appears to be just us for now."

He loosens his tie and flashes me a smile. "Let's fetch our things, then."

"In just a moment?" I place the lantern aside and drift closer to him. We've scarcely had a moment to ourselves all day, save for a few brief minutes this morning.

James' smile doesn't falter, but he takes a step back. "Before it gets too dark and we lose our light, sweetheart."

Something about the dismissiveness in that comment takes the breath right out of me, my hand dropping limply to my side. I could point out we're doing all of this in the dark, but the coldness of his words is enough to tell me it has less to do with the dark and something more to do with…I don't even know.

Still, if he wishes to get our things from the carriage, then I'll head outside with him to do just that.

It's not as if we brought much. We have our holy water from Reverend Thomas, our Bibles, crucifixes, some spare candles, all stuffed into our individual packs along with a spare set of clothing and medical supplies in the event of injury. Anything else is unimportant in the grand scheme of things for tonight. I even thought to go to the kitchens and request a few snacks, packed neatly, and I pull them out and slide them over to James in hopes it might warm his chilly mood.

Thankfully, it does immensely brighten his expression as he practically pounces on them. "You're too sweet to me, dear William."

Perhaps I was imagining his distance a bit ago. "Eat your fill while we wait or else you might have to share it with the others."

James scrunches his face and has a seat. "Only if they want their hands broken."

With a chuckle, I leave James to enjoy his snacks whilst I set to lighting candles around the house. Spirits don't, by and large, seem to care about lights at night, so no reason to suffer by lingering in the dark.

For the better part of an hour, we linger in silence with James licking sandwich crumbs from his fingers, hunched over a few slips of paper and a pen in hand, while I sit across from him with a book. The sound of the mare outside draws our attention, her hooves slamming into the ground and her whickering high-pitched and frightened.

In unison, we set our things aside and rise to our feet. I wait for the paralysing sense of fear to settle in. And it does, to a degree, but at the same time…the alcohol has done a good job of dulling it, making it manageable. I feel as if I'm viewing all of it from behind a piece of sheer muslin. I don't hesitate to move after James and head for the door; my heart is racing, but I'm able to somewhat focus through it.

At first glance, everything is silent and still save for the horse throwing a fit. I advance out into the cold and go to her, hushing her soothingly. The wide, frightened look in her eyes and the quivering of her muscles suggests she would bolt in a second if she could get free.

The horse barely settles enough that I'm confident I can leave her side and hurry after James, who's begun to circle round to the other side of the house. Everything is deathly quiet, unnervingly so. It doesn't mean nothing is out there, really. Just that whatever it is doesn't wish to be heard.

Around the side of the house, James halts so abruptly I nearly bump into his back.

"Our friend appears to have returned." He nods at the footprints not unlike those we encountered the other day. In the slush and mud, it's difficult to tell where the tracks came from, only that whoever made them appears to have lingered here, just outside one of the kitchen windows. Yet I see only prints coming toward the farm and none away.

"This is getting ridiculous," I mutter.

James sighs, squaring his shoulders to look around. "They've got to be around somewhere. They can't have just vanished into thin air."

The window is still closed. Whoever it is didn't manage to get inside—at least not through here. I've got quite good at sensing these things, following that subtle twinge inside my gut that tells me where the dead are, but the alcohol has muddled my ability to focus after all.

A faint and yet somehow deafening creak overhead makes me go still. Fear slithers under my skin.

We slowly look up.

There, crouched against the rooftop and looking much the worse for wear, is the reason we're still out here.

I can only guess the face we're staring into belongs to Abraham Fletcher. His eyes are wide and vacant, limbs coiled tight, joints creaking like a broken toy as he shifts toward the edge of the rooftop.

"There's our friend," James whispers.

It's all either of us can get out before Abraham lets loose a guttural snarl and launches himself from the roof, hands outstretched like a pouncing animal. His gaze is locked on me, rendering me frozen in place. I *should* be able to react in time, damn it all. Whether it's the shock or the alcohol or the fear that hinders my reaction time—

It does not even register that James has shoved me out of the way until I hit the ground, landing painfully twisted into a pile of firewood with my leg letting out a defiant jolt of pain as it angles in a direction it's not meant to go. A shout catches in my throat. I scramble to find my spectacles where they've been knocked from my face. "*James!*"

James is on his back in the mud and snow, too busy struggling with Abraham to answer. Even James, who is far broader-shouldered and stronger than I am, appears to be struggling to keep those gnashing teeth from sinking into him.

And I cannot find my damned glasses.

It hardly matters. I can see well enough for now.

I do not want to kill this boy. I do not want a repeat of Madeline, not if we have the ability to save him. But James' safety comes first. It will *always* come first.

I grab a chunk of firewood and swing hard, bringing it against the side of the Fletcher boy's head.

The sound of something solid colliding with his skull makes a deafening, wet crack. Abraham releases James and stumbles back, dazed but not downed. James immediately scrabbles away and upright, nearly losing his footing more than once. Breathless, he begins his scriptures, and I'm grateful yet again for his ability to memorise because they're fuzzy in my head as they always are in the heat of the moment. I do have the sense to pull the crucifix from my pocket and push it out in front of me, keeping it a barrier between him and us.

KELLEY YORK & ROWAN ALTWOOD

It takes a moment before Abraham twists in on himself, pained, and lets out a deep, deafening moan. Instead of sinking to the ground or letting down his guard enough that I can grab him, he runs. Damn it all. What's with these creatures *running* when we need them to be *still?*

James dashes after him without hesitation.

I start to cry his name, start to give chase. Except my twisted leg doesn't quite hold my weight, and it's all I can do to limp after them at a pace that will leave me far behind in a matter of seconds. Panic surges bright as Abraham and James vanish into the darkness.

If James is by himself, I cannot help him. I cannot protect him.

I press onward until they've completely disappeared into the woods. Without my spectacles, the world around me is a blurred mess of blues and blacks and greys, whorls of paint haphazardly thrown together on canvas.

"James!"

Nothing.

"JAMES!"

Still nothing.

I can't breathe.

What do I do?

Glasses. First, I need my glasses.

I limp back to the site of our scuffle, dropping to my knees, feeling through the dirty snow until my fingers close around the metal frames. They're filthy and cleaning them on my damp, equally filthy clothing is a chore as I hurry back in the direction they went, cramming the spectacles onto my face.

I haven't a clue which direction to go, just that I need to find James before something goes wrong.

I've scarcely dragged myself to the first row of trees when I hear the horses—plural, not just our mare—and Adelia calling my name.

I twist toward the sound, heart lodged in my throat and frightened to the point where I'm uncertain my voice will cooperate with me. Virgil and Adelia might otherwise be a sight for sore eyes, dismounting their carriage and rushing toward me, but right now, all I want to see is— "James." I point to the woods. "The Fletcher boy, he ran after him and I... I..."

Virgil clasps his hands upon my shoulders and looks me over. "Take him inside," he instructs Adelia, in an authoritative tone I've come to know well from him. Before I can protest or even send him with some of my holy water, he's released me and darted off into the woods.

Adelia comes to my side, taking my hands in hers. "Virgil will find him," she assures me. "We need to get you inside. You're limping. What did you do to your leg?"

"No, he can't..." I jerk a hand free, grasping hold of her arm. "He won't know what to *do* and James is—"

"*William*," Adelia says sharply. "Please, trust Virgil. You're only going to exacerbate your injury and you're of no use to James if you do. Come inside."

Dragging in a deep and quaking breath, I try to heed her words. Virgil may not be as experienced as us, true, but he *does* have experience; he isn't going into this blind, and if I had to trust anyone with James' safety, it would be him.

Still, I cannot seem to stop shaking from nerves as I let Adelia lead me back to the house. She pushes me down into a kitchen chair and attempts to check over my leg. I mumble that it's fine and shy away. Whatever I did to it doesn't appear to be serious, just a twinge that needs to work itself out. I don't even want to be sitting until James returns safely. "I'm going to strangle him."

Adelia has a seat in the chair across from me. "He's trying to help that poor boy."

"We don't separate when working," I snap. "It's a rule. After Whisperwood, it's always been one of our rules about this whole bloody business."

Adelia opens her mouth, sighs, and turns away to look for the door. "I'm sure they'll return soon."

I almost wish she would argue with me, just to give me something to focus on. Instead, I'm left to bow my head, hands fisted against my knees as I breathe in deep. "I'm sorry. I didn't mean to speak so harshly."

"You're worried," she says simply.

I don't even begin to know how to word it. How to say how much this job terrifies me, how great and crippling the fear is that something will happen to James, and without him, I...

I swallow hard and nod, hunching forward to press my face into my hands.

How much times passes, I'm uncertain, but it can't have been as long as it feels. Eventually, Adelia stands and says, "They've returned."

My head snaps up. I can just barely make out the sound of their voices—both their voices—and relief crashes over me. As soon as the door opens, I lurch to my feet to go to James. "Are you all right?"

He's dirty, his hair is a mess, and his expression is screwed tight in frustration, but otherwise he appears no worse for wear. "I'm all right. I'm afraid we lost sight of him, though. Fast little bugger."

Now that I'm reassured he's unharmed, I've half a mind to punch him. The anger swiftly edges out the worry. "That's it? That's all you're going to say?"

James pauses and blinks slowly. "Ah... How is your leg?"

My hands clench, expression twisting into something furious. "Have you lost your mind?! You *ran off*, James!"

My tone startles him into straightening his spine. "I

162

apologise? I didn't want him to get away again."

Anger has pushed me near to tears, coupled with the fact he doesn't seem to grasp *why* I'm upset. "Why do you make that apology sound like a question?"

"Because I feel as though you were wanting one but I'm uncertain as to why," he responds slowly. "We're working, William. I was doing my job."

"We do *not* split up, James Spencer. I've made that perfectly clear."

"Well, *you* couldn't exactly follow after, could you? What if this was the only chance we had before it was too late for him?"

"What if he'd turned back on you and attacked again?" I hiss. "What if there'd been more than him? What if he led you straight into a trap? We do not go where the other can't follow. I don't care for what reason!"

James' mouth draws tight, and his voice lowers. "This is not a fight you wish to pick right now, William. I apologised. It's done. Drop it."

I bristle at the seeming threat. "What is that supposed to mean?"

Instead of answering, James steps around me. "I need to clean up."

With a groan, I run my hands over my face and shove the front door closed. "Christ, I need a drink."

Behind me, James' steps come an abrupt halt. A moment of pause, and then, "I'm surprised you didn't bring any with you."

Facing the direction I am, I see the way Virgil grimaces and he touches a hand to Adelia's arm as though about to coax her outside. Before he has the chance, I turn to James. "Come again?"

"I find it hysterical you've the audacity to stand there and lecture me," James drawls, folding his arms, "when none of this would have been an issue had you not come to our job off your face with alcohol. You reek of it, do you realise? So who's the reckless one, exactly? Because I suspect being completely foxed while working is the epitome of recklessness."

My stomach knots as my heart plummets straight into it. Shame rolls over me like a wet, smothering blanket on a hot day, and with it, a layer of anger I am not proud of. "My alcohol consumption has nothing to do with what happened tonight."

James lets out a bitter laugh. "Oh, right then. So you standing there like an idiot as that boy threw himself at you was…what, precisely?"

Heat floods into my face. "*Fear*, because Lord knows it's not the first time such a thing has scared me half to death. For that matter, perhaps I wouldn't *need* to show up intoxicated just to function if it weren't for these fucking jobs!"

"Because God forbid you handle yourself for once, eh?" he snaps. "Never mind that I've been handing out your drugs at whatever ridiculous rate you require, without commentary nor judgement." He takes a step closer, putting us almost nose to nose. "Never mind that you know precisely how I feel about drinking outside of social situations. Never mind that I've never forced you to join me on these 'fucking jobs'!"

I rear back, the words like a sharp slap in the face. Of course James has told me I needn't come along, and yet I always thought it was him being kind, his way of gently letting me know he wouldn't hold it against me. Never did I think that, perhaps, it might be because he truly felt he didn't *need* me.

I cannot seem to find my voice. It's fled off into the darkness, leaving only anger and humiliation and pain in its wake. James may as well have cut my chest wide open to allow every niggling insecurity and fear about my laudanum and alcohol consumption spill out at my feet like an infection.

"I think you ought to go back to Evenbury," James says coldly. "I will handle this on my own."

Without waiting for a response, he storms off to the bedroom, door slamming behind him.

I watch him go, desperation biting at my heels to give chase to him, to throw myself at his mercy and beg him not to dismiss me in such a manner. But I stay put, rooted uselessly to the spot, feeling sick to my stomach and dizzy and like I want to crawl outside and lie face-down in the mud where I belong.

In the course of our relationship, James and I have bickered plenty over chores, finances, work, family... But I can count the number of large arguments we've had on one hand. Even those—aside from our blow-up at Whisperwood—were swiftly resolved. It takes a special kind of idiocy on my part for James to go off like that, to the point where it causes me to clam up and be unable to respond and create a cataclysmic breakdown of communication. James' temper is a beast when it's let loose, and it has a remarkable knack of making a person feel two inches tall.

Not that he said anything that wasn't completely true, of course. Were I at all capable of being normal and dealing with things, then none of this would be an issue, would it?

I become aware of Adelia and Virgil in the room, both silent observers—undoubtedly judging—and I cannot bring myself to meet their eyes. "I apologise for that display," is all I can manage, before forcing my legs to move so I can step outside.

For the better part of an hour, I sit in the cold, staring out at the woods as though expecting Abraham or the spirits will return. Hoping for it, almost, so that James and I can put whatever the hell that argument was behind us and work together, the way we always do. The way we're supposed to.

165

KELLEY YORK & ROWAN ALTWOOD

No such thing happens, of course. Virgil joins me at one point, but before he can get a word out I say, "Don't." He takes a deep breath, and eventually disappears back inside.

Christ almighty, what a failure I am. I'm angry with my inability to function, frustrated by it. As Virgil reminded me this morning, I tried to sober up completely during my fourth year at Whisperwood. With no access to my laudanum, with Charles Simmons no longer lording over me, and with the ghosts gone, it had seemed a logical thing to try to do.

What a glorious disaster that had been.

Final exams had left me a quivering, hysterical mess. There were days I could scarcely force myself out of my room. Days where I sat down, right in the middle of the hallway, unable to breathe and certain I was suffocating. The world had been too large, too loud, too frightening to deal with.

James had been so endlessly patient with me, even when I could tell that patience was wearing thin in places. He'd done his best, bringing me my schoolwork, making excuses for my absences to the teachers, sneaking me meals when I could not bring myself to go the dining hall to eat.

He'd been everything I needed him to be, and despite all that, eventually…I caved. I begged him for my laudanum because the alternative was so much worse.

Now, I wonder if I was wrong.

Did I not try hard enough? Did I not try long enough? Perhaps it needed more time to get out of my body. Perhaps I needed to be stronger, or perhaps, now that I'm no longer in school, it would be easier.

I press my face into my hands. My mind is running a hundred miles a minute, and I cannot make sense of my thoughts. As the night grows swiftly colder and I'm without a thick coat on, I re-enter the house. There are only two bedrooms; James has one, and the children's room is closed so I assume Adelia claimed that bed. So, I snag a kitchen chair, pull it over by one of the windows, and slouch down into it, figuring I will try to get some uneasy rest.

Thinking, over and over again, since Whisperwood there has never been an argument where James and I have gone to bed angry or hurt with one another.

I suppose we've broken that streak.

12

BEING hungover and having slept crooked in a chair all night leaves me aching and cranky. Not that I sleep much anyway. Frankly, we're all a bit on the grouchy side come morning, and one look at James' face as we settle down at the rickety kitchen table tells me now is not the time I ought to try to speak to him about much of anything.

Or maybe I'm being a coward.

From Evenbury, I brought along a selection of snacks and eggs and bread, enough to make us all a small breakfast. Adelia has undoubtedly never eaten so scantly in all her life, yet she doesn't so much as pull a face at the meagre offering. She was wise enough to dress down in a maid's dress yesterday, and I suspect it was easier to dress herself this morning without help than it might have otherwise been in her usual garb and corsets.

For that matter, I wonder how she fared last night. Virgil

slipped into the bedroom after James and, I suspect, demanded a place on the bed, however awkward that must have been. Adelia slept in the children's room with the door cracked open, and I'm feeling immensely guilty over not having checked up on her because I was so involved in my own self-pity.

No one says a word as we eat. Having James seated right across from me in such frigid silence is enough to drive me mad. I'm also distinctly aware I've gone more than a full day without my medicine and my body has begun to feel the effects. Perhaps not so drastically as it did the last time—I don't fear blacking out, for instance—but my hands have begun to quake and the headache behind my eyes is distracting.

I'm sure as hell not about to ask James for my usual morning dose.

Virgil is the one who finally breaks the silence. "I think two of us ought to try the woods again today. See if we can't find where that boy ran off to, or if the neighbours saw anything."

James takes a bite of his food but doesn't look up. "I'd be happy to look again."

I open my mouth to say that I'll go along, but the look Virgil shoots me suggests that I am not supposed to be one of the two.

"It might be best for you to rest that leg of yours," Virgil says. My leg feels almost completely fine and he must know that, which means he's sending me off for other reasons. "I suspect Mr. Foss will be on the lookout for Lady Adelia today, anyway, so she ought not to stay absent too long."

Adelia sighs in displeasure, but given that she doesn't argue, she must see the logic in that statement. "William, you could help me look through Father's library today. I want to see if I can find anything related to the history of this area. Perhaps something will give us an idea of what spirits could be lingering here."

I lock eyes with Virgil. He has some sort of reason for dismissing me like this, and I can only guess what that reason is. If he feels he's helping, if he feels James and I need time to cool our heads because working together while things are unsteady between us or—

My gaze drops back to my food. Not that I had much of an appetite to begin with, but now I'm certain I cannot stomach another bite. "Yes, Adelia. Of course."

We say little further. What food can be wrapped and brought back with us is packed up, and I busy myself transporting our things back to the carriage. As Adelia and I prepare to head out, Virgil catches me by the door, his voice low.

"Go into my room back at the manor. There's a bottle in there you may use."

My face flushes hot as I pull my arm free. "Pardon?"

He frowns. "You have that look about you, William. You can't just stop taking that stuff when you've been on it so long, and you know it."

"James gives me my medication now."

"Yes, well, he's not going to be there, so you'll need to be a big boy and take it on your own. Perhaps you don't trust yourself, but I think when it comes down to it, between your love and your drugs…you'll choose him."

He pats my shoulder and slips out of the house, leaving me with a headache forming behind my eyes and the urge to throw something at him. I know he's trying to help, but it doesn't feel helpful spreading temptation at my feet.

Arguing or no, I cannot leave without saying something to James. I find him still in the bedroom, fussing with his neckwear and packing his own bag. I watch him, resisting the urge to approach and nudge his hands aside to tie the cloth for him like I always do.

"Please be safe," I say quietly.

James' hands fall still, although he does not look up. "I promise."

I want to tell him I love him, that I'm sorry, that I promise to make things right, but my voice catches, and I suspect we haven't the time for a heart-to-heart right now. Instead, I swallow hard, bow my head, and say, "Thank you," before retreating from the room.

Virgil bids Adelia and me a safe trip as we board the carriage and set off to the estate. It's early, it's cold, and my head is pounding. The quiet of a chilly, empty morning in the countryside makes me homesick.

Adelia is so painfully quiet beside me that it forces me to dwell on how awkward this entire trip has probably been for her, particularly having to witness James and I carrying on as we were. "I owe you a sincere apology for last night."

Adelia glances at me. "You owe me no such thing."

"I feel that I do. I imagine all that was…uncomfortable."

"You needn't fret so much. I only hope you two can resume being on good terms."

"We'll be all right," I murmur, focusing on the passing scenery. "It's hardly the first argument we've had."

Adelia turns her gaze forward. "Well, that's all part of love, isn't it?"

My shoulders tense and I have to force myself not to simply pitch myself out of the carriage and hope I land conveniently under its wheels. I steal a look at her. She hinted before at suspecting something between James and myself, but this is a far more brazen accusation, and fear at being found out is embedded deep no matter how much I trust her to keep our secret.

I wish I were better at speaking, that I had the knack for words that James does so I might know how to verbalise to someone how I feel. There are so many things I've never been able to articulate to anyone, even to James, because whenever I've tried the end result is frustration and running circles around my own head while struggling to spit the words out.

Would that I could, I would try to confess properly to Adelia how desperate I am to make James happy, and that I sometimes fear I'm incapable of it in the long run. That I fear my presence is somehow holding him back from greatness.

I'll have to settle with quietly responding, "Yes, I suppose so," and allowing that to be enough of a confirmation of her assumptions. Which is, really, more than I've ever offered anyone else.

She reaches out then, giving my hand a gentle pat. "Everything will be all right. Please, no moping, hm?"

My expression softens the slightest bit. Adelia really is a remarkable woman, and her understanding is appreciated right now. "Thank you."

I shall do my best not to mope, as requested. We've things to do, after all. Such as sneak back into Evenbury and slip past Foss before he can come calling. We'll go our separate ways long enough to get washed and changed.

Before reconvening, I slip into Virgil's room and head straight for his medicine bag. As promised, there is a brand-new bottle of laudanum amongst his other supplies. I stare at it in my hand for what feels like hours, thinking I ought to leave it. Thinking I ought to take it. Perhaps take extra in case it ends up being a while before I can have more…except that's not really how it works, is it?

As I remove the dropper, I keep James' face at the forefront of my mind. Of the care and gentleness in which he tended to me the last time I messed all this up. Of how patient he was, all through fourth year, even when my attempts to be free of this ended in failure.

For James, I want to be a better person. I want to be someone he can rely on, someone he needn't worry about.

And right now, the best way I can do that is by taking only the prescribed dosage and no more. Enough to let me function. Later, when we've returned home, I will have to decide how to proceed, whether that means another attempt at going off it completely…but here and now is no place for me to be drugged senseless, nor falling over ill from withdrawal.

I take a single dropper full as prescribed, tuck the bottle back into the bag, and slip from the room to re-join Adelia.

She awaits me in the library where she greets me with a smile when I enter. "Ready for some reading?"

I grace her with a forced smile, still walking tightropes over my nerves, but I know it will pass. My medicine will kick in, and I'll have a few hours of reprieve. "Of course."

I slip out of my coat and set to researching, which feels monotonous and fruitless, but it's something for us to do, something to keep us occupied. I do steal repeated glances at the clock above the fireplace, noting the passage of time, anxiously awaiting James' return. Something could have gone wrong and we would not know it until it was too late.

Adelia never once comments on my distraction. The silence is eventually punctured by her clapping a book shut. "Well, this has been rather boring."

When she speaks, my eyes have roamed over to the clock yet again. "I also suspect you've been through this library many times over the years and already knew we'd find nothing of interest."

"Hmm." The twitch of her mouth suggests that I'm right. Likely, all of this was simply a ploy to keep me busy in James' absence. "The servants will have lunch ready soon. Hungry?"

Not in the slightest. "I can eat, if you wish."

"I do. Let's retire to the dining room, shall we?"

Yes, she's definitely trying to fuss over me without being so obvious about it.

It's only us for this meal, so the selection is small, which is fine by me. Less that I feel obligated to eat. For my part, I try my best to make conversation, distinctly aware of how terrible I am at such a thing without James there to seamlessly push a conversation along. I really do feel utterly hopeless and useless without him there, though perhaps it's largely my concern over him and Virgil making it difficult to focus on much else.

Speaking of Virgil—there's a subject I can linger on. "You and Virgil seem to be getting on well."

Adelia reaches for her cup but does not bring it to her mouth quickly enough to hide the slow smile. "He's quite adorable, isn't he?"

"Adorable? All the words in your vocabulary, and that was the first that came to mind?"

"Oh, I apologise. Should I have said delectable? Enthralling? Alluring?"

A laugh escapes my throat without my meaning it to. "Are those all words you'd use to describe him? Honestly?"

Her eyes positively sparkle in amusement. "Endearing and ridiculous, to boot."

Not at all what I would expect a woman to think of Virgil, whom I see as a friend but a very stuffy, no-nonsense sort of fellow who acts quite like a mother hen to those around him even when they're his peers.

Still, I admire Virgil in many ways. He's steadfast, loyal, level-headed, and concerned about what is right and fair above all else. Perhaps these are things Adelia has discovered about him, as well.

"I suppose I needn't put in a good word for him, then."

"Is that what you'd do? Aren't you a good friend."

"For most people, no. For Virgil, yes." I reach for my cup—water this time, no alcohol, although I'm itching horribly for a drink. "Virgil was a great help to us at school, and he didn't have to be. And...well, I don't have many friends. In fact, aside from James, he might be the only one I consider as such."

"You appear to be in good company, then."

"Mm. Perhaps I ought to warn you, though; I suspect Virgil is very much the marrying type."

Her brows lift. "Proper gentlemen usually are."

"Yet you've expressed disdain at the idea of marriage."

"I've expressed disdain for the idea of any man ordering me around," she corrects.

"Virgil does seem less prone to bossing you around than he does anyone else."

Her smile is amused. "That is part of his charm."

The fact that Virgil has clearly won over Adelia's affections so easily is immensely endearing. I doubt Lord Wakefield will see it that way. Virgil comes from a lower-middle class family and now, knowing he's dropped out of school and the line of work he's found himself in... He's hardly of status to be courting a Lord's daughter.

I also doubt Adelia would give a damn.

I'm getting ahead of myself, at any rate. They've only known each other a few days. Who knows what will transpire after the job has been completed and they have to return to their own individual lives?

Life has a habit of getting in the way.

13

AFTER lunch, Adelia and I retreat to the drawing
room. It isn't until nearly an hour later that the
doors heave open and James steps inside, Virgil
in tow. In an instant I'm out of my seat, resisting the urge
to throw myself at James and kiss him in relief. Certainly, it
shows on my face. I wring my hands together to keep from
reaching for him. "Everyone all right?"

"All right," Virgil agrees, moving immediately to the
fireplace to warm his hands before it. "It's begun to snow
again. We lost the tracks."

James' grin is strained. "Unfortunately. I'm afraid we're
left to run in more circles."

"I told you," Virgil shivers as he attempts to shake off the
cold, "I still think you ought to try summoning them. Miss
Bennett can do it, can she not?"

I pull out a chair for James, beckoning him over so he can

have a seat near the fire. "Yes, and frequently she cautions us against trying such things ourselves. She says we're not experienced enough should something go awry."

James doesn't look at me, really, but he does take the offered seat with a heavy sigh. "You're welcome to try, Virgil. Nag the spirits into cooperation."

Virgil's face twists, unimpressed. "Is it really any more dangerous than digging up a grave in the dead of night while an angry spirit damn near killed you both?"

He has a point, and we *are* running out of options. I look at James, who finally has his eyes on me and an amused smile adorning his mouth. "Here I am, for once in my life, trying to be reasonable, and Mr. Curfew here is lecturing me."

"I'm listening if you have a better suggestion," Virgil mutters.

I sigh. "There's an endless list of things that could go wrong. And—please, no offense—but especially with two amateurs who are not versed in this sort of thing. Makes it all the more dangerous."

"True," James agrees. "This is a task we would have to perform alone."

Adelia and Virgil both take on the same affronted look. Adelia protests, "Surely you could school us on whatever precautions to take. You said it yourself, this is new for you, too."

"But we've seen it done numerous times," I point out. "And I'll not have any blunders on our part result in harm to either of you."

"Are you certain? It wouldn't be wiser to have back up in case of trouble?"

It's difficult to explain without sounding cruel. James and I work well together. We're used to this, to stepping into situations that are unsafe and knowing we have each other's backs. Having to worry about the safety and wellbeing of two additional people, however? I cross my arms and lower my eyes, deferring this decision to James. For all I know, he may be too angry with me still. After last night, I wonder if his faith in me has been shaken.

Yet he answers without hesitation. "Certain. We'll be fine. We know what we're getting into and how to get out of it should things get out of hand."

With a displeased sigh, Virgil turns back to the fire. "Fine. But if you aren't back first thing in the morning, we're coming for you."

"Deal." We'll be done one way or another by then, won't we? I rest a hand against the back of James' chair. "In the meantime, I had the cooks set aside some leftovers from lunch for you."

Just like that, James perks up in his seat. "Oh, thank God. I was beginning to think I'd starve to death."

My expression softens. "I figured you might."

Rather than usher them into the dining room, I request the servants to bring the food to us. Shortly thereafter, they wheel in a cart of tea and leftover sandwiches and biscuits. While James and Virgil eat their fill, I fetch from my room one of my journals, poring over the various notes I've made from Miss Bennett, some of which have been observations of her séances. It isn't much, but hopefully it will be enough.

After eating, James slouches back in his seat with a heavy, pleased sigh and a hand against his stomach. "Delicious. Now, if you all will excuse me, I think a wash and a nap are in order."

I glance up, aching to go with him. A nap curled up together sounds delightful, but I'm attempting to give him space. "I'll wake you for dinner."

He does smile at that. "Try to get some rest yourself, dear William."

Rest? I don't feel as though I can.

Though that is, apparently, a feeling that changes. Long after Adelia has coaxed Virgil away to go for a walk in the gardens and go over the notes I've offered, and I'm left in the library with her father's books, I become aware of just how tired I am. I can scarcely keep my eyelids open. With some reluctance, I drag myself to my room, strip out of most of my clothes, and fall into bed for a few hours.

Honestly, I would sleep right through dinner were it not for a servant coming to wake me. My eyes feel like sandpaper and my throat is dry and my body seems to have realised how tense I've been, because it aches. I shake the tension out of it, readjust my clothing and hair, and go to knock on James' door to rouse him for dinner.

Wakefield will be returning the following day, Foss informs us. His business in London took a bit longer than expected. No matter for us, really. After dinner has been had, I'll make sure we have snacks and a breakfast to bring along with us before James and I head out.

The trip is a quiet one. It isn't until we're halfway along that James blithely remarks, "If this doesn't kill us tonight, do you suppose Miss Bennett will?"

To have James finally break the uneasy silence pops the lid on the back-aching weight I've carted around all day. Doesn't mean things are fine again, but… Small steps. "Only if we tell her."

"Doesn't she always know when we do something we're not supposed to do?"

"Fair enough." She is good at that, isn't she? A woman far wiser than her thirty-something years, Miss Bennett has seen a lot and knows a lot, much of it intuitive. She stresses that to us often; *Focus on what your gut is telling you, boys. That sixth sense will never steer you wrong once you learn to listen to it. Of course, seeing as you both listen about as well as stray dogs, it might be a bit yet...*

I wish I knew how to keep the conversation going, but anything I think to say catches wrongly in the back of my throat. For the remainder of the ride, I choose to stay silent.

Once we've arrived, however—after we've brought in our things, done a thorough search of the outside and inside of the house—I'm again trying to think of a way to make small talk. Instead, what comes out is a rather pathetic, "Are you still angry with me?"

James pauses in the removal of his greatcoat, sighs, and drops it onto a peg beside the door. "No. Are you still angry with me?"

Was I ever angry? I suppose that I was, although that anger was sparked by something much deeper. Fear. I light the candle on the kitchen table, keeping my head down. "No. I'm not even certain anger was the right word for it. I was just…scared."

"I *am* sorry for that, darling," he says gently. "Sometimes, though—sometimes risks must be taken in our line of work. Particularly when it has the potential to save someone."

I know that. *Logically*, I know that. But my heart and mind are hardly on the same page, and I doubt any amount of getting used to this job will change that. It's one more reason I don't want to be in this line of work, because none of it is worth it if something were to happen to James.

"Yes, well, you were right, in any case. Had I been clearer-headed, I'd have been able to keep up with you."

James leans into the sideboard near the stove, arms crossed. "Are you willing to tell me now why you've taken to drinking so often?"

"Is it really that often?"

"It used to only be socially. Lately, it's been with meals, sometimes before bed. I know you've been sneaking off for it occasionally, too."

My shoulders hunch. I can't bring myself to look at him. Do I even have an answer that I can articulate? "I don't know. Or perhaps I do, and I simply cannot..." I drag in a deep breath, tipping my head back to gaze at the ceiling. "I swear to you, James, these things I do to cope, it is not because I enjoy them. I just need something to get me through the day."

"Is it because of the work?"

"It's because I'm *me*. Because I'm—I don't know. Because something does not work right in my head, or..." I find myself growing increasingly frustrated even trying to explain it, because it sounds so foolish. Mother always thought so. Father wouldn't even hear of it. Had I pressed too insistently that something was wrong, they likely would have had me tossed into Bedlam like some defective toy. Hell, they already sent me to school just to be rid of me, and they'd sounded relieved when I propositioned the idea of me leaving home after graduation. They were glad to give me money in exchange to have me out of their way so that I could go off and be someone else's problem.

I finally turn to face him, desperate that he, of all people, will understand. "The world gets so bloody noisy and close and I feel as though I cannot breathe and it's all just...too much. Everything is too much."

James' expression is nothing shy of sympathetic and understanding. I think he must know what it's like to some degree. I've seen him have similar moments, when he's woken from nightmares, when something has dredged up memories he wishes to forget. Not often and perhaps not always as fierce, but...

"How can I help?"

I brace my hands back against the table. Isn't that the question of the day? "You do help. Tremendously. Yet the longer it goes on and the worse it gets, I wonder if maybe this is simply how it is for me. Maybe I will spend my life teetering between being too sober and too intoxicated to function while struggling to find a middle ground."

James tips his chin down, the muscles in his jaw clenching and unclenching in thought. "Would it help? If you didn't have to do this?"

My shoulders square. "We embarked on this journey together. I agreed to it, and I do not back out of my commitments. I've always known you'd not hold it against me if I chose not to take these jobs."

"I don't want this to be an *obligation* to you, William. I don't want it to be something that chips away at your very being and drags you down. I want you to be happy and well, to look forward to whatever you wish to do in life."

What would the alternative be? To sit at home while James is off risking his life? If anything were to happen to him because I wasn't there, I couldn't live with myself. "My happiness is being with you. If… If I've been a burden, if I've complained too much, then I'm sorry."

His brows furrow. "That's not at all what I'm attempting to say."

"Then what are you trying to say?" I ask slowly.

"Merely that if this life is too much for you, I understand. Not just the job. All of it. The secrecy, the isolation, the danger… You *like* women. You have the ability and the option to live a normal, better life elsewhere, holding a normal job and doing normal things." He hesitates, finally forcing his eyes to meet mine. "I would understand."

182

I blink once, trying to absorb exactly what James means with that statement. Not referring just to the job, but to him, too?

Have I truly driven him to think that? To think having him in my life somehow makes things worse, that I would be better off without him?

Oh, God, if I've said or done anything to make him think leaving him would ever be an option, that I would consider it, even for a moment...

"James..."

He's trying to avoid my gaze, trying to act casual, but I can see the storm brewing in his eyes and the worry etched into his brows. "We should get this over with, hm? Time to talk things over later."

I've not been blessed with the power of words. Not with things that are personal to me, at least. Speaking of my family, my past, of home, of things I think and feel—they're such elusive creatures to grasp. There is a lot I've never told James. Perhaps a lot I never will because I prefer to bury it in the dark and not shed light on it ever again.

And I see what James is doing now, attempting to give me time to mull over what he's said. But, oh, I loathe leaving things unresolved. I step over to him, linking my fingers with his, squeezing tight and hoping the smile I offer is at all reassuring.

"Are we ready to do this?" I ask.

"Not at all." He brings my hand to his lips to kiss it. "Let's do it anyway."

14

WE seat ourselves across from one another at the table, candle centred between us, hands linked. Miss Bennett says it's better to have someone close to the deceased present, or a possession that was important to them in life. I'm hoping being in their house, on their blood-soaked floorboards, will do.

We've watched a séance be performed more than once. We've participated in them. Actually performing a summoning for unwilling spirits is different from merely encountering them by chance, or even goading them into showing themselves. This? This is pulling them from wherever it is the dead go when we cannot see them, from some realm invisible to our eyes. Sometimes, they aren't pleased when that happens. Something about the circle helps keep us safe, and we are not to break it until the spirit leaves or has been dismissed.

I close my eyes, chin tucked toward my chest. Deep breaths.

"We are here to speak to the Brewer family. Flora, Hugo, Jules, Lottie, Douglas, and Alice. We need you to be seen and to be heard."

Moments tick by. The house remains silent. A howling wind outside rattles the windows. I repeat the words again, this time omitting the names of the children, who I fear would not be as helpful to us anyway, and I'd rather we focus our energy on Mr. or Mrs. Brewer. We know Mrs. Brewer still lingers somewhere nearby after encountering her in the woods the other day.

I repeat again. And again.

The hairs along my arms begin to stand on-end, a familiar sinking sensation in my gut draws my attention. But this is different from normal; not a prickling feeling, a pulling, like something is in the room with us, but more like…

Pressure. Something bearing in on me from all sides, like sliding into a lukewarm bath that's just on the wrong side of too cold. It's a vaguely familiar sensation that I cannot place, a feeling of being dragged under while the rest of the world dims, a soft hymn in the silence lulling me into a false sense of calm while invisible hands wrap round the inner workings of my soul to cast me aside and take over…

James squeezes my hands. The warmth draws me back, my fingers flexing tight in return. As best as I can describe it, I push back against the force bearing down on me.

The world brightens back into focus and I suck in a sharp breath, lungs burning in protest as though I've not had proper air in ages. I don't know if I've been out of it for seconds or minutes. When I dare to open my eyes, it's to see someone standing in the darkened corner of the room.

James' gaze remains on me. "She's here."

I drag in another deep breath, shaking off the effects of… whatever that was I just experienced.

"Flora Brewer," I call, tentatively, hoping she'll not become violent like she did last time. "We need to know what happened to your family. Can you tell us who attacked you?" Not killed. Sometimes the reminder that they're dead sends them into a fit, and that is the last thing we need. The circle of our linked hands protects us, but it does not make us immune.

Flora Brewer shifts, subtly, slowly. A creak of flooring beneath bare, blackened feet. "*Fletcher boy. Madeline… Madeline… Madeline…*" Her voice snags on the name.

"Edison."

"*Edison,*" she agrees, voice crackled and scarcely a whisper. "*They took… They took… Oh, my little Jules, my sweet girl…*" Her tone turns raw and pained with loss.

James asks, "Do you know why?"

It's difficult to tell whether or not she fully grasps the question. Although I'm refusing to look directly at her mangled body, I can see from the corner of my eye she's wringing her hands together.

"*All my fault. All my fault. My babies, all of them. I just loved him so very much. Thomas, I'm so sorry, so sorry…*"

James and I lock eyes.

"Thomas? Do you mean Reverend Thomas?" I ask.

Flora Brewer lets out a shrill, wailing sob, hitting a pitch that sets my teeth on edge and makes my hands clench around James'. Her words become unintelligible, fragments of sentences that, when strung together, make no sense. "*A good man, such a good man, not like Hugo, but he just…*"

She trails off. Her restless rocking ceases and her head drops back, black and bloodied mouth open mutely as her eyes stare into nothing. Slowly, her head rolls to the side.

"*It's come back again,*" she whispers. Then she shrinks into the shadows and disappears.

James watches me until I give a curt nod. "She's gone."

186

He gives my hands one last squeeze before we break the circle. "Shall we, then?"

We fetch our greatcoats, ensuring we each have our holy water and crucifixes on our persons. I catch hold of him as he reaches for the door, knowing I cannot ask him not to run off, but—

"Please try to stay close?"

Try. As best as he can.

James touches my cheek, leans in, kisses me sweetly. "I will do my very best."

With the utmost reluctance, I release him. Once I've the lamp in hand, we step outside.

In the still gloom, I see nothing of note. James' better eyesight, however, lingers on something in the distance, and he points. "There's our boy."

I raise the lantern higher. I'm only just able to make out the shape of Abraham, and it's only because he moves, an inky blotch against a smudgy grey backdrop. "Let's see if we can keep on his trail this time, hm?"

James follows Abraham, and I follow James, watching our footing in the slush and freshly fallen snow. We travel beyond the clearing we came to the other day with Virgil and Adelia. Farther still. Widely spaced trees pass in blurs, shadowy sentinels that sometimes look like people from the corner of my gaze, and it takes everything to focus on Abraham, not to lose him in the night.

We hit an incline that takes some effort to scale. At the top, the trees thin out further for only a spell before cramming in close, more like a proper forest than the scant smattering of trees I've seen elsewhere here. No sooner has the ground levelled again than Abraham's tracks vanish. The snow here is thin, more mud and ice. I hold out the lantern to try to discern his footprints while we catch our breath.

187

When Abraham lunges from the shadows, we aren't entirely caught off-guard. James braces himself for the impact of Abraham's heavy frame barrelling into him.

I abandon the lantern, ripping a bottle from my coat. James' back is pressed to a tree, one arm braced against Abraham's throat, keeping his gnashing teeth a few inches from his face, but not preventing his fingers from grabbing at James—his hair, his throat. Uncoordinated and clumsy, but still dangerous.

Bottle uncorked, I empty its contents against the side of Abraham's face, fully intending to pry his grip free so James can focus on his scriptures.

Except Abraham isn't fazed. I may as well have flicked his nose for all the good it does.

I catch sight of James' eyes, growing wide, looking at me—past me—and his frantic voice: "*William!*"

Something solid connects with the side of my skull, knocking me clear off my feet and bringing the ground colliding with my face.

Fuck.

Vision blurred, I roll painfully to my side and then to all fours, grasping for my bearings. The world has become muted and far away. James' voice, too—I can hear him shouting, as though from the end of a long tunnel, underwater.

"William, *move!*"

Everything snaps back into clarity just in time for me to throw myself to one side, narrowly avoiding another deft swing from a short plank of fence post. It strikes the ground where I laid a second ago and splinters in half, much to the dismay of the man wielding it.

James is still contending with Abraham, so this man is...

I haven't the time to study his face. He's dressed in the

clothes of a worker, shoeless and jacketless, the cold not seeming to bother him in the slightest. His mouth twists into a vicious grin as he stalks closer. I scramble back, trying to get my footing long enough to stand. A low-hanging branch grants me assistance. I grab hold and lurch to my feet.

In my other hand, I clutch tight at another phial of holy water. The last did not work against Abraham and I don't know why, but I'm willing to try again.

"Prayer to St. Michael the Archangel," I grind out, summoning the words to the forefront of my panicked brain. "In the name of the Father, and of the Son—"

The creature lets out a vicious howl and makes a dash for me. I uncork the phial; the second he closes the distance between us, I splash the water across his face, into his gaping mouth.

This time, it works.

It does not, unfortunately, halt his momentum.

He staggers. I grab his shoulders as he claws at his own face, and I put out a leg to sweep his out from under him, to get him to the ground.

A simple misstep is both a blessing and a curse. The man lashes out blindly and I fall back. The ground gives way beneath my foot, sending me backwards. Out of reflex, I flail, catching hold of his outstretched arm.

We drop down the hill like stones in a pond. For a few alarmingly slow seconds, I am airborne, before I hit the steep decline with enough force to slam the air from my lungs. Momentum keeps us rolling, unable to grab at anything to slow our descent.

Until I collide with a fallen tree in my path.

A brief, splitting pain blossoms at the side of my skull, and then—

Darkness.

I OPEN my eyes to a brightly lit room.

No, not just any room. My room at Whisperwood.

The light is *too* bright, blowing out the colours of everything around me. I woke because I thought I heard James' voice, but I appear to be alone.

The door bursts open. A girl twirls her way in, making it a point to draw attention to the fluttering blue ribbons in her hair. I know her face almost as well as I know my own. I've seen it often enough.

"Charlotte?"

"Up, Will! Up! You promised we'd go to see Mr. Roberts' horses." She grins, missing a front tooth.

This is all wrong. My sister is ten-and-six now, no longer a gap-toothed seven-year-old. Still a vivacious, tenacious creature, but it isn't the same.

Still, I find myself sliding out of bed even as she dances

out of the room. Her laughter transitions from familiar and comforting to something twisted that makes my stomach roll with nerves. Somewhere in the distance, I swear I can hear James.

James.

He was fighting the Fletcher boy, and I was—

And we—

Separated.

I step into the hallway. Charlotte has vanished, though I think I hear her voice behind a closed door as I pass. I pause there, reaching for the handle, when I spot a figure at the far end of the hall.

James, standing with his back to me, head down and motionless.

I abandon the door to go to him.

At each door I pass, I almost halt, because the voices behind them are calling to me. Mother, Father, my older brother Peter.

"You've got to get your head on straight," Mother hisses. *"Don't embarrass the family, William."*

I am ten again, shaking with nerves, unable to breathe while she grips my arm tight enough to leave remnants of her fingerprints on my muscles. I try to calm myself. There's a dining room full of people—colleagues of father's, their wives, prominent members of society, all with their eyes trained on the hysterical boy whose mother is dragging him from the room.

Peter's voice is loud. It rattles around my insides with the taunting sound of his laugh. *"You're a bloody loon, Will. Stop your crying; you're acting like a woman."*

I am eight again. Peter and his friends have ripped the book from my hands and thrown it into the well, snatched the spectacles from my face, and are jeering as I grasp blindly

191

where they dangle the spectacles above my head. Peter says I need to toughen up. He shoves me to the ground and allows his friends to snap my glasses in half.

Father's voice is lower, less intelligible, but I catch all-too familiar words, *"…no son of mine…"*

I am fifteen again, my mouth full of blood, the air knocked from my lungs. I lie on the cobblestone streets with four boys surrounding me, driving their boots into my stomach and back while I clutch at my head and duck my face to protect it. They caught me kissing another boy near the docks and chased me down. I think they might leave me for dead until a constable on patrol comes across us and helps me home.

I do not tell Father the reason why I was at the docks, but he knows.

He knows. And he looks at me in a way that says, *you should have let them kill you.*

I grit my teeth and press onward, determined to reach James.

Yet the hallway seems to drag on endlessly. For every step I take, it extends another two, and no amount of running will put those doors—and my family—behind me. I call for him, but my voice is muddled, lost in the thickness of the air weighing in from all sides.

"Will, why are you always gone?" Charlotte whimpers from behind her door.

Stop it.

Stop.

"Peter says if you behaved better, Mummy and Daddy wouldn't keep sending you away."

STOP!

Finally, by some miracle, I burst through whatever invisible barrier had been preventing my progress. The doors fall away behind me. I crash to my knees, grabbing hold of James' arm.

Be all right.

James.

Please.

He turns to me slowly, chin tucked down, watching me there on the floor.

But his face is ashen, and his eyes are as empty as that of any corpse.

The world goes cold.

Too cold. My lungs burn with it.

James slips away through my fingers again.

My eyes snap open, and the cold is all around me. A faint, metallic tang sits upon my tongue. The forest is deathly silent. Snow has seeped through my clothes.

Every inch of me hurts.

Including, and especially, the side of my head.

Wincing, I bring a hand up to touch it, and my numb fingers come away stained red and sticky. My spectacles are long gone, lost somewhere in the sharp tumble down the hillside. I'm fortunate that the tree stopped my progress because I'm not even all the way to the bottom.

Someone is, though. Through the haze and darkness, I can make out a prone body at the bottom of the incline, and my breath momentarily seizes in my throat. It may not be James. It likely isn't. But it *could be*, and that's enough to have me dragging myself forward, easing down the hill to where the ground levels enough for me to stand without slipping.

It is not James, but the boy who fell along with me. His eyes are wide and unseeing, and his neck is bent at an unnatural angle. Another life we could have saved and failed to.

What's more, I think I might recognize his face. Dimly. Perhaps someone I spoke to at Lord Wakefield's party.

Nothing to be done for him now; I need to find James.

I turn around, head spinning, still trying to shake the fog from my brain and work some warmth back into my freezing limbs. How long was I out? It's snowing again, and it's still dark, but it's on the morning side of midnight, judging by the pre-dawn light hazing the sky.

Has James been searching for me? The fall was a long one, but only vertically. He could have spotted me from the top of the hill.

And if he hasn't found me, then…

I launch myself back up the hill as quickly as I can. There is no graceful way about it. The rocks and grass and snow make the ascent slow, and my palms are bruised and torn by the time I reach the top.

Back in the clearing, there is no sign of James. Plenty of signs of a struggle; the snow and dirt are disturbed, a few low-slung branches broken and littering the ground. But no James.

Panic seizes my chest so tightly I can barely get a breath in to scream his name. The plea vanishes into the night and receives no response. I cup my hands around my mouth and try again, louder, though my voice cracks from exposure to the cold.

He's gone. He did not look for me. Which could mean a million things, but none of them are good.

I'm moving blind through the darkness. There's no telling where my glasses got to and if they'll be in one piece should I find them. So, when I locate a moderately clean set of tracks leading away from the clearing, I have to move slower than I'd like to follow them.

Not just tracks, either. Drag marks.

Would Abraham have taken James away? He hardly seemed to have the mental facilities for such a thing. He'd attacked like a crazed animal. Except…not entirely, right? Because it occurs to me he led us away from the safety of the farm out into the woods, to where the other boy sat in waiting.

They set up a bloody ambush for us.

And…what, kidnapped James? To what end? None of it makes any sense.

I stumble through the trees and fields, following the tracks as far as they'll take me. I haven't a clue how far I go or what direction I've gone, but by some turn, the tracks eventually lead to the road…and then disappear. Did they board a carriage? A horse? That would be the reasonable explanation, yet if so, there are plenty of recent tracks and no way to know which ones to follow. Hell, some of them could even be from our own carriage on the way to the Brewer's the night before. If this is even the same road.

It's cold and I'm lost and I am not thinking clearly.

And I need to find James.

A wave of nausea sweeps over me. I double over, hands to my knees, head down, incapable of getting in a proper breath. My heart is racing faster than any horse ever could. I'm positive my trembling legs are going to give and I'll pass out right here on the side of the road.

It's all right, I try to tell myself.

I envision it in James' voice instead of my own. That flippant, easy smile and the low cadence of his words against my ear: *It's going to be all right, dear William. Steady on.*

Right.

Steady on.

The tremors don't cease entirely, but they become manageable and the sick sensation in my stomach slowly settles. I straighten, dragging in a few deep breaths. Trying to reorient myself. The sun will be rising directly before me, which means the Brewer's house ought to be…to the right.

I head down the road at a steady run until my lungs are burning and any remaining cold in my body is replaced with the urge to strip off my coat as heat floods my limbs. The scenery steadily becomes familiar again and, finally, in the distance I spot the farmhouse.

Although I know he won't be there, I check the house over regardless. Nothing has changed since we arrived.

From our things, I take the remaining two phials of holy water James left behind and add them to my own. I rip a blank page from one of James' notebooks, scribbling a note to leave on the table should Virgil and Adelia show up as they said they would.

I hope they won't need to read it. I hope by the time they've even woken to begin their day, I will have James safe and sound.

I don't bother with the carriage. There are saddles in the old stables, well cared for and of surprisingly good quality—or maybe not surprising, given their profession involved breeding horses—and saddle up the mare. By no means am I an expert rider, but I'm good enough. And a horse will carry me faster without a carriage to drag along.

With no tracks to follow, I have only one real lead. The man Flora Brewer kept speaking of when we summoned her.

Reverend Thomas.

16

NAVIGATING to the church is tricky in the feeble early morning light and me without my full ability to see. But the church bell tower is easy to spot from the road, even with my poor eyes, and it leads me most of the way there.

The church itself is dark and pounding upon the door yields no response. Of course. Reverend Thomas wouldn't be here at this time of the morning, would he? He doesn't live in the bloody church. I recall spotting a cottage not far from here, just across the way, and if I had to wager a guess I would say he likely lives there.

It's a modest home, probably only fit for one or two people, as I would expect a man of the cloth to live. My fist beats against the door, loud enough to rouse even the deepest of sleepers.

"Reverend Thomas? Reverend, please! Open up!"

Finally, from within, light flickers beyond a window and the door cracks open. Reverend Thomas blinks fuzzily at me, eyes heavy with sleep.

"Mr. Esher? What in the world—"

I flatten my palm against the door and push, helping myself to step inside and out of the cold. Any thoughts of niceties or politeness went out the window the moment James was taken from me. "What was going on between you and Flora Brewer?"

Reverend Thomas staggers back to put distance between us, confused. "Pardon? I don't—"

I slam the door shut and move toward him fast enough so that he skitters back until he's pressed to the wall. "*No.* No time for playing stupid. James is missing, and Mrs. Brewer's ghost kept repeating *your* name over and over again. I want to know why."

Thomas has his hands up between us, like I'm some sort of angry beast to be mollified. "Mr. Esher, please. If you'll allow me to speak…"

"Spit it out!"

"It wasn't me!" he all but shouts. "Yes, Flora Brewer was having an affair, but it was *not* with me, I swear to you."

I've never wanted to hit someone so badly, and maybe someone would think me a particular kind of terrible for striking a man of God, but I really could not care less.

"She said your name," I snarl.

"In what context, exactly?"

"She…" I hesitate, reflecting. Mrs. Brewer was not exactly at the height of sensical communication, and she'd not *specifically* said the man she loved was Reverend Thomas, but…

Slowly, the vicar lowers his hands. "Mrs. Brewer came to me some time ago and asked to speak with me," he softly explains. "She and her husband had been having some... marital difficulties. She let it slip that she'd been having intimate relations with another man."

"*Who?*"

"I don't know. She didn't offer the information, nor was I inclined to press her on it."

No. I cannot allow this to be another dead end. "*Think*, Reverend. If you had to wager a guess."

He shakes his head. "I could not. It could be any number of men in the community."

"What did you say to her when she told you of this?"

"I told her I'd keep her secret in confidence, of course, and encouraged her to find peace with her husband. Adultery is a sin in the eyes of God." He frowns. "We spoke of it a few times over the course of a couple months, so I couldn't tell you if she ever reached any kind of resolution."

I turn away, shoving my hands fitfully through my hair. "Was there *anything* else? Anything at all?"

He hesitates. His hands are wrung together, his face twisted in guilt. "This affair was not some short, one-off tryst, Mr. Esher. It went on for years."

"And her husband never knew?"

"Not so far as she told me, no."

An affair going on for years. Christ, what was going on in her own marriage? Was Hugo hurting her? Why did this new man not step in to defend her, if so? A woman leaving her husband for another man would have dragged her reputation through the mud, but even so.

I've a thousand questions and I don't think I'll get an answer for any of them. "What of the children?"

Reverend Thomas' smile is sad. "Ah, the children, yes. It should come as no surprise that when one engages in intimate

199

relations outside of their marital bed, they run the risk of bringing a bastard into the world. It just so happened Flora Brewer had more than one."

Dread sinks its teeth deep into me. It can never be simple, can it? My head throbs something fierce; a result of the lack of medicine, lack of sleep, and the deep bruise and gash I'm sporting, no doubt. Another dead fucking end until I can sort out who Flora Brewer was bedding.

The vicar seems to notice the blood-encrusted wound on my skull, and concern overtakes his gentle features. "You're hurt. Please, allow me to—"

I brush him off, heading for the door. "Never you mind me, Reverend. However, there's another body in the woods about two miles south of the Brewer's farm, at the base of a hill. If you want to help, do me the favour of finding out what family is missing a son or a brother."

17

BY the time I arrive at Evenbury, the sun has risen, and my headache has turned from a mild nuisance to a blinding pain. I stumble in through the front doors, only dimly aware of a servant catching me by the arm as I trip over the edge of an ornate rug in the foyer. He shouts—not at me, but elsewhere in the house—and moments later, Virgil has hold of my elbows and is escorting me somewhere.

Lord Wakefield has returned from his business in London, it would seem. As Virgil settles me in a chair in the parlour, Adelia and her father join us. Disjointedly, trying to think through the foggy-headedness, I recount what happened the previous night, as well as my early morning conversation with Reverend Thomas. Virgil hovers over me, tending to my injury with care, and the antiseptic stings but helps to clear my head, oddly enough. Or maybe that's the laudanum he slips me when the others aren't paying attention.

After I've finished speaking and the pain has subsided enough that keeping my eyes open isn't making me feel like I'm going to pass out, I look at the three of them, Virgil standing at my side, ready to fuss at my first sign of discomfort, Adelia seated near the fireplace, and Lord Wakefield beside her, staring into the fire with one hand braced against the mantle and the other stroking his jaw in thought.

Adelia looks to him. "Father…"

He stands. "I know. I will have a party assembled to search for Mr. Spencer, and to recover whoever it was you encountered in the woods. I assure you, we'll find him."

He exits, leaving the three of us to sit in silence. I sink further into my seat, exhausted and dirty and chilled to the bone and yet utterly heated with restless energy. I need to be out there, looking for James.

I have the perfect view of Adelia on the edge of her seat across from me, her delicate features pinched in concern. She meets my eyes and tries her hand at a smile. "Are you all right, William?"

I swallow hard and look away. "I'll be better when we locate James."

"We will find him," she gently assures. "He can't have gone too far."

No, I suppose not. But that doesn't mean he's in one piece. I've seen first-hand the damage Abraham Fletcher is capable of inflicting on a person. There's a family of evidence laying in the morgue. The thought of James on an autopsy table with those same disfiguring gashes rendering his body unrecognisable… I tip my head back and try to breathe through a fresh, cold wave of nausea.

"You should get some sleep," Virgil says. "We can wake you when Lord Wakefield has a party ready to go."

I sigh through my nose. Would I be able to sleep? I'm

exhausted and sore and foggy-headed enough that I might be able to. An attempt needs to be made, at least; I'd be useless to them as I am. "You'll wake me? You promise?"

Adelia rises, stepping over to place a hand against my shoulder. "Of course. The very moment."

"I'll try to nap," I grudgingly relent, rising to my feet. It doesn't even occur to me until I've made it upstairs that I should have thanked them both. I shall have to do that later.

Rather than retire to my own room, I find myself going to James'. The absence of him is something I feel so profoundly that I could rip my heart from my chest and it would hurt less. By no fault of either of ours, we've been separated. I have no idea where the love of my life is, and there's a very real, tangible danger present.

I may never see him again.

And...then what? What happens if I lose James? He's been my sole purpose for existing. The reason I get up in the morning. The reason I try to be a better person every day.

I recall the end of third year, after the whole mess with Mordaunt and King. James, not wanting to stay at school but not wanting to go home, had accompanied me back to my family's house for a few weeks. It had been a strained, miserable time for the both of us, and resulted in James almost having it out with my brother on more than one occasion over Peter's treatment of me.

But for my part, the entire thing had been bearable because James was at my side. The harsh words of my family had not mattered when I could turn and see his eyes locked onto me, reassuring, loving, never judging me for things I could not help.

A world without James is one I could not bear to face.

I strip out of my dirtied clothes and wash up, pulling on a fresh pair of trousers before collapsing into bed. The sudden lethargy that engulfs me must be from the laudanum; I suspect Virgil purposely gave me more than I needed just to help put me to sleep. Maybe I will not thank him after all.

It's a sleep that's over in a moment. In one instant I'm closing my eyes, and the next, I'm jolting awake and it's several hours later. I'm still muddle-headed, fumbling my way out of a bed that smells entirely too much like James, and over to the window to look out. Several men are milling about in the front of the house, with wagons, guns, horses, and hounds. Lord Wakefield's search party has assembled. Good.

Pulling on the remainder of my clothes, I begin to make my way out of the room in search of Virgil and Adelia, assuming they'll be going with us. I spot them at the base of the stairs, speaking in quiet tones with one another. At my approach, they simultaneously turn to regard me, and the look on their faces makes my descent slow.

"What is it? What's wrong?"

Virgil pockets his hands, clearing his throat. "No, nothing's wrong. Just... After talking it over, Adelia and I thought, perhaps you ought to stay here while the search party goes out. On the chance that James returns on his own."

I almost laugh at the absurdity of such a suggestion. "Excuse me?"

"You're worn down. You're injured, and," at this, Adelia gives me a pointed look, "I wonder just how well you see without your glasses."

A blush creeps up my face. "I can see well enough to function, and I might have a spare pair." Possibly. Maybe. Did James pack them? I'm not entirely sure that I did. They say you always forget something when going on a trip. "Surely you don't expect me to just *sit* here while he's out there in need of help?"

Adelia ascends a single step, one hand rested against the banister. "And what if he returns? It would make sense to have you here, would it not?"

"Then someone else can stay here to greet him," I respond hotly, almost dizzy with the notion. As though James is just going to march in that door… "James is out there somewhere. Lord knows if he's hurt, if he's frightened, if he's—" The words splinter in my throat and cause my voice to fracture. *If he's even alive.* "I'll go mad if you leave me pacing the halls here all day on my own!"

A few more steps up, and Adelia stands just below me, imploring with her eyes. "I'll stay with you. Please, William. I assure you, they'll leave no stone unturned."

I bite back a few unkind remarks toward the two of them that spring to mind, knowing such cruelty is spurred by my frustration and fear.

"I'll ensure someone reports back often," Virgil offers. "James is my friend. You know I'll not rest until he's found."

My jaw clenches. I grip the banister tightly and turn my gaze from the both of them. "Have it your way. But if he's not found by sunset, I'm going out to look for him myself. I'll not leave him out there in the dark on his own."

Adelia lets out a sigh. "Of course not. Thank you."

Virgil gives a nod of approval. "Then I'll be taking my leave to go with the others. Please be safe, the both of you." His eyes linger a few moments longer on Adelia when he says that, the knitting of his brows suggesting he's not pleased to leave us—or just her, maybe—here alone.

And we are alone. Mostly. A cook and one of Adelia's maids have lingered, preparing lunch since I've not eaten since the night before. Not that I have much of an appetite, but I force down what I can to avoid worrying Adelia.

Afterwards, I scour our luggage for any sign of a spare set of glasses and come up empty-handed. Wonderful. I'm going to be bloody useless out there at night, unable to see five feet in front of my face.

The house is so painfully silent, and I meant it when I said I couldn't stand puttering about on my own, so I stay close to Adelia all afternoon and evening, even going so far as to nap—uncomfortably, sitting up—in a chair in the den by the fire.

Twice now, Virgil has sent someone back to deliver us news that...well, that there *is* no news. Other than they've located the body I spoke of. A Mitchell Keiser, whose name doesn't ring a bell but apparently, I was correct in that he'd been in attendance at Lord Wakefield's party. What's more, he has a sister named Sarah who went missing at the same time. It does not bode well for us, but I don't care about any of that. If they have nothing of James, I don't want to hear it.

The moment the setting sun begins to bleed the sky in shades of orange and red, I start to grow more restless. Still nothing. In just a few hours, James will have been missing for a full day.

Close to dark, the sound of hoofbeats outside catches my attention. I lurch from my seat, not waiting to see if Adelia will follow, and hurry out into the foyer to fling open the front door. This time, it's not a messenger, but Lord Wakefield and one of his men dismounting their horses. Wakefield hands the reins over to the lad when he spots me, and gives me a tired, sympathetic look.

My hope sinks.

"Nothing, I'm afraid. We have most of the neighbours searching. Checked every building we came across—farm included."

I drag in a deep breath, unwilling to let that news shake

me. "If you'd permit me to borrow your horse, I'd like to go back out and look a while longer."

Wakefield gestures at the pair of horses they rode in on. "Of course. Though I'll warn you, many of the men are retiring for the night. Some volunteered to stay out. Mr. Edison, for one, and your friend Mr. Appleton. But without light, it's going to be difficult to find much of anything."

"I'll take that chance." I don't give a damn if I have to go by myself and run circles through the hills.

I turn away to retrieve my coat hanging near the door.

Adelia has, in fact, followed after me, and her brows are furrowed. "Will you be able to navigate all right in the dark?"

As I pull on my greatcoat, I flash my best charming smile, which is really no rival at all to James'. "I'll stick with Virgil. He'll be my eyes."

Adelia looks unimpressed. "And how do you plan to find him with your remarkable sight, William?"

"It's not dark yet, is it? Though if you keep me talking much longer, it will be."

Wakefield steps over the threshold, peeling off his gloves. "Nathaniel here can take you back to the others, if you'd like," he suggests, referring to his companion—a gentleman not much older than Virgil, I think, with skin and hair and eyes of a colour that reminds me of Benjamin Prichard. Wakefield is likely unaware of why, precisely, Adelia is so disgruntled. Indeed, she looks very much like she wants to stamp on his foot and scold him, but instead she turns away.

I give a nod of thanks to Wakefield and start for the door. Guilt has me sighing and turning back to Adelia, however. Stepping up behind her, I take her shoulders gently, leaning in to press my cheek to her temple. "I'll be all right. I promise, if Virgil deems it too dangerous to continue, I'll come back with him."

Adelia makes a noise at that, though she does relax a little under my hands. "You'll hear about it if not."

I give her shoulders one last squeeze before pulling away. I can only imagine how frustrated she is, feeling trapped in the house, knowing her father would not permit her to join me. Were the matter not so dire, I'd try to sneak her out again, but as it is I feel too much time has been wasted.

Riding on Wakefield's horse, I follow Nathaniel across the property at a steady trot. It's closer to dark than I expected, and it's a good thing he leads the way because by the time we find the last few members of the search party, visibility is next to none. I spot them from a distance only by the little flicker of lantern-light against the inky blackness of the rolling hills and trees.

When we're close enough, Virgil draws his horse up alongside mine.

"Nothing?" I ask.

"Not a bloody thing. The dogs had his scent for a bit by the farm but lost it near the road."

"That's where I lost the tracks earlier. I suspected whoever took him continued on by carriage."

"A possessed man driving a carriage? That would be something to see."

"They're not as instinct-driven as I initially thought." I coax the mare into keeping pace with Virgil's as we continue on. The remaining members of the search party have formed a line, combing down the hill and keeping lookout for anything out of the ordinary. I can see what Wakefield meant, though; there's little to see once the sun has gone down. A blanket of snow and black trees beneath a glittering sky. "You'll recall back at Whisperwood, the ghost knew exactly what it needed me to do. However…"

Virgil squints off at nothing in particular. I think. For all I know, he could be looking at something I can't make out. "You have some sort of theory about that, it sounds like."

"My theory," I say slowly, "is actually Adelia's original theory, that the possessed are being controlled."

"Controlled?"

"I brushed it off at first, but I'm beginning to think she was onto something. Multiple spirits. Multiple possessions. Working together, no less? Setting up an ambush and kidnapping someone? Violent spirits act on emotion, attacking out of fear and anger. They don't *strategise*. Even Nicholas Mordaunt's spirit was easily distracted and tricked."

"Then you believe the Brewers were targeted?"

I shrug. It sounds silly when worded like that. Earlier, as I restlessly paced the library of Evenbury, it was the only thing that made sense. If they were not acting of their own volition, then they were obeying orders. Orders from who or what, I haven't a clue. The idea is not that far-fetched. Miss Bennett herself has summoned spirits, has drawn them into her own body to have them speak through her. I've witnessed it countless times. I've been controlled by a spirit who wanted to guide us to an answer, as well.

If a medium can summon a spirit into their own body, who's to say they could not summon one into the body of another?

As we continue the search, I mull over these thoughts aloud with Virgil, who in turn nods quietly and takes it in, brows furrowed, but not coming up with any counter-argument.

It isn't long before we've combed the entirety of the hillside, and the next, and the next, and the rest of the men are beginning to wane, returning home after promises of picking up the search in the morning. Mr. Edison is the last to go, giving an apologetic tip of his hat before manoeuvring his horse to head back.

Even Virgil has begun to grow tired, his horse anxious and fussy, and it's only a matter of time before he says, "I think we ought to stop for the night."

My jaw clenches. "Just a bit longer. We've headed this way awhile, maybe if we—"

"William. Please. We're not getting anywhere. It's too dark, it's beginning to snow heavier." He tips his chin skyward. "A good night's sleep will do us well, then we'll have daylight on our side and more men in the morning."

James *cannot* be out there on his own all night. It isn't fair. It isn't right. It isn't…

I give a yank on the reins, turning, looking out over the blurry dark mess of grass and trees and snowfall all around us, chest tight with the thought of where James is. What if he's injured, waiting for me? What if I rest, and find him in the morning, and something awful has happened because I wasn't there fast enough?

It occurs to me that he said the same to me, once upon a time, nursing his guilt over not having been there quickly enough for Oscar Frances. I'd only been able to moderately sympathise with that then, but I fully grasp the depth of it now.

But I also made a promise to Adelia. I cannot push Virgil—not that he'd let me even if I wanted to. He knows as well as I do that I can't be out here on my own, so I've little choice but to turn back to him with a defeated slump of my shoulders.

We ride for the estate, which is settled and silent when we arrive. All but the one or two servants who live on-site have gone home until the early hours of morning. One of them blearily comes out to greet us and take the horses, having received instructions to wait up for our return. I suspect Wakefield has long since gone to bed himself.

There's light seeping from under the parlour doors, and

inside we find Adelia dozing by the fire. At our entrance she rouses, smoothing her hands down the front of her skirts and turning a tired, inquisitive gaze our way.

"Well?"

Virgil goes to her and shakes his head. "We will resume in the morning."

I lean against the doorframe, arms crossed. "Which means we all ought to get some sleep."

Adelia's lashes lower as she rises to her feet. "Something will turn up. He couldn't have disappeared."

"No," I agree. "But if Madeline and Abraham were able to go missing for months, obviously whoever took them is adept at keeping them hidden."

Virgil and Adelia exchange uncertain glances, and I imagine they're trying to think of some way to refute that. Something to make me feel better about this whole miserable affair. No such phrase exists, I'm afraid; it is what it is.

There's a very real chance I've lost James.

But I will do as James would do. So long as hope remains, I refuse to let the overwhelming despair swallow me whole.

SLEEP does not come easily. I could medicate myself to rest better or steal downstairs to get a drink. I do neither of these things. I would rather toss and turn for the rest of the night and be able to get up with a clear head should anything happen.

For the first few hours, tossing and turning is precisely what I do. Although my head is no longer splitting, I'm still fending off the bruises, aches, and pains from my tumble down the hill. Coupled with the fact that every time I close my eyes and begin to drift off, nightmares of James laying bloodied and torn asunder in the snow have me jerking back awake in a cold sweat.

During one of those moments I lie awake, staring out the windows, which have frosted over, and listen to the sounds of the house that have begun to grow familiar during our stay. I wonder if I should have returned to the farm tonight and stayed there. Clearly, Abraham and that dead boy were after us. Perhaps I could have lured Abraham back and got a second chance at apprehending him.

Ha. As though I could handle something like that on my own.

Eventually, my eyelids grow heavy again and begin to fall shut. The quiet wind outside, the creaking of old walls, the shift of fabric as I move my restless legs...

Then, an unfamiliar sound. A thud, a slam, a crash. Faint. Not anywhere in my room nor even in the hall, but...below, I think.

And, accompanying it, that frigid sensation of something *impossible* and *wrong* lurking nearby.

I throw back the blankets and crawl out of bed, making quick work of yanking on a pair of trousers and a shirt in exchange for my nightshirt, and fetching my crucifix and phial of holy water. Just as quickly, I hurry downstairs.

The sounds continue. Shuffling, moving about, coming from the parlour. My heart hammers away in my chest as I approach the doors, hand upon the knob, pressing my ear to the wood to listen.

Silence.

I know I did not imagine it.

Cautiously, I twist the handle, and push open the door.

The embers of the fire in the hearth have long since died. At first, the room is too dark to make out anything beyond the doors leading onto the terrace and gardens; the curtains flutter in the breeze, which has also upset stacks of papers on Wakefield's tables and desk. The only movement.

It isn't until I step further inside, willing my vision not to be so uselessly blurry, that I notice the man.

James.

I choke on the sound of his name. Knowing, even as I rush toward him, by the gut feeling tugging at my insides that something is *wrong*, and I cannot seem to help myself. I need to see his face.

"Darling," is the word that makes it past my lips. I halt just shy of him, able to make out his profile. The slope of his nose, his lips, the curve of his jaw, the tumble of his mussed hair hanging in his eyes and the fresh scratches down his face and neck from his tussle with Abraham.

At the sound of my voice, James turns, moonlight cast across his face and the haunted, milky whiteness of his eyes. There is no reaction there. He looks right at me without seeing, and every nightmare I've had over the last day slams into me full-force.

Just like Madeline. Just like Abraham and Mitchell Keiser.

Without thinking, I lift my hands to his face, aching for some sort of recognition to register in his features. His skin is cold to the touch, but the gentle flutter of a pulse still thrums beneath my fingertips.

"James," I manage, shaking out my voice to keep it calm. "It's me. It's William. Please, I know you're still in there somewhere."

Nothing.

No reaction. Not so much as a blink. I might as well be throwing my voice into an empty room.

It's foolish to have expected more. It's foolish to have let my guard down, even for a moment, because in the next—

I don't know where Abraham comes from, but there he is, knocking me away from James with enough force that there's nothing I can do but land heavily, crashing into one of the low tables which cracks and topples beneath the assault, sending papers and knick-knacks and empty glasses scattering.

Abraham makes another lunge. I roll left, away from the broken table, coming face to face with the fireplace and the steel tools arranged neatly beside it.

I grab the handle of the fireplace poker and pull myself off the floor. Beneath the broad swing of Abraham's arm, I drive the razor-sharp end of the poker into his right shoulder, deep. He does not register the pain.

I heave my weight forward, driving him back as he tries to grab for me, keeping distance between us so he cannot get his hands on me. There's a closet nearby, and I force him toward it—at least, up until he plants his feet into the rug and resists. The poker begins to slide through his shoulder with a sickening sound, and he grins.

I brought two of the remaining phials of holy water with me. It didn't do us a lick of good back in the forest, but I've no other option. I fumble one-handed to get the bottle. The cork has been jammed in too far; I can't get it out with my teeth, can't relinquish my hold on the poker to mess with it.

Abraham shoves his way closer still, teeth gnashing.

With a grimace, I shove the bottle into his mouth, and slam the heel of my hand against his chin. The bottle shatters between his teeth.

That, he feels.

Abraham's head wrenches back, a gurgling caught in his throat. But he stops resisting, and it's just enough that I can throw myself forward and shove him back and into the closet, poker and all, and slam the door to trap him inside. The old trick of grabbing a nearby chair and jamming it up and under the handle ought to do. At least for a time.

Breathless, I stagger back, having all but forgotten that Abraham is not the only person I have to contend with. I whirl back toward the windows.

James is gone.

The parlour doors stand wide open. I *know* I closed them when I entered the room.

215

Abraham claws at the inside of the closet door, but the attempts are weak; the holy water will keep him subdued, but for how long, I do not know. I don't have time to find out. As I hurry from the parlour, I shut the doors and lock them, hoping they'll slow his progress should he break free. I'd rather he escape back outside than have him running loose in the house.

But now, I have to find James. Again.

Logic says he would have gone upstairs. I need to alert the others, except if I begin causing a scene and shouting, it will lure everyone into the halls. Right now they're behind closed doors, and they're safer that way.

I hurry upstairs, attempting to focus on that feeling just beneath my skin that I know will lead me right to James if I can focus on it enough. It takes me not to my section of the house, but to the halls containing Adelia and Lord Wakefield's bedchambers. Only a single sconce remains lit in each stretch of hallway, their flames turned low to the barest of glows, doing little to illuminate the numerous shadows in which a person could hide.

The sound of steps up ahead, just around the corner, catch my attention. With bated breath, I square my shoulders and march for it, rounding the corner in preparation for another fight.

Instead, I nearly collide right into Lord Wakefield himself. He blinks and jerks back, bleary-eyed and startled in his nightgown and robe.

"Esher! Christ almighty, you gave me a fright. What are you—"

"Have you seen anything?" I ask urgently. "Heard anything?"

His brows furrow. "I was having a difficult time sleeping and heard a commotion downstairs. Was it you?"

I open my mouth to respond to that, but movement at the

far end of the hall draws my attention. The faint flicker from Wakefield's candle catches the whites of James' eyes, and my heart skips.

The second James moves, I throw myself forward, shoving Wakefield and myself through the open door of his bedchamber and heaving it shut behind us. Followed, not a moment later, by the sound of James' body slamming fitfully against the other side. I lock the door, though James doesn't appear to have the thought to try the knob. Instead, it's just the sound of his angry snarling, and nails dragging down the wood.

I lean into the door and squeeze my eyes shut, heart threatening to break to pieces. "James, James *please*. Don't do this. I need you to snap out of it!"

I'm met with nothing more than James continuing to strike against the other side. Yet it seems to be strong enough to hold for now. I twist around, slumping back against the wood, eyes closed, trying to figure out what to do.

And just as suddenly—confusingly—the banging stops. The hall goes quiet.

Not necessarily a good thing. If I can hear James, I know where he is. If I cannot, there's no telling if he's still standing right out there, or has retreated to the shadows, or gone off in search of another living, breathing body to attack.

If James hurts anyone, he'll never forgive himself.

"That was—that was Spencer," Wakefield whispers.

"It would seem that way."

"Has he gone...?"

My eyes open to regard him. "I don't know," I begin to say, though the words fade at the end as my attention is drawn elsewhere. Beyond Wakefield, to the paintings above his fireplace mantel.

They're no different than other paintings in the house.

217

Some of landscapes, others of people. In particular, I'm drawn to the largest one in the centre, a beautifully crafted portrait of a young girl with rosy cheeks and bright blue eyes and honey-coloured curls framing her face. The painting is clearly of a younger Adelia, but I have seen another such girl before.

Laying in a morgue in the town.

Younger, but the face, the cheeks, the eyes…

I step further into the room, staring up at the painting, taking in all the details.

"Mr. Esher?" Wakefield asks, voice pitched with concern. "Are you all right?"

I drag my gaze over to Wakefield. Same cheekbones. Same eyes. Long lashes and that shade of hair… Flora Brewer did not have hair like that. Neither did her husband. Slowly, I turn to him, taking in the sight of his honeyed hair greyed at the temples. God. Why had I not seen it earlier? It was right in front of my damned face.

"It was you. You were bedding Flora Brewer."

19

I T'S the first time I've seen Lord Wakefield look shaken. His eyes have grown wide, and the colour has vanished from his face. "I beg your pardon?"

"Mrs. Brewer was having an affair. Some of the children did not belong to Hugo Brewer."

It's a bold accusation to make without solid, tangible proof. But then shame and pain and regret etches into the lines of his face and I know beyond a shadow of a doubt that I'm correct. He could deny it all he wants, but the truth of the matter is clear, and I can't believe James and I didn't notice the signs sooner.

It also occurs to me, as Wakefield attempts to conjure what to say in response, that I don't have time for his explanation right now. Every second I waste here is an increasing risk of losing track of James again.

"Stay here," I instruct, voice hard. "Keep the door locked and watch the windows. Find something to arm yourself with."

"Wait, what are you—"

I don't give him a chance to finish before cracking open the door and slipping into the darkened hall. There, I wait until I hear him click the lock back into place.

Everything is silent again. No James. But I don't believe he's gone far.

Something moves to my left, behind the dim glow of the gas lighting at the end the hall. I have a single phial of water on my person. The idea of using it on James, of causing him pain, is one I'm going to have to contend with at a later time; I need to restrain him no matter the cost. I would expect him to do no less were our situations reversed.

"James," I call softly, uncertain whether what I saw was him or a wayward spirit. I follow shadows and a sixth sense through the halls, occasionally catching sight of something, always just ahead, just past the short threshold of what I'm able to clearly see.

Finally, the halls open out into the top of the double stairwell leading down into the foyer. The sconces here have been put out completely for the night, but the tall windows let in just enough moonlight that I'm not stumbling entirely blind.

Which means I see James half a second before he's on me.

Even on an ordinary day, James is stronger than I am. Now, there's an inhuman aspect to his strength. The ease in which he bears down on me until I'm crowded against the railing, bent back and over it until I'm clinging to the front of his shirt to both keep from plummeting backwards, and to keep him at bay so he doesn't give me an injury matching the one I received from Madeline.

I open my mouth to shout his name. The sound swiftly turns to a sharp yelp as James sinks his teeth into my arm, hard enough to draw blood even through the fabric of my shirt. My fingers spasm in reflex, nearly losing their hold. If he keeps on, we're both going to topple down to the ground floor and I don't fancy a broken neck for either of us.

I cannot reach the bottle in my pocket. Frantically I try to recall the verses James has drilled into me time and again, but what comes out of my mouth instead—

"How do I love thee? Let me count the ways. I love thee to the depth and breadth and height my soul can reach, when feeling out of sight."

A poem. One of the first I recall James reciting to me, one I could recite in my sleep because I can hear it in my head, in his voice, and the words come tumbling inelegant and hurried from my lips.

James sneers though he releases his bite on my arm and instead clamps his fingers about my throat to shove me further back.

"—To the level of every day's most quiet need, by sun and candle light."

Then something in his expression shifts, a key clicking a lock free. His grip on me relaxes, and the colour begins to freckle back into his eyes.

"William…?"

His voice is hoarse and quiet, confused, but it's most definitely James, and I could cry out for how relieved I am. As he begins to pull back, I'm able to straighten up and grab hold of the railing to ensure I won't be sent over it to the floor below.

Before I can respond, I realise the battle is not over. James retreats a few paces, a hand in his hair, shaking his head. The noise that escapes his throat is guttural and pained. Even as I reach for him, James wrenches back and out of my reach, turns, and tears down the stairs.

By the time I've stumbled blindly down to the foyer after him, the front doors stand wide open, and James has disappeared into the night.

221

ABRAHAM is silent.

He must still be in there because the door is wedged firmly shut and I see no evidence it's been tampered with. I'm not about to open it and take a peek, however.

Lord Wakefield, Virgil, and Adelia have joined me in the parlour, oblivious to the boy trapped nearby. They each have a seat while I linger near the hearth, soaking in the heat from the fire.

Virgil frowns. "You're bleeding."

I glance down. My sleeve is stained an impressive shade of red where James bit me, but it's nothing compared to what Madeline did.

"It's nothing," I mumble. "James is always hungry."

It's a stupid attempt to lighten the situation, even if I feel anything but uplifted. Virgil and Adelia's eyes widen as it dawns on them what I mean by that remark.

"James is—" Virgil starts.

"Yes. The good news is he came back to himself, if only for a moment." I pocket my hands, leaning a shoulder into the mantle. "He's still in there, and that means…"

"You can save him?" Wakefield asks.

"That's the idea." And I'm not going to entertain any other thoughts on the matter. James will be saved. I'll see to that.

My eyes settle on Wakefield, who has made it a point not to meet my gaze once since I left his bedchamber earlier. "So…are you going to tell them, or shall I?"

Adelia looks to her father. "Tell us what?"

Wakefield slouches forward, elbows on his knees. I've never seen him look so dishevelled and uncertain of himself; he's a man who exudes confidence and hasn't balked at anything during this entire ordeal. Not even being chased into his room by a possessed man seems to have shaken him quite like the truth does.

For several long breaths, the room is silent save for the steady ticking of a clock and the crackling fire. Just as I'm about to let loose the truth, Wakefield finally straightens his spine and speaks.

"I was the one Flora was having an affair with."

Virgil's gaze snaps to me. Adelia's holds fast on her father. "Pardon?"

Wakefield clenches his jaw shut tight, watching her, but at a loss for what to say. If he hasn't the courage to speak, then I'll do it for him. I have no time for his hesitation, not while James is still out there.

"Your father was the one bedding Mrs. Brewer. I feel a bit foolish I didn't notice it sooner. Buying their land to help them financially, hiring investigators to look into her death…"

His hands wring together tightly. "It is not something I'm proud of, Mr. Esher. But yes. I did what I could for the Brewers

223

because I cared for Flora a great deal. They were attempting to get their horse breeding to turn a profit, and they were at risk of losing their farm. So, I purchased the land and charged them half what the previous landowners were, and I made an investment to get their business going."

Adelia, to her credit, maintains a quiet and cool expression save for the slight narrowing of her eyes. Virgil appears to be piecing things together, and he glances over, studying Adelia's profile. "Is that why Flora Brewer's ghost attacked Adelia in the woods the other day?"

Wakefield startles. "You went gallivanting off into the woods, Adelia? When?"

"And the children," I press on, ignoring his question. "They were yours. Some of them, at least. I realised it when I saw that portrait of Adelia in your room. Some of Flora's girls look just like her at that age."

Colour flushes to Wakefield's cheeks. "Flora swore they were not, but..."

"But you knew. She could deny it all she wanted for the sake of her marriage, for simplicity, whatever. But *you knew*."

Before Wakefield can respond, Adelia rises abruptly to her feet, mouth thin. "We've other matters to concern ourselves with right now, do we not?"

I incline my chin toward her. "This has everything to do with current affairs, Adelia. Why do you think Flora's spirit attacked you? What made Abraham and James come all the way out here to break in and, seemingly, target your father? Prior to this, they'd only ever come near the farm."

She shoots me a sharp look, and it occurs to me what a shock this is for her. I don't for a second think she had any idea about any of this.

Taking a deep breath, I duck my head. "The point I was leading up to... You might have been correct, Adelia, that the possessed are being controlled. It would also seem a possibility that whoever is controlling them is purposely targeting people. I think Lord Wakefield was the target tonight. Abraham and James came in here and James immediately went in search of someone specific while Abraham distracted me."

"Speaking of," Virgil interjects. "You said James fled, but where did Mr. Fletcher go?"

Ah. Yes. That. I pause and turn my head to the closet door. Their gazes go with me.

"Who would care to target my father?" she asks, glancing back to me. "None of the Brewers are alive to try to extract revenge."

"Correct." I push away from the fireplace and meander over to the closet, studying it. "People were being targeted prior to the Brewers' deaths. I think whoever wanted your father dead wanted Flora's family dead, as well."

"And Madeline and Abraham before them," Virgil murmurs.

"So the real question is—do the victims have anything in common to make them targets, or is it random?" I roll my stiff shoulders back. "Abraham here might be able to shed some light on it for us."

Adelia folds her arms, a bit of thoughtfulness creeping into her pinched features. "How can you ask him?"

I don't know that I can, but I have to try, don't I? For James' sake. "I would attempt to exorcise the spirit. Reverend Thomas might have the rite of exorcism in his possession."

Adelia scoffs. "I'm not so certain that man knows how to be that useful."

I raise an eyebrow. "If anyone has a better idea, I'm happy to hear it."

"Do you not know how to do it?"

"Exorcisms are performed by ordained clergymen, Adelia."

"And yet you and James routinely put spirits to rest. I'm not so sure there's a vast difference between the two. Besides, aren't you an atheist? Why would you think only a man of the cloth to be capable?"

My cheeks warm a little in embarrassment. "This entire situation is very new for me. We've not had to deal with this before."

"Well…" Virgil starts to say. Despite me levelling a warning scowl in his direction, because I know what he's going to say, he continues, "We *have*, but it was just once, and the spirit left of its own volition."

"It also was not a very malicious spirit, when all is said and done," I point out dryly. The victims of Whisperwood had been dangerous, yes, but not *malicious*. There's a difference.

She tips her head. "I didn't ask if you've done it before. I asked if you knew *how*."

A pause. "I mean… In theory, on paper, I… Perhaps?"

"Then you will have to do your best, William," she says. "Virgil and I will assist however we can."

My face blanches at the thought of attempting this on my own. Perhaps she's right in that a priest is not necessary, but that doesn't mean *I'm* capable of doing it, either.

Wakefield's eyes widen. "Now, wait a moment! I don't think this is something a young lady ought to be getting tangled up in, darling. Let's leave this to the professionals."

Adelia's posture snaps straight and she turns to Wakefield with a steely gaze. "Beg pardon, Father, but I will do my part to bring an end to whatever you've brought into this house, and I will thank you to let me do it in peace."

Wakefield startles, clearly at a loss. What he does not do, however, is argue, although I imagine he wants to. I'm not about to give him the chance, regardless.

I gesture to the closet. "We need to get Abraham out of there. Suggestions on where we can restrain him?"

Adelia turns her attention back to me. "The cellar. Single exit, no windows large enough for a man to crawl through."

"Right, then. My Lord, if you would see if any of your employees are yet on-site who would be willing to assist? The more of us there are when that door is opened, the better. And you might want to fetch some rope."

Dealing with Abraham Fletcher is not unlike wrangling a wild animal. Within the hour, Virgil, Wakefield, Foss, his servant Nathaniel, and myself, are opening the closet door. Abraham, who seemed to have gone almost catatonic left in the darkness on his own, immediately jerks to life again the second he sees us.

It's with a lot of brute strength—and not without a few bites and scratches to our own persons—that we wrestle him to the ground, binding his wrists behind him and his arms to his sides, and drag him down into the cellar. The cooks and maids and other servants who'd arrived in the early hours of morning to begin their work had been promptly cleared out to ensure as few injuries as possible.

Nathaniel and I chain Abraham to a solid fixture upon the wall, giving it a few sharp tugs to ensure it will hold against his struggling. And struggle he does—particularly when Wakefield is in the room. The moment I usher him out, Abraham settles, instead grinning horribly at any of us who venture too close. Adelia, in a moment of brilliance and after seeing Nathaniel nearly get a bite taken out of him, procures a piece of chalk and draws a safety line across the floor.

As for me—well, I suppose I'm really going to try this. Better test it on Abraham than on James, though I'm aware it isn't a very fair method of thinking. *It's all right if I botch this because I don't know him*, isn't it? Tsk.

227

I have little in my notebooks about possession. Not like this, anyway. It's occurred to me to send a telegram to Miss Bennett and ask for advice, but I know what she'd say. *Get a priest.* At least I was able to offer a few key passages to my companions that should prove useful for this endeavour.

As I stand at the far end of the cellar behind that chalk line, arms crossed, with Virgil and Adelia at either side, I comment, "I feel it fair that I warn you: I have absolutely no idea if I can do this."

Adelia, dressed for the day in her maid's dress and flat boots, folds her hands neatly together and watches Abraham impassively. "You must be exhausted, William, being so negative and pessimistic with yourself all the time."

"I consider myself a realist," I say dryly, rolling up my sleeves with a bit of a wince. "And *realistically speaking*, I probably cannot do this."

Virgil folds his arms. "He's the only way we're likely to get answers about James. Consider that your motivation."

"But no pressure. Right." Deep breaths. "I suppose the both of you flipped through those notes on banishing? Any questions?"

"No," they say in unison.

It's simply not possible to cram experience and hours upon hours of lectures by Miss Bennett into a meagre few minutes, so here's hoping the notes were enough, that our quickly discussed plan will actually work.

With an unsteady, tired breath, I steel myself. "Grab him."

Abraham is tied, and not nearly as much of a threat as he once was. Still, Virgil and Adelia advance with caution, circling to either side of him. He snarls, teeth snapping inches from Virgil's face. Together, the pair grab hold of the ropes binding his arms to his sides; a kick to the back of his legs sends him to his knees. Once he's there, I step up, bottle of holy water in hand. I dampen my fingers and press the sign of the cross upon his forehead. He strains against Adelia and Virgil's grips, hissing. It's working this time. Good.

I slide open the notebook, removing a few pages tucked within. Unfolded, they contain prayers written in James' hand. Prayers I can recall just fine on my own but never when I seem to need them most. Some of these even appear in the rite of exorcism, but I can't help but think this would have a better result if I had the rite in its entirety. "St. Michael the Archangel, illustrious leader of the heavenly army…"

It's an odd thing to speak with conviction when the words mean nothing to me. They sound hollow and weak coming from my lips. When James recites these same words, you can feel the faith and the strength and the confidence emanating from them, and I'm positive that's why it works for him. My abilities lie with drawing the dead to me. James… James is the one good at putting them to rest.

But I try. For James, I try. Picturing him, knowing he's out there somewhere, counting on me to be able to do this, sparks a fire in my heart that gives power to my voice.

I don't give a damn about spirits or possessions or God. This is going to work because I need it to. Because *James* needs it to.

"The Lord has entrusted you to the task of leading the souls of the redeemed to heavenly blessedness."

The water may have done nothing, but the words are starting to. Abraham squirms until Adelia and Virgil have to press him face-down to the cellar floor, Virgil with a knee against his back to keep him pinned. Abraham snarls and howls, head wrenching side to side, eyes rolling into the back of his skull. He gnashes at nothing, unable to twist enough to get a hold of his captors.

I reach the end of the prayer. Stop. Drag in a breath.

Adelia says, "Again, William. And again. Until it works."

And so I do.

ORNING turns to afternoon. Lunch passes us by. My voice has long gone dry and rough and the cellar is muggy, reeking of sweat and something deeper, something sickeningly sweet and rotten, like a corpse left out in the sun.

I've recited the prayers so many times that Virgil and Adelia have begun to speak the words along with me.

We hurt. We're exhausted.

But so is Abraham.

The spirit inside him pants and groans, whispering quiet, unintelligible things now and again. For a time, he goes deathly still and quiet. Then in one last burst of energy of a creature in its death throes, he convulses, nearly throwing Adelia and Virgil off him. He thrashes, howls with the undercurrent of a voice not his own, and the room trembles. Crates and barrels and stored furniture and fixings rattle and shake.

Then he goes still, slumping to the floor, eyes closed.

I drop to my knees, shaken, and scoot closer, pressing my fingers to his throat. His pulse is faint and thready, but present.

"He's alive," I say, aware of the shock in my own tone.

Despite her weariness, Adelia does not relinquish her hold nor move away. I can see the dampness upon her brow, the faint quivering of her arms. "Is it gone, then?"

I try to focus. Really focus. My head is a muddled mess at the moment, a mixture of exhaustion and hunger and no medicine. "I don't know. I think… Maybe…"

Abraham jerks slightly. His eyes flutter open, unfocused and blurry, but very much a warm hazel and no longer the milky white eyes of a corpse. He inhales, a tired look of panic washing over his features as he gazes around the room.

Adelia slowly uncurls her hands. "Mr. Fletcher?"

Still bound and limited in his movements, Abraham rolls part way onto his side to look up at her. "Lady Adelia," he says hoarsely. "What… Where am I?"

"You're in my cellar. Are you all right?"

He stares at her distantly, attempting to sit up and finding his range is rather limited, which, in turn, seems to make him panic. A justifiable reaction, I think. "I… I was… What am I doing in…"

"He's likely in need of water and food," Virgil says. "Lord knows when the last time he ate or drank was. I also need to look at that wound."

I close my eyes and press the heels of my hands against them, trying to make my head clear. "I think we could all stand to eat and get some nourishment. Let's see about getting him untied and upstairs."

We set to getting Abraham's bindings off him. As he tries to get to his feet, his legs shake beneath him and he has to lean into Adelia and me for support just to get across the room and up the stairs.

231

Per our instructions, the kitchens are still free of people. All the better. Wakefield himself is likely somewhere nearby, fretting over his daughter. I'll send someone to give him news that she's well in short order. One thing at a time.

Virgil pushes aside a pile of potatoes in the middle of being chopped earlier this morning so that Abraham can have a seat on the table. Before long, Virgil's cleaned, stitched, and bandaged the puncture wound from the fireplace poker. We've got a cup of water placed in Abraham's hands, and Adelia helps him take a few careful sips. Soon, he's swallowing it down in eager, thirsty gulps.

I try to be patient, but the questions are itching to burst free. Chances are he remembers little about his time possessed, but if he has anything to offer, anything at all, that might lead me to James… "Mr. Fletcher, do you recall what's happened to you over the last several months? Or even the last few weeks?"

Abraham stares down into his empty glass as though he's not sure how it got to be that way. "I was… Madeline and I— we were wrong, you know. He warned us about it."

Virgil frowns. "Who warned you about what?"

"Sinning. That's what we were doing." He looks to Adelia. "A man and woman should only lie together if they're married. It's only proper."

He's making little sense, though given the context— "Do you mean Reverend Thomas?"

"What's he got to do with this?" Adelia asks.

"He warned us," Abraham repeats. "He said not to leave, but we did. We tried. We were punished. That's what The Order does."

The Order. I glance at the others to see if that name means something to either of them, but their stares are just as blank as mine. "Mr. Fletcher, you'll need to slow down a bit and start from the beginning."

"He's got to fix it all. Right the wrongs, for God." Abraham doesn't seem to hear me in the slightest, his shaky hands turning the cup round and round as he stares down into it. "No. No. No. It's all right. You don't understand, but you will. He'll come for those who need to be punished."

Adelia rests a hand against his arm. "Abraham, deep breaths. You're rambling. Are you saying Reverend Thomas is responsible for this? For what's happened to you?"

A chill settles in my veins at those words. That can't be right, can it? Adelia has made it clear she cares little for the man, but perhaps her bias is showing. Perhaps…

Perhaps the holy water wasn't working because it wasn't holy water at all.

Abraham chuckles, shaking his head. "You're not *seeing*. It's more than that. Bigger."

Something in the sound of his voice has taken on a colder edge and makes the hairs on the back of my neck stand on end. I pluck the cup from his grasp. He stills.

I ask, "What's he done with James?"

Slowly, Abraham's eyes roll up, the colour vanishing from his irises. A smile drags the corners of his mouth into a wicked smile.

"He's a sinner, too, dear William."

Before I can respond, Abraham grabs the knife from the half-cut pile of potatoes, and swings.

I grab Adelia and wrench us back, narrowly out of range, but his focus was on Virgil, not us. Virgil doesn't dodge quickly enough. The blade slices through his shirt and skin, the upward stroke catching his shoulder, glancing off his clavicle, and cutting a deep, thin line up his jaw and cheek.

Virgil recoils in pain while Abraham leaps from the table and knocks past him. He makes a mad dash for the door in the same breath Adelia is yanking free of my grasp to rush to

233

Virgil's side. I hurry to do the same, noting the blood coating his hands as he presses them to his face.

"Virgil—"

"Go," he hisses, jerking his head to the door. "We can't lose him again!"

I hesitate only a second, looking to Adelia and back again, before rushing out the door.

It's evening. I still have daylight, and it's been snowing enough that I can make out the hurried prints of Abraham's departure heading in a straight line away from Evenbury.

If I lose him this time, if he returns to Reverend Thomas, if he's able to tell him what we now know, then James—

I shove the thought from my head, charging onward. Just past the manor and the gardens is swamped by trees for only a short distance. It opens soon enough into wide swaths of hillside, the occasional farm and manor dotting roads in the distance, trees scattered haphazardly across the landscape in small clusters.

And in the open land, I can see Abraham, a blurry figure running through the snow up ahead.

I have no hopes of catching him, but if I can follow him to wherever he's going, all the better. If Reverend Thomas is involved, then it's just as likely he's headed for the church.

I run until I'm certain my lungs are going to burst. My legs are going to give out, and I am struggling to maintain my footing. The rolling landscape slopes up sharply before me and I push onward, using my hands to clamber up and over the ridge to where the ground levels again.

I don't know how long I've run, but I know I'll not be able to run much farther.

Though it looks like I won't have to; up ahead is Abraham, poised in the snow, his corpse-like gaze levelled right on me.

Except he isn't alone.

234

Beside him is a girl. Sturdy, dark-haired, dressed in the clothes of a worker. I remember what Nathaniel told me: the possessed boy, Mitchell Keiser, had a sister who also went missing.

"You must be Sarah Keiser," I say, more to myself than to her because I doubt she can hear a word I say.

I have only a single phial of holy water—what I sincerely hope is *real* holy water, but I've lost count—left on my person, and I plan to save that for James. I'm worn down, physically at my limit…and I am most definitely outnumbered. Lovely.

They sprint toward me. Exhausted or not, I have no choice but to run.

I'll not lead them back to the estate. I pick the route that appears to be the flattest—not that I'm the best at telling as much without my glasses. The ground is wet and slick. Abraham and Sarah may be tireless, but they're subject to the same difficulties with gravity that I am, and I try to utilise that.

Except, as we run through a cluster of trees and come out the other side, the texture of the ground changes. Not snow. Not grass.

Ice.

A lake, frozen over. What's more, I can feel a stitch beginning to form in my side, along with a sharp shooting pain up my leg.

One misstep, one limp, and Sarah slams into me from behind. We pitch forward. I hit the ice on my shoulder and we go sprawling away from one another. The ice groans and crackles beneath the assault. I look down, brushing aside a thin layer of snow; the ice is thin enough I can see the water beneath, and my breath catches.

Sarah begins to clamber to her feet with a delighted, shiver-inducing laugh, and Abraham barrels out from the trees and onto the lake right along with us.

I can hear it—the cracking. Splintering.

Mustering my waning energy, I heave myself to my feet, trying to gain traction, but unsure where the lake ends and solid ground begins. I can't see a bloody thing. I can't stop to try to figure it out.

Abraham goes in first.

The ice around his feet gives beneath him, and in the second it takes me to glance back twice, he's there and then gone, into the freezing dark water. From that gaping hole, the ice splits wide, an open maw to swallow us whole.

Only by some heavenly mercy do I manage to breathe in before I'm plunged into darkness.

The world goes blindingly, breathtakingly silent and cold. Every muscle in my body locks up in protest, and it's all dark. So dark.

Fingers latch around my ankle, and then my shirt, and I cannot see properly in the murky, pitch-black water, save for the brief glance of a wicked face trying to drag me down, down, down.

It's too small to be Abraham. Sarah, then. I grab a handful of floating tendrils of hair and pull as hard as I can, until I can get a leg up between us to plant against her torso and kick. It's enough. Her grip isn't strong enough. She releases, and she vanishes into the depths.

I try to relax, to allow my body to find its way back to the surface. My fingertips touch solid, unbroken ice above my head, and panic seizes hold. Have I really strayed that far from the opening? I haven't the air nor the strength to search.

Relax, darling. Steady on.

James still needs me. I cannot give up yet.

I press my palms to the ice. There's light, just that way. I drag myself toward it, and a moment later—

I break the surface of the water, gasping in air until it bloody hurts, and clutch at the ragged edges of ice. I can scarcely feel my legs. I need to get out. Except when I try to pull myself up, the ice crumbles and gives way beneath me, dropping me right back down.

Fuck, fuck, fuck.

"*William!*"

Virgil's voice. I scan around until I spot him and Adelia, almost straight ahead, dismounting from a horse. They begin to rush for me but Adelia grabs his arm, halting, pointing—I think—to the lake. I cannot hear a word they're saying.

I can *see* in the next moment that Adelia puts her back to Virgil and, at first, I haven't a clue what they're doing. They're pulling off her outermost skirts, bodice, corset…stripped down to a scandalous few petticoats, chemise, boots, and scant little else.

"Be still, William, I'm coming!" Adelia calls, as though I can do anything else but cling for dear life and try to keep my legs moving, try not to relinquish my hold. I cannot feel my fingertips any longer where they're digging desperately into the ice.

Adelia begins to walk out onto the lake, leaving Virgil behind holding an array of garments and staring helplessly after her. She moves with caution, watching her steps. I choke on the sound of a helpless near-sob, struggling to focus on my breathing, to not panic.

As she draws nearer, Adelia sinks down to her knees and then to her stomach, scooting the last few inches to the edge of the ice and extending her arms out toward me. I can see her shivering already, cheeks and lips flushed, yet her voice remains even-keeled and reassuring.

"Take my hands. I want you to listen to me carefully. Relax.

237

Kick your legs to try to put your body horizontal in the water, can you do that?"

I'm certain if I move, I will be sucked right back down and will not come up again. I close my eyes a moment, forcing myself, one hand at a time, to reach for her. Adelia closes her fingers around my wrists, the left and then the right, and her skin is a blossom of warmth against my skin.

"I can't feel my legs," I manage through a jaw clenched tight to keep my teeth from chattering.

"I need you to try, William. Focus on me. You can do it."

I swallow hard and nod. I will my legs to kick, uncertain at first if I'm even getting anywhere with my attempt. But after a moment, I'm able to dig my elbows onto the shelving of ice. Slowly but surely, I'm dragging myself—with Adelia's assistance—out of the water. She inches back as I emerge, never faltering on her grip. Only when we've cleared the gap in the ice by a few feet does she sit back. "Do you think you can stand?"

I'm not honestly sure, but I have to try. I give a tight dip of my head, releasing one of her hands to plant it against the ice and slowly leverage myself up. My legs are weak beneath me, devoid of feeling, but I'm standing, and if it gets me off the lake that much faster, all the better. Adelia puts an arm about my middle, helping me along.

Soon, the creaking ice gives to solid ground, and a rush of breath escapes me. Virgil immediately steps forward, having lain the garments over the horse's saddle, to gently take my elbow and help guide my shivering form.

"We need to get somewhere warm," Adelia says.

"The church," I manage. "We need to find Reverend Thomas."

"*You* need to get out of those clothes and into something warm before anything else," Virgil says.

"There's no time. If he finds out we know, if he flees before we have a chance to confront him, we lose all hope of finding James."

"Where's my shawl?" Adelia picks her way over to the horse to rummage through the garments.

"Dare I ask why you needed to remove most of your clothing?" I say.

"Had the ice broken and I'd fallen in, I would not have wanted to contend with all those garments, thank you very much. Now, I believe you were right; we should be going." Rather than using it to regain some semblance of modesty for herself, Adelia drapes the shawl around me. It's a meagre comfort given my own dripping clothes, but I clutch it around myself tightly with a murmured thanks.

Virgil exhales heavily, but he's outnumbered, so he doesn't argue. Instead he tries to help Adelia make sense of her clothing to get dressed again. He insists Adelia and I take the horse, helping me up into the saddle where I huddle and shiver and attempt not to get Adelia soaked by leaning into her for warmth.

"I don't suppose either of you know which direction that is from here."

Virgil points off to the distance. "That way, isn't it? We saw the bell tower through the trees."

I puff out a breath and gesture for him to lead the way. He'll have to keep pace alongside us, one hand on the horse's neck, which means we're stuck moving slower than I would like. It's still faster than I'd be able to move on foot right now, so that's something.

To Adelia I say, quietly, "Thank you."

She ducks her head. "I'm just glad you're all right."

"I'm glad you have impeccable timing." My gaze flits to

Virgil. From this angle, I can't make out the injured side of his face. "Is he all right?"

Her voice lowers. "I made quick work of bandaging what I could in what little time we had. There will be scarring, I think."

I could almost laugh and congratulate Virgil on joining the club. He's officially a ghost hunter now, I suppose. Scars to match mine and James'. Instead, I just feel angry and saddened; never had it been my intention to drag him and Adelia into this, and yet I'm aware that I could not be doing this alone, either.

We ride in silence. By the time the church comes into view, we're moving by the orange glow of sunset, the wind has picked up, and while the sky is gloomy and overcast, there is no snow yet. I hope that luck holds a bit longer.

Some semblance of feeling has worked its way back into my legs so that I can slide from the saddle unassisted, but I still cannot shake the chills wracking my body. We tie the horse to a nearby post, proceeding with caution to the church doors. Virgil pushes them open a few inches, just enough to peer inside, and then more so we can enter.

The chapel appears empty, void of movement save for the flickering of candles and lamps along the walls. We close the doors behind us. I strain to hear, to sense, to feel anything off, anything lurking about the shadows, and feel nothing.

"I think we're alone."

For now, at least.

Down the centre aisle, we scan between the pews for anyone—anything—that might be lurking. At the far end, to either side of the altar, are doors leading elsewhere. I recall Reverend Thomas stepping into one of those rooms for the so-called holy water upon my last visit here, so that's the direction I go.

Through the door sits the vestry, one wall lined with books, another with a desk stacked with papers and more books, and a fire filling the four walls with warmth. I let out an involuntary noise of relief and immediately drop before the hearth and hold out my hands as close to the flames as I dare.

Adelia sinks to my side to do the same. Virgil disappears back out the door, returning a few moments later with a wool blanket to drop about our shoulders. "The other room is clear, as well. We appear to have the place to ourselves for the time being."

I swallow back the fear of what that might mean, if Thomas has already left, if he took James with him...or worse. "I don't suppose you found spare clothes with this blanket."

"Afraid not, but you really do need to get out of those wet things."

"I'm not strolling naked around a church, Virgil. Even I have some respect for sacred places." I glance around the room. "Should we go through his things to see if there's anything of interest? Something about 'The Order' Abraham spoke of?"

Adelia hunkers down, unmoving. "He's foolish enough that I wouldn't put it past him to leave something of importance lying around."

I glance askance at her. "You've certainly got opinions about him. What is it about him you dislike? Prior to all of this, I mean."

She studies the fire. "Have you ever read the Bible, William?"

Eyebrows raised, I drag my corner of the blanket closer around myself. "Yes. I mean, not from cover to cover, but... Why?" Like any boy from a proper Christian family, I attended church every Sunday with my family growing up. And at Whisperwood, too, for that matter. Certain things are drilled

241

into a boy's brain. Rather than solidify my faith, however, it only served to weaken and then completely destroy it. Too many questions unanswered, I suppose.

"If you've read any at all, then you know that the son of God, his own flesh and blood, spoke of love." She shifts to look over at me. "He preached of understanding and forgiveness, of the importance of being a good person. Reverend Thomas spouts nonsense, doom and gloom and our damned souls, how the slightest infraction makes us somehow unworthy of God's love. He claims himself a faithful servant of the Lord yet preaches the opposite of all that Lord is supposed to stand for. Why would anyone like him, I wonder."

I study the cast of firelight across her face, cracking a brief smile. "I don't know why hearing you say that is so surprising. It shouldn't be."

"Please don't mistake me," she says with an indignant sniff. "I think the whole idea of some being in the sky dictating everything is absurd. I'm simply saying if you do believe in it, you should not use people's faith and hope as a tool of fear to rule over them. He's a hypocrite, and I despise hypocrites."

I steal a glance over at Virgil, who is still busy rifling through papers and books upon Reverend Thomas' desk. Never capable of being still, is he? "Care to join our theological discussion, Virgil?"

He does little more than briefly lift his head. "I'm not an atheist, if that's what you're asking."

"Now *that* surprises me. You're a man of science."

"Science and faith are not mutually exclusive, William," he says with the patience of someone who's had to explain such a concept to people before.

"I suppose all men must have flaws," Adelia says with an exaggerated sigh and a twitch of her lips.

Virgil turns to us. "I suppose so. Also, there appears to be nothing of interest here. What's our next course of action?"

I wish I could think that far ahead. "We'll search the church one last time and then go to Reverend Thomas', see if we can't find something there."

Virgil nods. "If you two have warmed up enough, we should be going."

I'm not sure I have. My clothes are still wet and clinging and I would love to get out of them and into something warm, but we hardly have time to worry about it right now. Not to mention, sitting by the comfort of a fire has invited lethargy to settle into my bones and tired muscles. We get to our feet, discarding the blanket on the floor. It hardly matters if Reverend Thomas finds it here now. "Let's be on our way, then."

Adelia stretches her arms above her head, touches a hand briefly to my arm in a comforting gesture, and heads out of the den. Back in the church, she and Virgil make for the pulpit to search, and I give pause as a faint, dark sensation surfaces beneath my skin.

Something's coming.

"Hide," I call to them in the same instant that the church doors begin to creak open. For the space of a breath, they freeze, and then they scurry to the right, darting into the other room. I could duck back into the vestry, where I would be effectively trapped with no other doors or windows.

I drop down behind the first row of pews instead, listening to the sound of the doors groaning open and footsteps entering the church. Multiple pairs. Can I steal a look without being spotted?

"I know you're here, Mr. Esher," comes a voice. Reverend Thomas. "If you wanted to see Mr. Spencer that badly, you need only have asked."

My heart damned near stutters to a halt. Risky or not, I lift my head enough to get a glimpse. Just enough to see Reverend Thomas moving slowly down the centre aisle. At one side is Sarah Keiser, sopping wet and disgruntled.

At his other side is James.

And they're headed this way.

I scoot down and around the end of the bench. I could potentially avoid them, slipping between the pews and the wall, and make a run for the exit. But I'd be leaving Adelia and Virgil trapped in that room, and if James or Sarah give chase, I'll never outrun them in my fatigued state.

The steps stop, a few benches away from where I'm hiding. I focus on my breathing, attempting to be as quiet as possible.

From the other room comes a dull thud, the sound of something dropping or, perhaps, a window being yanked open.

Reverend Thomas says, "Go."

James and Sarah move to obey, rushing for the door. Virgil and Adelia can handle one of them, but surely not both.

I press a hand to my pocket. The phial is still there; I'd been afraid I had lost it in the lake. The crucifix, however, is long gone.

Breathing in deep, I lurch to my feet.

"James!"

Like a flipped switch, James pivots at the sound of my voice, eyes locked onto me and a snarl upon his face. The moment he sees me is the moment I know he'll give chase.

If I go outside, I stand no chance of outrunning nor overpowering him. Instead, I dash the short distance to the nearby stairwell and make a run for it up the steps.

The staircase winds upwards in a tightly coiled spiral. James crashes up the stairs a few feet below me, just uncoordinated enough to slow him, but not by much. I take the steps two at

244

a time, working my aching, weak muscles to go just a little bit further. A little more.

Steady on.

A faint beam of light awaits me at the top. No sooner have I reached the end of the stairs then I'm eye-level with the massive silver bell of the bell tower, its rope trailing down and into the stairwell shaft to make it easier for a bell ringer to ring without actually crawling into the tower—which is precisely what I do, scooting around the massive bell.

The tower is smaller than I expected. Stone archways taller than I am open out into the countryside all around me. And from those archways, as I risk a glimpse over the edge, is a nice long fall and certain death waiting in the church graveyard below.

My vision swims, the ground below spinning slowly. I turn, pressing my back to the narrow stone wall between archways, and pull the holy water from my pocket.

James crawls up through the stairwell opening. I wrap my fingers tight around the phial. He straightens, rolls back his shoulders, and slowly turns to lock onto me. Everything James has ever represented to me—safety, comfort—is missing from his sneering expression and glazed eyes.

But he's in there somewhere. I proved it back at the estate, and I will prove it here.

"I know some part of you can hear me, and I need you to fight as hard as you can."

He lumbers closer, and I allow it. Shoulders pressed hard back into the cold stone, I brace myself. Running will do no good. If I've learned anything, it's that running only spurs them to attack. In this confined space with a sharp drop to either side of me, there is no margin for error.

James halts in front of me. Everything Miss Bennett has taught me about using my other senses is on high alert right now; everything about James that is wrong burns into those senses like fire.

"You can hear me, you know me," I repeat, even as James' fingers grab hold of my jaw and wrench my head to one side, baring the still-healing bite mark on my neck from Madeline. At this angle, he could tear into me like a rabid dog, and I'm not certain there's anything I could do to stop it. I could be the next body lying on a table at the morgue.

He does not bite. But he grips, and he holds, and he waits. Seconds later, I realise just what it is he's waiting for; Reverend Thomas ascends the stairs, ducking around the bell with practised ease and dusting off his clothes.

"Mr. Esher," he greets me, cheerful, warm, almost fond.

I would spit at his feet if I could. "Reverend."

"You've made this entire endeavour difficult, I'm afraid to say." He reaches to his belt and slides a knife from it, tracing his fingertips along the flat of the blade. "Which is a shame. I had a good feeling about you and Mr. Spencer. Two young men, helping restless spirits find peace… A noble cause, isn't it?"

I click my jaw shut as James' grip tightens, speaking through gritted teeth, "Clearly not noble enough for you."

His smile fades. "No amount of noble causes can excuse two men who choose to lie together, Mr. Esher."

My blood chills.

There is no possible way he could know. Haven't we been careful?

Except…

I close my eyes, thinking back to James kissing me in the church the other day. It had been foolish and careless; I'd thought as much at the time. And then I'd brushed it off as inconsequential. No one had been around.

We'd slipped up. Just like I'd always feared we would.

"Mr. Spencer was quite adamant about keeping you safe, I should say," Reverend Thomas continues. "I believe his exact last words were, 'if you hurt him, I'll kill you.' I don't believe he'll be doing that after all."

I envision James, captive and being subject to whatever kind of unholy ceremony Thomas used to force a spirit into his body, and still...*still*, worrying only about me. Red flashes across my vision. If I could get a hold of him, I am not so certain I could resist the temptation to fling Reverend Thomas from this bell tower.

"This is what you do, then? You play judge, jury, and executioner and...what, turn innocent, living people into monsters?"

"Hardly innocent." He shoots me a dagger-edged look. "Madeline and Abraham, bedding outside of wedlock. She was with child, you know. That's why they planned to leave. And, oh, Flora Brewer... I warned her time and again to cease her affair, and instead she brought several bastards into the world. Hugo was no innocent, either; he had quite a temper on him."

"And the children—"

"Bastards, as I said." Another smile. "Not their fault, but nothing good comes from such a union. A few less sinners in the world."

It occurs to me that this man fully believes everything he's saying. Every person he's responsible for murdering, he did so in the name of God. He sees himself as nothing but righteous.

I exhale slowly, trying to keep my heart from racing, my nerves from spiking in an anxiety-ridden panic. I have questions, but I don't think keeping him talking is going to work for long, and to what purpose? I don't know when anyone will arrive to help. I don't know if Virgil and Adelia are hurt, if they've successfully eluded Sarah.

247

More than anything, I need to subdue James.

I open my eyes and look at him. There's no recognition there. I'm going to remedy that.

"Not a one of us is without sin, Reverend," I say.

Then I grab a fistful of James' hair, yank his head back, and drain the holy water into his snarling mouth.

"Kill him!" Reverend Thomas bellows.

James doesn't pull away, but he does not obey, either. He rips free of my grasp, a gurgling howl escaping his lips, raw and pained and heart-breaking. But that means it's working.

I grab his face in my hands. I think of the prayers, of James coaching me through them, again and again, of the gentle sound of his words and his endless patience with my memorisation.

When I envision them that way, in his voice, they come back to me as clear as day.

If conviction is what is needed to drive the spirit from his body, then that's what it's going to get.

"Come to the rescue of mankind, whom God has made in His own image and likeness, and purchased from Satan's tyranny at so great a price."

As I begin to speak, James buckles back so quickly that when Reverend Thomas advances to try to grab me, James slams into him, nearly sending them both to the ground. Reverend Thomas catches himself on the bell, which sways faintly beneath his weight. The knife in his hands clatters away and out of reach.

James staggers, hands over his face, screaming. Endlessly screaming. It sounds less like him and more like something else—something inhuman and dark and familiar in the way it makes the hairs on my arms stand on-end. A sound reminiscent of a dark night at Whisperwood and burning flesh permeating my senses.

248

A spirit twisted and made wrong and ugly.

A spirit withering away. Resisting.

He isn't watching where he's going. I throw myself across the distance to grab him, hands fisted in his dirtied, torn shirt, dragging him back from where he's ventured too close to one of the ledges, and I keep the words coming, loud enough to be heard over the piercing wail. James sags against me before his legs buckle. He goes to his knees, and then to his side, writhing and gasping for breath.

I don't falter in my words. Not until I catch sight of Reverend Thomas rushing up behind me, knife in hand, and I have to whirl on him to make a mad grab for his wrists. The blade glances right, off my shoulder, just barely breaking skin. I use the momentum to twist his wrist sharply to one side; he cries out but manages to maintain his hold on the hilt, wrenching free and leaping back to put distance between us.

Reverend Thomas is a lot of things, but he is not a fighter. In a battle of me versus him, I would bet money on me. Except that I'm reaching my physical limit, and he's the one who is armed. I can hardly catch my breath, and my vision, which had cleared for a while, has begun to swim again.

"Is this really what you want to do?" I ask. "You've avoided spilling blood yourself all this time by using others under some ridiculous notion you're doing God's work. But murder is still murder, Reverend Thomas. Do you think your God will forgive you if you kill me?"

There it is. A flicker, however brief, of hesitation flashing across his face. Long enough, strong enough, to make his gaze drop to the knife in his trembling hand. I did not need to truly convince him—all I needed were those few fractions of a second.

Mustering the last of my energy, I close the distance between us, and he has just enough time to brace himself to be struck. Except instead of trying to put enough strength behind a punch, I grab hold of a fistful of his hair and slam the side of his skull into the church bell.

The sound reverberates—quite literally—in a dull, melodic boom that makes my ears hurt. Reverend Thomas himself lets out a strangled little sound just before he hits the floor. I stoop and retrieve the knife from his slackened grip, and take several slow steps back, ensuring he is not, in fact, getting back up any time soon.

From James' corner comes a noise. The sound of a low, guttural growl and a groan, and I know my work is not done yet.

I drop to the ground, dragging James' head into my lap. I've no holy water left. No crucifix. No Bible. Nothing but words and my hope that it will be enough. Adelia said she didn't think I needed faith in God to drive out a spirit; just confidence and conviction that I can.

I only hope she's right.

"It's all right, love," I mumble, tired, low, as comforting as I can manage. "Everything's all right. I've got you."

Holding onto James, stroking back his hair and bowing over him…I pray.

THE sun has long since dipped beneath the horizon, though the sky still possesses a deep violet hue, flecked with only the brightest of stars. Even the early night sky seems to dim when the spirit finally leaves.

I see it. Feel it. Taste it, even; salt and sulphur. A shadow drops across the tower. Briefly, vaguely, I make out the shape of a person taking form at James' feet. I cannot even determine if it's a man or a woman. Something made of raw emotion, twisted to suit Reverend Thomas' needs. It looks at me, eyes nothing more than deep-set shadows in its mangled, skeletal face.

I drag in a slow, deep breath. "It's time for you to go."

And it does.

I drop my chin, sweat beaded on my forehead and the back of my neck, exhaustion set in bone-deep. James breathes in slow, and although he feels cool and clammy, his pulse is steady. I need to get him back to Evenbury.

The moment I begin to move, James stirs, a plaintive groan escaping his lips that stills my heart. His eyes flutter open, dazed and disoriented. When they come to rest on my face, he mumbles hoarsely, "May I have pancakes for breakfast?"

My vision blurs. The relief is so strong that it comes in the form of a laugh as I take his face in my hands and bend down to press a flurry of kisses across his forehead. "I'll make you all the pancakes you want, you ridiculous man."

James offers a soft sound at that. I feel his fingers touch fleetingly to my jaw before falling away again. When I draw back, his eyes have drifted shut and he appears to have fallen asleep.

No sooner has he settled than I hear my name echoing up the stairwell. Virgil.

"I'm here," I call back, voice fracturing in the middle, worn from use.

A moment later, Adelia appears with Virgil just behind her. They both look quite a sight, dishevelled, hair a mess. Adelia presses a hand to her bleeding arm and the earlier wound on Virgil's face and shoulder has bled through the bandaging. But they're alive, and any injuries appear minimal.

"What happened?" Adelia scurries around the bell, taking in the sight of Reverend Thomas prone on the floor, and James in my lap. "Is he—"

"He's all right," I assure. "What happened to Sarah?"

Virgil comes to my side and drops to a crouch, checking over James. "Restrained downstairs. You were able to dispel the spirit?"

"Yes. For sure this time." I try not to feel guilty about that. I've failed Abraham in that regard, and I suspect he's long gone, floating at the bottom of a lake. But perhaps I can save Sarah. One less child a parent will have to bury.

"Thank God." Adelia's hand comes to rest on my shoulder. "We should get him back home and see to dealing with our good vicar there."

I couldn't agree more.

252

23

BY the time Virgil and Adelia assist me with getting James out of the bell tower, Lord Wakefield has arrived, flanked by Mr. Foss and several other men, many of them armed. I leave it to them to retrieve Reverend Thomas and Sarah, who are loaded up into one of the wagons to be brought back to Evenbury.

Everyone is so full of questions that neither Virgil, Adelia, nor I have the energy to answer right now. Reverend Thomas wakes during the trip back, hopefully with a headache, and remains in the cellar with two men posted on guard outside, awaiting the arrival of the constables to take him away. This isn't the first time we've had to figure out what to tell police, but this time, I think the truth is going to have to be what we go with. When an entire community agrees on what happened, well…

For my part, I have Sarah Keiser brought to another room. Dispelling her dark spirit is easier than James'. Maybe I'm getting better at this. Maybe it's just luck.

I leave her to sleep while I get myself a bath. Every scratch and bruise and muscle twinges in protest beneath the hot water, and the warmth is a reminder of how tired I am and how much I would like to sink down and fall asleep myself. By the time I've emerged, dressed, and permitted Virgil to bandage my wounds, Adelia comes to inform me that Sarah has woken.

"She's coherent?" I ask as we head down the hall.

"More or less. Frightened. She doesn't remember much."

"No, I expect she wouldn't." Frankly, I hope she never does. I wouldn't want her nor James to recall what they did, how it felt to be a puppet. My own memories of my short time spent under possession are spotty. Sometimes, I think I can recall a flicker of something. A voice, a thought not my own, but those recollections are fleeting and like ghosts themselves in how elusive they are.

Adelia raps lightly upon the door and waits for Sarah to say, "Come in," before we step inside. It's a guest room not unlike my own, with some extra lamps for added light. I wonder if that was at Sarah's request. Looking at her in the woods, I'd taken her to be Adelia's age—young, but an adult. Now that I see her, clear-eyed and huddled in a robe beneath several layers of blankets, I realise she must be several years younger than I previously thought.

"Evening, Miss Keiser," I say with a smile.

She watches me warily; she doesn't know me, of course. Not an ounce of recognition on her face. "H'llo."

"Would it be all right for me to sit and speak with you for a moment?"

Sarah curls her fingers into the blanket but nods. Once Adelia takes a seat on the edge of the bed with a comforting hand on Sarah's arm, and I've pulled up a chair for myself, Sarah says, "I'm afraid I don't remember much to be of any help. Did I do something bad?"

"No," I say quickly. "No, you did nothing bad. It wasn't really even you. Did Adelia tell you what happened?"

"A bit." Sarah glances shyly at Adelia. "She says I was possessed. By a demon?"

"I'm not certain if demon is the right word." I lean forward, elbows on my knees, trying to think of how best to explain it without getting into a drawn-out lecture. "You see, sometimes when someone dies and the circumstances of that death are violent or bad, the spirit remains. Not everyone can even see them, most of the time. What Reverend Thomas did was to summon some of those restless spirits and force them into a living body."

She frowns, troubled. "Why would anyone do that?"

I could tell her what I know, that Reverend Thomas thought himself some sort of judge of humanity. I wonder what he thought Sarah and her brother's sin was. I don't think it prudent to ask her after all she's been through, despite my curiosity. "He wanted control of them, is all. But he's in custody now and I can assure you he won't harm you again. The police are likely to have questions when they arrive. Do you think you'll be able to speak with them?"

Sarah watches me, her brown eyes strikingly clear. "I can try, but I don't remember much, as I said."

"What's the last thing you recall?"

A pause. Her lashes lower. Adelia gives her arm a squeeze, and that appears to give her the courage to begin speaking.

Sarah recounts to us the events leading up to her

possession. She and her brother had been visiting a neighbour. During their walk back, Reverend Thomas rode by, stopped, and offered to take them the rest of the way, saying that they ought not to be walking by themselves in the dark. They'd had no reason to not accept the invitation.

Thomas instead brought them to the church, where Abraham was waiting to apprehend them. Mitchell was knocked unconscious, and Sarah was small enough that Abraham had little trouble restraining her.

From there, Sarah's memory is spotty. She doesn't remember how, precisely, the vicar did what he did. She recalls dizziness. A sense of being outside of her own body, of having something intruding on her entire being. Although she finds it difficult to describe, I can imagine it perfectly. I felt it at Whisperwood. I felt it at the farm when we summoned Flora. I can only compare it to the sensation of lying in bed with your eyes closed, in that peculiar stage between sleeping and waking, and feeling someone cold crowd in beside you, pushing you further and further to the edge of the mattress until you have nowhere left to go.

I shiver at the thought of anyone going through that, and at the idea Miss Bennett does it willingly.

By the time she's done talking, Sarah has worn herself out. I could ask her a thousand more questions, but Adelia levels a flat look at me that suggests I ought to leave well enough alone. I thank Sarah for her help and advise her to get some more rest.

Adelia remains with Sarah while I slip out. We had James put in his room, and I personally saw to washing him up a bit and getting him into a clean nightshirt so he would, at least, wake feeling moderately more human.

It's to his side that I return after procuring a tray of food from the kitchens, knowing he's going to be famished when he wakes. Standing in the doorway and watching him there, sprawled on his back with a hand tucked against his cheek, a sense of peace washes over me. The scene before me is reassurance that he's all right. The uncertainty about his well-being had me so tense, so terrified, that I don't know how I coped with any of it.

I haven't a clue how long he'll sleep, but I plan on remaining at his side while he does. I take a seat beside him, slouching back against the headboard, grateful to be warm and still for a change.

Falling asleep is not what I'd intended, but at some point, I must have dozed off. Because when James does stir from his rest, I jolt upright with a crick in my neck. I touch his hair, wanting him to know I'm here. "Hello, darling."

His lashes flutter open and he turns toward the sound of my voice, even as his mouth curves up into a sleepy smile. "Hmm. I had the oddest dream."

"Did you now?" I murmur, carding my fingers back through his hair. "What about?"

He tips his head into my touch. "I dreamt that I was so hungry that I tried to eat you."

I chuckle softly. If he doesn't remember the details of the last few days, all the better. I'm not certain he needs to have all that on his conscience. "Well, as you can see, I'm here and not on a dinner plate."

"Mm." James rolls slowly onto his side and closes his eyes, curling against me. Silence for a moment, and then, "I don't know what you did or what happened, but…thank you."

I swallow hard, unable to keep my voice from wavering. "Everything is over. We completed our job. I'm just… immensely relieved you're all right."

257

"Don't speak too quickly. I might die of hunger."

"A good thing I prepared." I slip out of bed, fetching the tray from the top of the nearby dresser. It's hardly a four-course meal, but there's fruit, bread, some dried meats and even a few biscuits, along with a glass of water. James pushes himself up to sitting, and his face lights up. He catches hold of my hand and presses a kiss to the back of it. "You're too good to me. I'm going to get fat," he declares happily, predictably reaching for one of the biscuits first.

"All the better to keep me warm at night."

It's good to see he's already feeling like himself. I recline back while James eats, simply watching him through half-lidded eyes. I've almost started to doze again when a soft knock at the door jars me back to full consciousness, and a second later Virgil pops his head in.

"You're awake."

"Observant." I sit back up.

"The police have arrived." He eases into the room. "They're speaking with Lord Wakefield and Adelia now, and I suspect you'll be next."

My favourite thing, speaking to the police. I heave a sigh, resisting the urge to crawl beneath the blankets and tell him no. I've had my few hours of rest, and our job is not *completely* done yet. I get to my feet, offering James a reassuring smile. "Afraid they'll want to speak to you, too, when you're feeling up to it."

James wrinkles his nose. As I exit the room, I hear him exclaiming to Virgil, "Good Lord, what happened to your face?"

I'm very unsuitable for company, arriving downstairs in rumpled clothes, my hair a mess, and shoeless. The two constables in the kitchens with Adelia and her father give me a once over when I enter the room, and I decide I really don't give a damn about appearances. I think I've earned the right to look as worn out as I feel.

The constables, as it turns out, are polite enough gents. They've already spoken to several people, from the Wakefields to Mr. Foss, Nathaniel, and some of the other servants, so much of what I say is a repeat of the story they got from Adelia and Virgil. Only once I've finished do the two exchange looks. One of them—Constable Michaels—rubs the back of his neck.

"Er, see, it's a bit peculiar, all of this. Trying to put this into any kind of a report…"

I smile tightly. "I suspect you'll hear the same from anyone you ask here. Though if you needed an easier story to spin: Reverend Thomas is responsible for the murders, as well as the kidnapping and attempted murder of Sarah Keiser."

"Your associate was abducted, too, isn't that right?"

My mouth twitches. James is not going to want to be dragged into legal affairs where it can be prevented. "That's correct. He's a bit indisposed at the moment, although I'm sure he and Miss Keiser will be glad to give you their version of events once they've had a bit more rest."

"Nonsense," says James from behind me. "No need to keep these nice gentlemen waiting."

I turn to see him strolling into the kitchen, all smiles, hair stuck up in every direction. He didn't bother to dress, only pulled on a robe over his nightshirt. He looks more a fright than I do. In this lighting, I can better see the array of bruises blemishing his skin; results of being tossed around and scuffling the last few days. I suspect if one were to line up Adelia, Virgil, James, and I, we rather look like we've been at the wrong end of a mugging.

Adelia covers her mouth to hide a smile while the constables look him over, somewhere between concerned and startled. Constable Marshall clears his throat. "If you're feeling well enough, we'd like your version of events."

What James proceeds to recount to them is, of course, no different than what I've said—at least up until our paths split, and I find myself diverting my full attention to him as he speaks.

"Mr. Fletcher rendered me unconscious in the forest when William and I were separated," he says, nodding to me. "I've vague recollections of being dragged through the snow, but I didn't fully come to again until Reverend Thomas had me bound in the cellar of his home."

My stomach lurches.

Reverend Thomas' cellar. I was there, and James was right under my feet, and I had no idea.

I slowly brace myself against one of the prep tables, sick with the notion that I could have saved James so much sooner, perhaps prevented his possession altogether, had I just pushed Reverend Thomas a little harder.

James gives a dismissive wave of his hand. "I'm afraid after that, I don't remember much until waking in the bell tower. I'm certain you can find plenty of evidence at Reverend Thomas' home, however."

Adelia and Lord Wakefield, too, have snapped their gazes to James in surprise. "We can take you there," Adelia offers, and I see it for what it is: an opportunity for us to investigate for ourselves. To try to make some sense of what was being done to Thomas' victims.

The officers are kind enough to wait while I argue with James upstairs about him staying behind. He needs his rest, and I prefer one of us to remain in the house with Thomas should anything go awry. Virgil offers to stay with him, so it's Adelia and I fetching our coats and boarding a carriage to ride over there, following the officers' wagon.

In the stretch of time we're left to converse, Adelia recounts her and Virgil's encounter with Sarah. The girl had nearly broken down the door to get to them and, determined to capture her alive, they willingly allowed her in, prepared to tackle her to the ground and bind her. Neither of them had been fully prepared for how strong she would be, how relentless in her pursuit. But they made it out alive, so clearly, they didn't fare too poorly.

"How is your arm?" I ask.

"Just a scratch." She touches the spot, hidden from view by the sleeve of her dress. I imagine it's been bandaged by now. "I suspect it will scar. I shouldn't complain, though."

It's likely she's thinking of Virgil with that statement, of the gash across his face and shoulder. A flare of guilt rears its head. Were he not here at my request, Virgil wouldn't have been injured at all, although he'd likely reprimand me for that line of thinking. Besides that, I cannot envision how all of this would have played out had Adelia or Virgil not been here.

We roll up to Reverend Thomas' in short order. As I exit the carriage, I glance to the church across the way. A shiver slides down my spine and I turn my gaze away and follow Adelia toward the vicar's front door.

The constables trail us inside. Everything is as I remember from the other night, although to be honest, I'd not been paying close attention to details. Everything about Reverend Thomas' home is as I would expect from a man of the cloth. Tidy, neat, sparse, with little more to adorn the walls than religious symbols. A crucifix hangs over each doorway, a painting of Jesus above a desk in the small study, and an old, well-loved, leather-bound Bible on the dining table.

It's in one of the larders that Adelia locates the entrance into the cellar. A rug used to cover the door has been shoved back, the hatch opened wide, and I suspect in his hurry to find us at the church, he'd not thought to lock it up before leaving.

We exchange looks. As she calls for the constables, I brace myself and descend the steps into the darkness. It's hardly the first time, and a dark cellar is significantly less intimidating than the belly of a haunted school.

As far as cellars go, this one is mustier than most, and a foul odour hits me about halfway down the stairs. I go still, clamping a hand over my nose and mouth. A dim light flickers from behind me as Adelia follows in my steps, an oil lamp in hand. I offer a hand of my own out to help her the rest of the way down; almost immediately, she recoils with her nose wrinkling.

"What is that God-awful stench?"

"He kept people locked up down here. Not sure we want to know." It isn't the smell of death, that's for sure. Adelia presses the hem of her sleeve to her nose and lifts the lamp high as we move further into the room. When the constables follow, there are more mutterings about the smell.

As my eyes begin to adjust to the dim light, details of the room become more apparent. Aside from items tossed down here for storage, shoved up against one brick wall is a small table and chairs, bowls of half-eaten sludge that was probably porridge at some point, and a few candles burned down to pitiful nubs.

The far end of the room has been completely cleared save for a few chamber pots nestled into the corner and some ratty, threadbare blankets strewn about the floor. Hanging from the wall, embedded into the old brick, are shackles with enough chain for their wearers to walk, perhaps no more than three feet in any given direction. I remember the bruising on Madeline Edison's wrists and ankles. The same bruising I saw on James while he slept…

He truly was down here while I stood directly over his head. Had he been unconscious then, I wonder? I'd have heard him if he'd called for help. Surely Thomas had not yet had a chance to possess him, or else he'd have had James come after me then when I was still unsuspecting and reeling from my fall.

Adelia touches my arm, pulling me from my thoughts. "This isn't the time to be wallowing in guilt, William."

I make the mistake of breathing in deep, so my, "I know," comes out with a cough.

As the constables take note of the state of the cellar, of the obvious location of where Reverend Thomas kept his victims, Adelia and I search for any sign of *how* a vicar from a quiet little community could have possibly done any of this.

There are no markings upon the walls nor floors. No books or documents detailing his methods. Nothing denoting any kind of black magic or Satanism. Miss Bennett might have a much better idea, but not a lot of help when she's not here to see it all. I commit what I can to memory instead, wishing I'd had the foresight to bring Lord Wakefield's camera along.

Once we've assured ourselves there's nothing of interest in the cellar, we bid the constables farewell for now and take our leave back to the estate. James will be eager to hear news of what we found, and I don't want to keep him waiting.

"**Y**OU'RE supposed to be resting," I say when James greets us like an overeager puppy at the door. He's bathed and got himself dressed, although he's forgone his tie and his hair is still a disaster. I've spent enough time with my partner to know when he's manic and in need of sleep, and the anxious way he paces the parlour coupled with the shadows under his eyes tells me he needs more rest.

"He's been hounding me to speak to Reverend Thomas," Virgil says dryly.

James rolls back his shoulders with a long-suffering sigh. "And *Virgil* has been nagging me ever since you left, William. It's been horrible."

"Good, you need to be nagged at sometimes. Christ, James, sit down; your pacing is making me nervous."

With a huff, James drops gracelessly into the chair beside mine, and his fingers ghost the back of my hand, taking hold of my shirt sleeve. He wants to touch me and knows that he shouldn't, and the urge to simply grab his hand in mine is overwhelming.

It's then that I notice Virgil and Adelia watching us, and I could almost take the looks on their faces for concern. "What is it?"

They exchange glances before Adelia says, as delicately as she can, "Reverend Thomas knows about the two of you, doesn't he?"

Instinctively, my spine goes rigid and I draw my hand away from James, who sighs and says with ease, "He does, yes."

"And that doesn't concern you? What if he tells the police?"

With the commotion of everything else, I'd not honestly thought about such a thing. A sinking feeling of dread encompasses me.

James is unflappable. He reaches the distance between us and reclaims my hand—properly this time, his fingers lacing with mine—and flashes a confident smile at Adelia. "Do you really think they'll take his word over ours?"

"Maybe not," Virgil says softly. "But clearly we're concerned enough about it to bring it up."

James tips his chin up, defiant. "Even if they did, I would simply steal dear William out of the country where no one would find us. I worked awfully hard to get him, you know, and I'll not allow anyone to separate us now."

I can't take my eyes off this ridiculous man of mine. Were we not subjected to an audience, I'd be kissing him senseless. As it is, I can't help but squeeze his hand tight, and I suspect the look on my face is utterly sappy and adoring and my cheeks are undoubtedly cherry-red. He has that effect on me more than I'd care to admit.

"I only wish you to express some caution," Virgil says with a frown.

James waves him off. "You fret too much."

"I fret because you give me reason to. *You,* especially, are not subtle, James."

"We appreciate the concern. Truly, we do," I interject. "I promise we'll be careful. Though perhaps it wouldn't hurt to have a conversation with Reverend Thomas before they come to take him away?" I take the silence of the room as agreement. We're all exhausted and want nothing more to do with this whole affair, but they must know I'm right.

Together, the four of us relocate to the cellar, entering with caution. Reverend Thomas is seated at the far end of the room. Not bound, likely because there are men posted outside and Nathaniel here, standing guard. It doesn't appear as though he's even tried to get up to wander around.

Adelia nods to Nathaniel and gives him permission to step out so we might speak with the vicar alone. Nathaniel hesitates, but bows his head and slips away.

The cellar doors fall shut. Thomas lifts his head to regard us, a pleasant smile upon his face. "Good evening."

"About to be not so good once the constables come back," James drawls, pocketing his hands. "I hope you realise it's likely the gallows for you. Or spending the rest of your life in prison; not sure that's any better."

"Are you here to try to frighten me, Mr. Spencer?"

James' eyes narrow and a sneer begins to form on his face. I press a hand to his chest to nudge him back as I step forward. "No, actually. We came to ask about the process you used to force a spirit into an unwilling person's body."

Thomas' smile widens a notch, but it doesn't reach his eyes. His lips remain pressed firmly together in defiant silence.

Nowhere in my mind had I thought this would be simple, of course. "All right. What about The Order? What can you tell us about them?"

Still nothing. Reverend Thomas gazes back at me impassively.

Behind me, James lets out a frustrated huff of breath. "Now, look here. You're responsible for the deaths of *several* innocent people—"

"Not a one of them was innocent," Thomas interrupts. "Not Flora Brewer, not Madeline Edison nor Abraham Fletcher. Not even Flora's bastard children."

James' shoulders lift, fury lit bright across his face as he steps forward. His temper is too short for this, I realise, especially running on frayed nerves and little sleep; James can't abide by innocent people being hurt. The memory of Oscar Frances still burns too hotly in his mind.

I place myself between James and Reverend Thomas, palm pressed flat against James' chest to command his attention. "Step outside. Let me handle this."

"What?" James' gaze snaps to me. "No, he's—"

"*Let me handle this,*" I repeat.

James hesitates, muscles in his jaw twitched tight as he grinds his teeth. He spares a brief look at the vicar before he does as I ask and retreats from the room. Virgil follows, bless him, undoubtedly to try to calm James down. I'm fortunate today; normally, James' temper is not so easily quelled. I wouldn't put it past him to hit Reverend Thomas out of anger, but it wouldn't make him feel any better.

Adelia steps up beside me, her presence significantly calmer than James', although I suspect she's merely better at hiding her anger. These were people she knew and cared for, after all.

She says, "The Order. I want to know what it is, and why you were working for them."

Thomas rolls his gaze ceilingward. "You've been running all about the countryside these last two weeks, Lady Adelia. Very unbecoming for a lord's daughter."

"I'm obliged to show you how unbecoming I can be if you refuse to cooperate," she responds coolly.

"Now, that *is* a threat. Shall you pluck off my fingernails, or place my legs in a vice?" He smiles again. "Somehow, I feel you two are not the sort to stoop to such levels. While this one—" he pins me with a stare, "—is already bound for Hell, I believe you are still in God's good graces."

My muscles screw up tight as I resist the urge to strike him. I'd be lying if I said it wouldn't make me feel better. Were James still missing, I dare say the only way Reverend Thomas would be leaving this room would be with a broken jaw.

"You've kidnapped and murdered several people. I don't think the constables will mind if you have a few broken fingers," Adelia says. It's an empty threat, but it's all we have right now.

Reverend Thomas' doesn't so much as flinch. "By all means. Have at it. I have God on my side, and with Him I can endure whatever punishment you might seek to throw at me."

Christ almighty, he really does believe it, doesn't he? He believes everything he did was in the name of a higher power, that it was all justified. And if he does, I'm not certain any amount of torture would make him talk.

Adelia seems to have reached a similar conclusion, because she lets out a frustrated huff. "The constables will return in short order," she snaps. Then she whirls on her heel and manages to make stomping out of the room look elegant.

At her departure, Reverend Thomas returns his attention to me.

I make one last attempt to ask, "What is The Order?"

He responds with a curt laugh. "You have no idea what ire you will invoke if you continue asking those questions. They have eyes everywhere."

"This is me not caring. What is it? *Who* is it?"

The vicar merely bows his head, but his eyes roll up, never leaving mine. "That isn't really why you're still here, Mr. Esher. That's not what you're wanting to ask me."

I cross my arms. He's correct there. While The Order is something I fear we're going to need to investigate further, my immediate concern lies with James and me. Protecting *us*. "Is there a point to asking if you plan to divulge my and James' relationship to the authorities?"

"To what end?" he asks. "The only true judgment that matters is God's, is it not?"

I'm not buying that, as much as I wish I could allow it to put me at ease. "If you really believed that, then you'd not have doled out your own punishment to all those people."

He smiles, saccharine sweet. "Then I suppose you'll just have to find out what I will and won't tell them, hm?"

The cellar doors open once more and Nathaniel returns, likely at Adelia's behest. "I apologise for interrupting, Mr. Esher, but the constables have returned."

My jaw clenches tight. I have little grounds to ask them to keep him here further. All I can do is re-join the others and watch as Reverend Thomas is shackled and led to the wagon outside, as silent as the grave.

I never want to see this man again unless it's swinging from a noose.

IF I never have to see this farmhouse again, I'll die a happy man. As it is, when we arrive, James and I sit in the carriage and simply stare at the building for several minutes, working up the nerve—and the energy—to go inside.

I'd tried to insist he stay behind to rest. He's been up and going, going, going, since waking this morning, but James is never one to sit idle. He's also being a bit clingier than usual, so I suspect the events of the last several days have him more rattled than he'd care to admit.

Odd how the Brewers' farm feels so much less ominous now despite the lingering spirits. I can feel them, a faint crawling sensation beneath my flesh. As we let ourselves in and James stills and draws in a slow, deep breath, I think he must feel it, too.

This time, when I call for the Brewers, they flicker into view at the corners of my vision. Still absent is Mr. Brewer, I realise, but one thing at a time. There's a sort of calmness to their presence now. The fear I felt from them before has gone.

James leans against the wall, hands pocketed, watching one of the children seated on the ground not far from his feet—a tiny girl with braided hair and a mauled face that once looked much like Adelia at that age. What happened to this family was not fair, and although we couldn't save their lives, I'm glad we could at least help them find peace. I always wonder if these moments remind James of the friend that we couldn't save, if he finds any solace at all in what we do.

"Go ahead, William," James says. "Send them off."

Send them off. I wonder where it is they go when they leave here. Do they still wander on some plane of existence? Simply…out of our sight? We already know not everyone can see them even as they are, and that with practise, James and I have grown more attuned to their presence. We know some people have more natural talent for it than others. It's possible, then, we simply push them on into another realm where we cannot see them.

I still have so many questions I'm not certain I will ever get answers to until the day I draw my last breath and find out for myself.

I face the Brewers and, as I speak, their attention diverts to me. "Flora Brewer, Jules, Lottie, Douglas, Alice… Reverend Bernard Thomas is the one responsible for your deaths, and justice has been dealt to him. You're safe, and it's time for you to go."

They disappear into the shadows, the only sound of their departure that of a relieved sigh beside my ear. Everything in the house feels different with their absence. Quieter. Safer. It is now just a house littered with bad memories and nothing more.

James breaks the silence, voice low and soft as it fills the emptiness.

"*Pale rider to the convent gate.*

Come, O rough bridegroom, Death."

I close my eyes, silent for a spell. "We're missing one."

"Hm?"

"Hugo Brewer. He wasn't here."

"That's because you sent him off already, darling." James pushes away from the wall. When I look to him and frown, he smiles. "Who do you think was possessing me?"

My eyes widen. "You could tell?"

"A bit. It was…just a feeling. I'm not sure I could explain it, but his anger, his sadness… It was palpable. It lingered even after he was gone."

My stomach turns with the thought of it. Do such emotions linger with Miss Bennett, too, I wonder? She opens herself willingly to the deceased. The willpower that woman must have in order to repel the spirits when she wants control again… Is that something James and I could ever hope to learn? "You never should have had to go through that."

He shrugs. "It's part of the job, dear William. All of it is. It's why I would understand if you decided not to do it anymore."

Those words drag me back to the last real conversation we had in this house, how James more or less told me he'd not fault me if I were to leave him for a more "traditional" life. After he disappeared, I replayed those words in my head, again and again, lamenting how I allowed it to end. Had the worst happened and I never saw James again… I would have had that as our last conversation—him thinking I could ever choose a life other than the one I've built with him.

"About what you said before," I begin slowly. "I've thought

a lot about it."

James fixes me with a stare that I think is not as confident as he wants it to be. "Have you? I meant what I said."

"I don't doubt that, but I fear I did you a great disservice by allowing you to walk out of here that night without telling you how wrong you were."

He frowns. "Pardon?"

This is the difficult part. Talking out the thoughts in my head. There are things I'm not certain I could bring myself to tell anyone—even James. Things that I could mention only in passing, never in detail. Yet I can't truly express to him the impact he's had on me without him knowing at least something about what I've come from, what my life was like before him.

Perhaps some dark secrets *have* to come out to air sooner or later.

"It was my mother who got me started on the laudanum," I begin.

"Yes, you've told me that."

"I knew I relied on it too heavily. The summer before my third year, I attempted to go off it on my own and... Well, you've seen how poorly that goes. Mother and Father thought me impossible to deal with. Either I was taking too much and they accused me of being useless, or I was not taking it enough and they thought me too over-sensitive and prone to hysterics."

James gives a tight, humourless smile that I've seen plenty of times before, the smile that suggests I've given him another reason to dislike my family.

I continue, "One afternoon, they went to a dinner party for a business partner of Father's. I desperately wanted to go, but I'd been struggling the days prior. Mother feared I'd have one of my 'fits' and embarrass them, so they left me home.

273

"While they were gone, I snuck into Father's study and took the revolver from his desk. I thought to use it. I thought…surely it would be better for everyone all round if I were gone. Better for them, and myself. If I was never going to get any better, then what purpose was there to continue on?" I gesture vaguely, struggling to push the words out because it's humiliating, exposing myself in such a way to someone whose opinion matters so greatly.

James' arms slowly drop to his sides.

"…At any rate, clearly I changed my mind at the last second and decided I would give it one more go. 'One more school year,' I said. If I couldn't make things better, then the next summer, I would do it. But do you know what? I'm glad I waited." I move away from the table and step up to James, lifting my palms to cup his face. "Because it got better. Because there you were, and *you* made it better. You made *me* better, sweetheart."

His eyes have glazed over, and the smile that twists at his mouth is more sad than anything else. His arms instantly go around me, dragging me to him. "You're such a fool," he murmurs, but his voice is so gentle and without an ounce of reprimand or disappointment.

I wonder if he thinks differently of me now. If the idea of me standing there in Father's study with a gun pressed to my temple and sobbing like the bloody world was ending makes him think less of me. Nothing had mattered more to me in that moment than making everything just…*stop*. Cease. Quiet.

To this day, I don't know what it was that changed my mind. A sudden, exhausted sort of calm had swept over me, enveloped me in its arms, sapped me of all energy to do much of anything—including pulling the trigger.

I put my arms around James without hesitation, nestling

my face into his neck. "You are my everything, James. For as much as I struggle, as difficult as things are for me that are so simple for everyone else—I'd not trade *you* for any such normalcy. You are what makes me want to be a better man. I'm sorry I've been failing at that."

James shakes his head, pressing his lips to my neck and sniffling quietly. "I worry for you, darling. I want to be able to help."

That's the difficult part, isn't it? Because I don't know what will help anymore. I fear driving James away with my stormy, unpredictable moods and my inability to function the way others can. I worry about what happens if, someday, I do have to step back from this job and let him go it alone—or with another working partner. Oh, it makes my blood boil just thinking about it.

For now, though, I just want to hold onto him tightly, tipping my head to press kisses to his jaw and face. "You *do* help. You and your ridiculous business names and poetry and eating biscuits in bed…"

James pulls back with a sunny smile upon his handsome face and a faint sheen of tears in his eyes. Always so emotional, this man of mine. He ducks his head to capture my lips with his own and murmur warmly against them, "I love you, you know. One day, I'm going to get you to understand how happy you make me."

I permit those words and the kiss to chase away the remaining unease from everything we've faced since Mr. Foss showed up at our doorstep. Everything is all right. Maybe not *fixed*, but it will be. I'll make sure of that. "Please tell me we've finished with this bloody job."

He laughs. "Yes, I think so. Let's go home."

WE intended to return to Evenbury just long enough to say our goodbyes and retrieve our things before being driven to the train station. The solemn faces awaiting us outside the manor certainly don't bode well.

James approaches Adelia and Virgil with a smile and his hands in his pockets. "The spirits have been dealt with. What's with those looks? Are you that sad we're leaving?"

"Reverend Thomas is gone," Adelia says.

James and I come to an abrupt halt.

"Pardon?" I say.

"Gone as in…taken off to the nearest gallows, right?" James asks hopefully.

Adelia frowns. "*Gone* as in the constables' wagon was hijacked on the road, and Reverend Thomas was taken."

A chill goes through me from head to toe. "And the constables?"

"Alive, by some miracle," Virgil says. "They saw a horse on the side of the road and its rider on the ground and stopped to have a look. Whoever it was knocked them unconscious. When they woke, the man and Reverend Thomas were gone."

Small blessings that the officers weren't merely left for dead. But then, what of Reverend Thomas? On the one hand, if he's no longer in custody, he'll not have the opportunity to spill my and James' secret.

On the other hand, we no longer know where he is, and who else might find out should he decide to run his mouth.

Or who else might fall prey to his twisted idea of doing God's work.

A servant slips past us from inside the house, carting along our trunk to load it into the carriage. The four of us crowd closer, self-conscious now that we might be overheard.

James murmurs, "He spoke of The Order. Obviously, he was a member of…whatever it is. Do you suppose—?"

"That they rescued him?" Virgil asks.

I add, "Reverend Thomas did say The Order has eyes and ears everywhere. But rescue him to what end? Would he have been of some use to someone?" They're useless questions none of us have answers to. Merely frustrated speculation. What I do know is that James and I will have our work cut out for us, trying to investigate this organisation. If it has something to do with summoning spirits, then stopping them certainly falls into our realm of expertise.

James smiles weakly. "We'll hope Miss Bennett has some insight for us, hm?" He glances over his shoulder. "Now, I think our driver is waiting for us and we've a train to catch."

I turn to Virgil. "You're sticking around?"

"I've talked him into spending an extra day or two, just to help wrap up the inquest and answer any medical questions

277

they might have." Adelia gives a wide smile that tells me all I need to know about why he's really staying. Virgil bows his head, ever so sheepish.

"Keep him out of trouble then," I say, amused, casting a glance to the driver awaiting us by the carriage. I'll admit, I'm sorely going to miss being tended to, not to mention the hot baths and full meals.

Adelia catches hold of my hand in hers. "I should be the one telling you two to stay out of trouble. If I have to come rescue you, I'll make certain you regret it."

I smile, bringing that hand to my lips to kiss the back of it. "I'll do my best, but I'm afraid trouble follows James everywhere."

"Terribly rude," James mutters.

Virgil folds his arms across his chest. "The truth can be brutal."

"Now, you look here!"

With a roll of her eyes, Adelia loops her arm with mine and leads me away a few paces, leaving the two of them to playfully bicker. "In all truthfulness, I will miss you both. I'm afraid Father won't be up for having you back as guests, given that you know about his affair…"

"To be expected, but we're not going to spread his secrets around. I hardly see what good it would do." I come to a halt and look down at her. "The next time your father has business in London, perhaps you could pay us a visit. Aside from that, I suspect we'll work together again in the future."

Adelia's brows lift. "Do you now?"

"You're going to become an investigator, aren't you? I look forward to being able to consult you on cases."

She laughs and glances away, looking equal parts pleased and uncertain. "We shall see."

I hardly think I need to tell Adelia she's capable of anything she puts her mind to; she doesn't need my validation. Or anyone's, for that matter. But I know the obstacles she faces—namely, her father, and society as a whole—that will make her goals difficult to achieve.

Mr. Foss approaches to inform us it's time to depart. Adelia bids us farewell, rising on tiptoe to place a kiss on my cheek. When I turn to Virgil to offer out a hand, he takes it, followed by a frown as he pulls me closer and wraps his other arm tight round my shoulders in a brief, awkward hug.

"You know where to find me should you need me," he says before pulling away.

I chuckle, more out of surprise than anything else, because displays of affection from Virgil are as rare as unicorns. "What's all this, then?"

Except I know he's referring to the laudanum and our previous conversations. I know he's offering his help, however he can, and the long look he proceeds to give me reaffirms as much.

So my expression softens, and I give his hand a reassuring squeeze before stepping back. "Thank you, Virgil. For being here, for everything. I don't know what we'd have done without you and Adelia."

"Died, probably," Virgil says solemnly and without humour. I can't tell if he's joking, but he's probably right so I laugh all the same.

"Come now, dear William," James calls, giving Adelia and Virgil one last smile and nod. "I don't know about you, but I'm eager to get home."

He hops up into the carriage and I follow suit, settling in beside him. "Ready to begin planning that holiday of ours, are you?"

"Indeed I am."

As the carriage begins its trek away from Evenbury, I lean my shoulder into his. "Good. I think we've more than earned ourselves a vacation."

James grins a mile wide, filled with the brilliance and liveliness of a child, as though the last few weeks hadn't nearly killed us more than once. "And cake?"

I laugh loudly enough that our driver undoubtedly overhears me. "Yes, darling. All the cake we can eat."

WHITECHAPEL

ONE of the things I appreciate about Aunt Eleanor is that she knows when to not ask questions.

When I show up at her home one rainy afternoon without warning, she only peers into my face for half a moment before stepping aside and saying, "Come in, Preston." She doesn't ask me what I'm doing there, if there's anything I'd like to speak about, or how long I'm staying. She only asks me if I'd care for some tea or a light lunch and then leaves me be.

It's just what I need, that silence. In fact, it's why I came here instead of heading home where Mother would immediately notice something off and come at me with a hundred questions.

I don't know what I would say, anyway; I can't begin to sort out the chaos of my current state of mind and I find the subject matter too delicate to discuss with…well, anyone. Even a beloved aunt, an oddity who I know deep in my heart would never ultimately judge me for whatever I brought to her table.

Over the next several days of my visit, Aunt Eleanor goes about business as usual, keeping busy between clientele, matters of the house, and needlework. I assist her where I can, of course, because I am a well-mannered person and I'm rather invading her space, but most of what she does has no need for any other involvement and so I'm left to my own devices.

My time is spent in a largely unproductive manner. I get up in the morning at a respectable hour, clean myself up and dress, tend to any chores that need to be tended to, exit the apartments when Aunt Eleanor has clients, and then I…

Sit around.

Stare out of the kitchen window.

Dwell.

I think of Benjamin.

Despite it all, I'm sorry to have left him alone. I worry about what he's going through, what he's thinking and feeling right in this very moment. It has to be difficult for him, and it will only grow tougher still. He's been thrust into a position— no, into a life—he is woefully underprepared for, and forced to interact with a previously absent father who now wants to take the reins. From what little I've gleaned of Franklin Hale, he is a cold and demanding man. Not the sort of person one could ever imagine having helped create someone as soft and sweet as Benjamin.

I wonder how he's faring. Has he started his new job yet? I wonder if the work is difficult or if it's something he enjoys. I cannot for the life of me imagine Benjamin stuck indoors all day, overseeing factory workers or organising files or…

whatever other mindless tasks are involved in office work. It isn't that I think he'd be terrible at such things—he always had an organised mind—but I can't envision such things being engaging or fulfilling for him. I can't imagine he greets each day bright eyed and with excitement, bubbling over at the thought of puttering around with paperwork.

More than that, Benji is alone, and that worries me.

I don't think for a moment he will ever have a strong, warm relationship with his father, and he has no other family, no friends that he's spoken of. Has he made any? I hope, of course, that he has, but I know him to be so shy and quiet that it's not likely unless someone approached him and insisted. What are the odds there?

No, it's far more likely that he's sticking by himself and— what if someone is giving him trouble? What if someone is cruel? Benjamin has always been so terribly gentle, a human being too sensitive for his own good, and I just...

I know I worry too much, but when it comes to him, I cannot help it. I never dreamt we'd be in this situation. Perhaps I should have, perhaps it was the only reasonable outcome, but he'd grown to become my closest friend in our years together at Whisperwood. No, more than that—he'd become the most important person to me, someone I held dear.

I suppose I had just thought we'd always be together.

Lord knows I'd tried to keep it that way.

I have no idea what to do with myself now, or what comes next. Logic says I ought to return home, to help Mother and Father on the farm. It's unfortunate, then, that I have no interest in doing so. Even Father has always said I have stars in my eyes and a sense of wanderlust that cannot be quelled. I'm too independent and too eager in my newfound adulthood to find any real pleasure in running back to my family home.

No interest in city life, no means of starting my own farm or whatever else I might do and…

I don't know. I honestly don't. I'd never thought beyond that whole, *Benji and Preston together* bit and, without that, all I have right now is—moping, I suppose. That's what I've been doing, what my aunt has been allowing me to do without question.

It's time that I need, perhaps. Or I *hope* that I need. If I can just sulk myself out, let these emotions and disappointment run their course… Doesn't Aunt Eleanor always say that fate finds us one way or another? Perhaps the universe will reveal a path to me if only I wait and see.

How funny is it, then, that I'm thinking on that exact sentiment when James and Esher walk through the door. Those two seem to be at the centre of so much in my life; maybe some part of me was expecting them to arrive. It's good to see James' face.

They've been in Buckinghamshire for a while on a job, Aunt Eleanor previously told me. I can't recall how long it has been since I last saw them, though it has been several months. Upon spying them as they trudge through the front door, looking worse for wear, bandaged and bedraggled, I almost laugh.

"You two look like you've been getting into trouble."

James' head lifts at the sound of my voice. Through his exhaustion, he doesn't hesitate to offer me a bright grin. "Just a bit of it," he says, more energy in his tone than anyone else would possess. "But we won in the end, so that's all right."

I clap him briefly on the shoulder in greeting, and Esher as well. Esher, of course, reacts more like a normal person who has been away for a while on tiring work: with a muted nod and a weary glance in my direction. I can imagine he's more interested in sleeping for a week than any socialising.

That's fine, honestly; the hour is late enough. I offer to

fetch their things from the carriage and won't pester them with small talk, even though I know I could easily rope James into it and I'm so desperate for any sort of distraction. It won't kill me to wait.

In the morning, they still aren't in the best of shape, but they're certainly better than they were the night before. James, especially, seems to have bounced back with vigour, though I would expect no less from him. He gobbles down all his breakfast and whatever Esher doesn't finish of his own plate, going over everything they've been through in the past weeks.

I've never quite known what to think of the work James and Esher do. Prior to our third year at Whisperwood, I'd taken Aunt Eleanor's talk of ghosts with a grain of salt and a polite smile. Now, after having dealt with them myself, having experienced it… It's dangerous work, often thankless and even ridiculed. From what I've heard, the pay isn't even enough to cover a steady supply of food more often than not.

We've barely finished breakfast when my aunt, largely silent up until this point, turns to the pair of them. "I've a letter for you two. Another job."

James brightens. "What is it?"

"The client is in possession of a box that needs transporting," she says.

Esher's mouth turns down. "We're not couriers."

She taps her spoon delicately against the edge of her teacup. "I'm told this particular piece of cargo has a bit of a dark past. A spirit attached to it, perhaps. I've not seen it for myself, so I couldn't tell you more than that."

"And the pay?" James asks.

"Aside from all expenses of travel being covered… let's say it's likely more than you made from the job in Buckinghamshire."

285

I don't know how much that particular job paid but judging by the way James and Esher's eyes go wide as plates, I would say it's a lot.

"All expenses paid," Esher says slowly. "Where would we be going, exactly?"

Aunt Eleanor brings the cup to her lips. "America."

James blinks. "*America?*"

She nods.

I can see in his expression James wants to instantly say yes, how there are a million questions at the tip of his tongue. Where in America? What is the item? What is said to haunt it? Who wants it transported and to what end?

Before he says anything further, though, his gaze slides questioningly to Esher. Esher, who says nothing, but who is already watching James with a measured look. His expression is unreadable. To me, at least. He and James have been like that for years, able to hold entire conversations with their eyes. Whatever it is Esher is trying to communicate, clearly it works because James' shoulders slump.

After a moment, he nods mutely before swinging his gaze back over to my aunt. "America's a bit of a journey," he says. "And we've only just returned. We'd actually planned a bit of a holiday to unwind."

She shrugs. "I thought as much. You may write back and let them know they will need to look elsewhere."

A frown tugs at James' face. He hates denying anyone's request for help, has always been like that for as long as I've known him.

I find myself sitting up a little straighter and before I can stop myself, I say, "I'll do it."

Three pairs of eyes swing my way.

"You'll what?" James asks.

I shrug. "I'll do it. You two look like you need the time off. I'll give you a finder's fee, of course."

"It might be dangerous," Esher points out. "They felt the need to request someone with paranormal experience instead of tossing it on a ship like common cargo."

I offer him a nonchalant smile in response. "It can't be that bad. Besides, I'm not exactly in the dark. I've watched you two at work before, and I've spent a lot of time with Aunt Eleanor. When would I need to leave?"

Aunt Eleanor watches me, calculating. "Two weeks."

"All right, then. Surely that's some time to give me a few lessons? I can figure out anything else as I go along. I transport a package and keep it safe. How hard can it be?"

James shakes his head. "There's no telling how long you'd be gone."

"It's a good thing, then, that I'm in possession of free time and flexibility."

I know none of them want me to take the job, but in the end, what solid argument do they have against it? It needs to get done, and better by someone with a little bit of knowledge than someone with none.

"Then you have some learning to do," my aunt eventually says with some reluctance.

That gives us a solid week for a few courses, cramming in whatever information they think might be useful, and then to drill me on it. I'm a good boy and even take notes, though I honestly don't think I'll have use for most of it. If it makes them feel better, it's no skin off my nose, and on the off chance that something does happen…at least I'll be prepared.

I don't honestly know if this is the right thing to do, and it's such a huge task to take on in the swing of the moment, but perhaps this is what I was waiting for. Something to do, some direction to take, a purpose. Something that would get my mind off other matters. It has to beat sitting around, at any rate.

The day I'm due to return home so that I can spend some time with my family prior to meeting up with my contact and departing for America, James accompanies me to the train station. He prattles on during the trip in that exhausting and endearing way that he does. I don't know if he does it because he enjoys the simple act of talking or if he can sense something a bit off about me, but either way, I appreciate it. He gives me plenty to focus on, keeps me from dwelling (at least for now) on whether or not I'm making the right decision.

As we wait for my train to arrive, James asks, "Are you nervous?"

"Not in the least," I admit. And honestly, I'm not. Not about the job, anyway. Being away from my family, from Benjamin? That's another story.

"Good." He clasps my shoulder tightly. "You'll do wonderfully. Most of this line of work comes down to simple determination."

I smile at his reassurance. "Is that why you flourish at it, then?"

He laughs. "Likely." And then he pauses, peering at me closely in a way that makes my smile fade. "Did you let Benjamin know that you're leaving?"

Ah. Benjamin is a subject I've been careful to side-step this last week, and neither James nor Esher have prodded me on it. I look away. "I wrote to him last night."

James nods solemnly, lashes lowering. "Miss Bennett told us what happened. I feel horrid we didn't know sooner. Is he all right?"

The smile I offer James is a bit tight, perhaps more than I mean it to be. I don't honestly know how to answer that question. And that in and of itself hurts because there was a long period of time where I'd know without even having to think about it. It's been weeks since I last saw or spoke to Benjamin. I have no idea how he's doing, what he's thinking, how he's coping. I feel guilty that I haven't checked in on him more. That I haven't known what to say with how we left things.

I thought…perhaps the pair of us needed some space, that communication would only make things harder.

Besides, there is really no right answer, and I would be dissatisfied regardless of what he said. He's either miserable and I'm unhappy that he's unhappy, or he *is* happy and then *I'm* unhappy because his happiness would be in a life without me.

"Haven't you heard?" I ask, still holding a smile that doesn't reach my eyes and in a voice I barely recognise as my own. "Our dear Benji is getting married."

FROM THE AUTHORS

Someday, maybe we'll finish a book and be able to say, "Hey, at least nobody died!"

Maybe, but not likely.

While breathing life into the world of A Light Amongst Shadows was a huge undertaking, the limited scope of the setting allowed us to ease into the 19th century world without feeling too overwhelmed. There was still plenty to get wrong if we weren't careful, but by the end of the story, we were comfortable at Whisperwood.

A Hymn in the Silence yanked us right back out of that comfort zone. I have the utmost awe and respect for authors of historical fiction who can get all the details right. Clothing, hairstyles, homes, decorations, religion, weather patterns and geography, etymology of words and phrases… It was a struggle to just write and leave notes for ourselves of things to look up later, so we didn't get bogged down in researching during the early drafts. Examples of some of our notes: "Forensics? Were they using this terminology yet?" "What employees were working at a mortuary in a small town?" "How'd they keep the bodies in a mortuary from smelling?" "Best way to get out of ice if you fall in??" and my personal favorite: "No, Rowan, Preston can't be excited to go to America and be a cowboy because that word wasn't really in use yet."

As always, the language is a tricky line to walk. We're striving for a sense of realism of the culture and time while not going overboard with the terminology that might be too grating for some readers. There's no way to make everyone happy in this regard, so we just do the best that we can.

That's where our beta readers came in. Jon, our native Brit and history buff, was yet again our first line of defense. He's so incredible with his attention to detail and the time and care he takes in reading for us. We learn so much from him. A huge shout-out also goes to Jada and Karen; their sharp eyes were an immense help, and their cheerleading from the sidelines is a great motivator. We had Lacy again, too; she's been there for every fashion question I could think of. When I message her to ask, "How quickly could a woman get out of her clothes in freezing weather if it were a life-or-death situation?" she not only answers but sends me pictures and very specific examples to run with. Bless. And, of course, Jaime Manning. My darling friend and talented eagle-eye proofreader who manages to catch everything everyone else missed. Melissa Stevens of The Illustrated Author deserves a huge round of thank yous. Although I formatted this book on my own, Melissa not only answered every stupid question I had, but helped me any time I got stuck.

Indie publishing really does take a village. It's a community that comes together, and we really do have some of the most amazing friends.

Lastly, if you haven't already checked out Kelley's reader group on Facebook, you're seriously missing out. We post all kinds of news, goodies, behind-the-scenes stuff, and art...plus, group members get exclusive contests and chances to read things early. Nice, huh? Come join us by searching for "Kelley's Yorkies" on Facebook.

What's next in store? We've got tons
We hope you're ready.
I know we are.

Until next time,
Kelley and Rowan

Printed in Great Britain
by Amazon

86754730R00165